£1.50

Critical acc

RANDOM ACTS

Taylor Smith ... John Grisham. "It's a plausible comparison—though Smith's a better prose stylist."
—*Publishers Weekly*

"The mix of suspense, forensic science, romance and mystery make this a real page-turner."
—*Orange Coast*

THE INNOCENTS CLUB

"Smith's gloriously intricate plot is top-notch ... her writing is that of a gifted storyteller."
—*Publishers Weekly*

"Smith keeps the action going in a way that will remind readers of Robert Ludlum, but Mariah Bolt has more depth than many of Ludlum's protagonists. Let's hope we see more of her."
—*Booklist*

THE BEST OF ENEMIES

"Smith taps into the deep-seated fear that neither life nor love is predictable."
—*Publishers Weekly*

Already available in MIRA® Books by
Taylor Smith

COMMON PASSIONS
THE BEST OF ENEMIES
GUILT BY SILENCE
THE INNOCENTS CLUB
DEADLY GRACE

Look for Taylor Smith's newest novel

LIAR'S MARKET

Coming 2004

TAYLOR SMITH

RANDOM ACTS

First published in Great Britain 1999. Reprinted 2003
MIRA Books, Eton House, 18-24 Paradise Road,
Richmond, Surrey, TW9 1SR

ISBN 0 7783 0034 X

58-0803

Printed and bound in Spain
by Litografia Rosés S.A., Barcelona

This book is dedicated to:
Mildred and Jack Smith,
to honor their fifty loving years together;

and to Marilyn and Len—
we choose our friends, but fate chooses our relatives.
Lucky me, that fate gave me the brother and sister
I would have chosen for my best friends.

Heaven has no rage like love to hatred turned,
Nor hell a fury like a woman scorned.
—William Congreve, 1697

Prologue

He was bottled terror, ready to blow, and all the more dangerous for not looking the part.

Hundreds of people passed by him that Friday night in the Southern California mall. One or two even engaged him in casual conversation. But who would connect him *to the monster and the panic he'd unleashed?*

He leaned against a pillar, contemplating with disdain the churning human sea before him, a tidal wave of Christmas shoppers intent on long lists and busy schedules—little people leading dull, ordinary lives. Most of them too weary, stressed and preoccupied to take notice of him standing at the edge of the central atrium, sizing things up—selecting a target.

The teenage girls were another matter. Strolling in insular bunches of two, three and more, they were as intent on seeing and being seen as on spending their meager allowances and baby-

sitting earnings. He watched them lure awkward boys with their teasing, tortuous, sidelong looks, a ritual dance, primal as fear and twice as disgusting.

Suddenly, two girls with mascara-fringed eyes and tight T-shirts emerged from the throng and passed close by him, making shameless direct eye contact—flirting with more danger than they could possibly imagine. His nostrils flared at the scent of cheap cologne that wafted before them like some flowery advance reconnaissance unit. He toyed momentarily with the idea of taking one of them and teaching her a lesson she'd never forget, but wouldn't live long enough to remember. But they weren't what he wanted or needed.

He stared back until the silly things wilted under his blank, brutal gaze. They averted their eyes, arms crossing reflexively over tiny breasts, and hurried on. He continued to watch until they had disappeared down the mall's west wing. If they turned around or came back to spy on him, he had a problem. Would have to abort the operation.

No.

He wouldn't be deterred. Couldn't. He needed to act. To take control. Needed the addictive surge of power in his veins, like a heroin rush.

This time, it would be even better. The panic would be greater. This time, they'd know what they were dealing with, and that they were helpless to defend against him.

When the little snoops had disappeared at last, he turned his attention back to the ersatz North Pole erected in the mall's central court, where seasonal workers in green elves' costumes were trying to maintain some semblance of control over the confusion. Dozens of small children milled around, waiting for a chance to sit on Santa's lap and reveal their sweet, secret wishes to him. Eyes bright, smiles wide, they wiggled and chattered, oblivious to everything but sparkling lights and frantically gay music ringing out holiday tunes. He studied their faces, one by one. So enraptured. So innocent.

Such easy pickings.

His gaze shifted from the line for Santa to the children riding the reindeer carousel next to his throne. One of them, *perhaps. He liked the idea of his victim running a last, doomed race against the inevitable. The garishly painted reindeer seemed to glance sideways as they spun past him, their plaster eyes bulging in frantic, dumb perception of the danger he posed—straining at the bit to get away, only to orbit back once more into the inescapable pull of his will.*

Ride! he thought, smiling to himself. Ride like the wind, for all the good it will do.

His appraising eyes gravitated to the tiniest of the children bouncing, chattering, giggling as they waited to see Santa. He studied plump hands tugging grown-up sleeves. Scrutinized round, pink mouths from which spilled pure, high-pitched voices. Examined chubby legs scrambling on metal guardrails.

Which one? he asked himself, mentally pawing them—touching, sniffing, squeezing soft flesh like ripe fruit in a market. Evaluating.

Choose carefully, he told himself. The target had to be perfect for his purposes. As young as possible. Beautiful, but pliant. A baby girl, this time, he thought, though a boy would have done just as well. He wasn't particular. All that mattered was that the sacrifice be worthy of his cause.

Today, he liked the idea of bows and curls. Large, dewy eyes. Pink, unblemished skin. Every daddy's little dream girl.

Suddenly, his gaze connected with the wide, blue eyes of a toddler—barely one, he estimated. She was in her mother's arms, curly blond head resting on the woman's shoulder, staring sleepily at him while her small, moist mouth worked at a tiny, pink thumb. He smiled back at her, entranced. Grateful.

She was the one. She was offering herself to him. She understood.

Part I

Bicoastal Blues

1

Claire Gillespie could sleep through shrieking sirens, cats in heat, domestic donnybrooks, the unearthly 3:00 a.m. clangor of garbage trucks, and the occasional eruption of gunfire in back alleys near her New York apartment. After half a decade of chasing stories cross-country for the weekly newsmagazine that issued her paycheck, napping when and where she could—cavernous airports, packed red-eye flights, nondescript hotel rooms—her Kansas-bred sleep patterns were pretty much invulnerable to assault. With one exception. A ringing telephone was Kryptonite to her superhuman powers of repose. A knife through the heart of blessed oblivion.

So, inevitably, the phone's first ring woke her that Saturday morning—more or less. At the second, she flung her right arm out from under the covers and fumbled blindly toward the side table, knocking over the water tumbler she'd apparently been sober enough to remember to fill last night, though not quite sober enough to remember to drink—too inexperienced at it to have gotten the drunkard's tricks down pat. Through dense mental fog, she sensed a titanic hangover bearing down on her at top speed.

"Damn!" she muttered as her hand found the portable phone and its On button, then dragged it back under the blankets to her ear. *Now* she remembered why drinking to forget was such a poor idea. She'd deal with the spilled water later—if she survived.

"What?"

"Well, a cheery good morning to you, too!"

Claire replied with a two-step grunt. "Oh—Serge." Sergio Scolari, national editor for *Newsworld.* "What time is it?" Her voice rasped like gargled gravel, and her tongue felt as if it had licked an ashtray. "Did you foist one of your smelly cigars off on me last night?"

"It's nine-thirty, and they're not smelly, they're Davidoff. What's more, you swiped, I did not foist. Not at ten-fifty a pop."

Claire heard the sulk in his tone. Typical. Flamboyant, independently wealthy, but cheap in ways that always surprised her, Scolari begrudged every wasted penny, his or the magazine's—a miserliness that probably endeared him to the publisher even more than his instinct for newsstand-dominating cover stories. Scolari wore bespoke Armani. He traveled first-class. Yet on those rare occasions when he treated his hopelessly middle-class colleague to dinner at one of his chichi haunts, Claire noticed that he never failed to carry off his leftovers—wrapped by kitchen staff in some arty sculptural concoction of tinfoil, maybe, but a doggie bag just the same. Like he didn't know where his next meal was coming from. Go figure.

Scolari would never have parted willingly with a Davidoff, but pride required that she plead not guilty. ''Baloney. I don't smoke. I quit.''

''Tell it to the silk blouse you burned a hole in.''

Claire forced open one gritty eye and raised her aching head an inch or two above the pillow, only to experience a moment of panic.

I'm blind!

Then, logic kicked in, and her free hand dragged the sheet off her head. She cast a bleary glance around. Various items of clothing marked a wayward trail across the dusty hardwood floor—gloves, coat, scarf, heels, black skirt, hose—all abandoned en route from the front door to the sofa bed she vaguely recalled wrestling open last night.

She peered nervously at the door, but all four locks and bolts were securely fastened. She breathed a sigh of relief. Despite her less-than-optimal state last night, her instincts had obviously remained on full alert against the ominous presence she'd felt dogging her footsteps for weeks.

The red silk blouse she'd worn to the Christmas party at Scolari's East Central Park penthouse had been tossed at about the halfway point between front door and sofa bed, landing on her desk. Even from her skewed perspective, Claire could see the stippled brown edges of a dime-size burn hole in one sleeve. The blouse was draped across her open laptop computer like some funereal banner on a tombstone. Fitting, she thought, since the notes on her hard drive were the only memorial she could give Michael Kazarian—a maddeningly incomplete testament to a slain hero whose image haunted her, day and night. At the thought of him, Claire felt the ache return with a vengeance—a dull, hollow throb deep inside her that alcohol briefly numbed, but obviously couldn't cure.

She dropped her head back to the pillow. "So waking me at this ungodly hour is payback for swiping one of your cruddy cigars, Serge? You think a ruined eighty-dollar blouse and fertilizer breath aren't punishment enough?''

''You tell me. You're the one inflicting this punishment on yourself.''

''Give me a break. I was feeling festive. It's the holiday season. First time I've smoked in months,'' she lied.

''I'm not talking about smoking, and you didn't look festive, you looked lousy.''

''Thanks a lot. See if I squeeze into heels and panty hose for you again, buster.''

Claire rolled over and stumbled out of bed, holding on to the phone as she shuffled in her underwear toward the bathroom, floor grit sticking to her bare feet. How long was it since she'd swept? She had no idea.

''I wanted to make sure you got in okay last night,'' Scolari said.

''No problem—but I don't believe for a minute that's why you called.''

In the bathroom, against her better judgment, Claire risked a look in the mirror. Bad move.

Holy mother of God, Gillespie, what a mess!

Her eyes—Prussian blue, Michael had called them, whatever that meant—were bloodshot and ringed with dark circles. Her skin was drawn and pale as milk, her unruly black curls sticking out at all angles, weeks overdue for a trim. She looked like a hungover Celtic Medusa.

Scolari assumed an aggrieved tone. ''You doubt my sincerity?''

Claire sighed. ''Putting you on speakerphone here, Serge.'' She punched a button on the base of the phone, set it on the windowsill and pulled a scrunchie from a basket to tie back her tangled mane. The sky beyond the window was gunmetal gray, sleety rain tattooing a rhythm on the pane. ''I know how your mind works,'' she said. ''You think you're going to catch me at a weak moment, convince me to reconsider and go out to L.A. to cover that baby-snatcher story.''

Over the past few weeks, three Southern California babies had vanished, boldly kidnapped in broad daylight from crowded public places, the most recent abduction having occurred just last night. In the absence of ransom notes or bodies, police and FBI officials suspected an underground adoption ring. The entire state was seized by panic.

''That's partly why I called. I really was concerned, though.''

''Yeah, right.'' Claire squeezed a line of toothpaste onto her toothbrush.

''I booked a flight for you,'' he added helpfully. ''Delta 176 out of La Guardia. Departs at noon, but the weather's lousy, so you'll have to hustle.''

''I told you last night, Serge, I'm up to my eyeballs on the Kazarian project. I've got an interview set up for later today with Ivankov that it took me weeks to wangle. By the way, if I should happen to disappear, could you make sure the authorities trawl for my poor, battered body off Brighton Beach?''

''That's not funny, Claire. Look what happened to Kazarian.''

''I know, but I'm not getting anywhere talking to the cops or the FBI. I want to see what Ivankov has to say for himself. Don't worry, I'll be careful.''

''I'd rather you were in L.A.''

''I can't do anything out there the locals can't.'' Claire leaned over the sink, engaging her toothbrush in a savage effort to undo the damage wrought by the allegedly pilfered cigar.

''They've run into a brick wall. The FBI's moved in and put a lid on statements to the press.''

''See?'' she mumbled, frothing at the mouth

like some mad dog begging to be put down. ''So what's the point of me—''

''This just came over the wire—they found a baby's body last night in an aqueduct east of L.A.''

Her head snapped up. ''One of the missing kids? Aw, damn!'' Toothpaste spattered the mirror.

''They think it's the second one who was taken, the Morales baby. Ten months old.''

''Drowned?''

''They won't know till the autopsy.''

Claire shook her head, then rinsed her mouth and splashed cold water on her face. ''That's horrible, but it's still no reason for me to go off half—''

''That's your buddy running the FBI investigation out there.''

Claire sighed. This is what came of trying to impress the brass with your sources. ''Not *my* buddy, my dad's. And Sprague may have opened a few Bureau doors for me in the past, but he's not going to cut me any slack on an active case. This is a strictly by-the-book G-man, Serge. Even his own stiff-necked underlings call him Button-Down Dan.''

"You have a better shot than anyone else I've got."

She ran a towel across her face, then tossed it into an overflowing laundry hamper. "Serge, you *promised* me some downtime to work on the Kazarian project."

"Doesn't sound like there's a story there any time soon, though. And you really do look like hell, Claire. What's with you? I've never seen you like this—tense, avoiding people—"

"I came last night, didn't I?"

"You were here in body, but the spirit never did put in an appearance. Don't try to kid a kidder, bub. I spent too much of my life living a lie not to recognize the symptoms in someone else."

Claire arched one eyebrow, only to discover even that was painful. How could eyebrows hurt? "You think I've got my sexual identity in a closet here?"

"That's not what I mean. You've lost weight, got tension lines in your face—"

"Oh, well, lines. That's just middle age creeping up. Happens to the best of us. After thirty-five, it's all downhill—isn't that what you told me on my last birthday?"

Claire reached for her bathrobe, but froze at the sight of the pale face, ravaged eyes and quivering body in the full-length mirror on the door. She turned to face the image head-on—a tiny, trembling Gibson girl, born too late to be fashionable in an age of heroin chic. Tending to round if she wasn't careful. Not at the moment, though. Scolari was right; she could see her ribs. Claire grimaced. Those hips were still there, however, perched atop legs that barely lifted her over the five-foot mark. Threatening to balloon like her mother's, though held in check for the time being. Becoming a nervous wreck had its upside.

"Have you heard from the schmuck?" Scolari ventured.

His loyalty brought a smile to Claire's lips. "Not since I signed the divorce papers. Anyway, it's old news."

She meant it. Alan had lost interest in their marriage long before the final split that past spring. The only surprise was that it was her sister he'd left her for—but that, Claire thought, said as much about Nicky as it did about Alan. Not her favorite people, but she had no intention of brooding over them.

"Is this about Kazarian, then?"

She was slipping into her bathrobe, but her hands paused on the belt. "What do you mean?"

Scolari hesitated, as if torn between discretion

and curiosity, but curiosity finally won out. ''Were you involved with him, Claire?''

She closed her eyes, feeling sick.

Fight it!

''He was a source. A terrific source, Serge, but that's it. Besides which, he was married.''

Not that he told me. I had to find out at his funeral. Dammit, Michael!

''You haven't been right since he was murdered.''

Claire yanked the belt tight and passed the back of her hand across her eyes, brushing away tears that had no business being there, cursing Scolari's nosy probing. She didn't need him in her private affairs, digging at raw wounds. But he was a friend, she reminded herself, trying to help. ''It hit me, I guess.''

But why so hard? Because Michael came to trust me, against his every instinct? Because he lived on the edge, and died alone? Because I violated my own rules by getting involved with him? Or because I was the cause of his death?

''It's the loose ends that are driving me nuts. Some scumbag shot this incredible guy—'' She'd said too much, Claire realized, but she stumbled on, oblivious to the catch in her throat that had nothing to do with cigars. ''Then stuffed him, bleeding, into his own car, blew it up and watched him die.''

''No word on the investigation?''

''*What* investigation? Does this make any sense to you? An undercover federal agent is violently murdered, and here we are, three months later, and nothing?'' Claire shook her head disgustedly. ''The Bureau should have been all over the mob Kazarian infiltrated, but after an initial flurry, the investigation's fizzled out, far as I can tell. No indictments, no arrests. Why not? Did somebody get paid off? And while we're at it, why was he murdered in the first place?''

''Maybe the mob found out he was a fibbie?''

Claire felt the guilt wash over her once more.

He let down his guard—because of me.

She and Kazarian had recognized each other at a *blini*-and-*borscht* joint frequented by the immigrant Russian gang they were both investigating—she for a *Newsworld* feature, he for the FBI. They'd said nothing at that moment. Afterward, though, he'd sought her out, reluctantly at first, only to be sure she wouldn't blow his cover. More willingly later, as if he craved the relief of dropping the stressful charade for a few hours. Their time together had been spent in carefully chosen locations, far from prying eyes. Maybe not carefully enough, though.

"Ivankov's mob wouldn't even have had to know he was a fed," Claire said. "They knew a reporter had been nosing around down there. If they thought one of their own was talking to the press—"

Her voice caught again. Sinking to the floor and leaning against the tub, she wrapped her arms tightly around her knees.

"Oh, hell, Serge," she whispered. "I think I got him killed."

2

Bone-cracking cold gripped half the country that Saturday morning. On the eastern seaboard, ice-crusted power lines had tumbled, leaving households from Maine to Rhode Island freezing in the dark. Blinding snowstorms were blanketing the Midwest, and six people had already died in traffic pileups or from shovel-induced heart attacks. In Florida, orange groves stood in frost-tipped ruin; tourists in Orlando, caught off guard, envied Mickey his gloves and Goofy his knitted hat.

Hard to believe, Dan Sprague mused as he drove up Wilshire Boulevard, bright sunshine dappling his windshield. Here in Los Angeles, the air was clear and mild, blowing inland off a gentle Pacific breeze. Palm trees were draped in glittering garlands, and mock-Dickensian shop windows dusted with fake snow, but temperatures were expected to hit eighty by noon. Even after six years in the city, this winter balm struck him as surreal and vaguely unsettling. Angelenos took their creature comforts for granted, but he mistrusted such complacency. It was when you let your guard down that fate had a habit of blindsiding you with disaster.

One of the radios on his center console crackled, and Dan reached over to adjust the volume. He was monitoring LAPD and county sheriff's traffic, as well as his own FBI frequency. So far, things had been quiet—a couple of domestic disturbance reports; a drunk sleeping in the doorway of some coffeehouse just opening for the day; a dog running loose down Sunset Boulevard—but it was only a little after seven, and thieves and gangbangers tended to be late risers. The pace would pick up as the day wore on. One thing you could count on if you carried a badge in L.A.: a daily fix for the adrenaline craving that was as much a part of the job as doughnuts and bad coffee at midnight. Even a paper-pusher like himself got enough excitement to feed the need—although, Dan thought, he would have forgone the buzz today in favor of a little more sleep and time with his daughters.

He propped his left elbow on the open window, hand stifling a yawn. He'd driven this route in the opposite direction just a few hours earlier when he'd gone home to make sure the girls were in safe and that the house was still standing. After crashing for a brief bout of restless sleep, he'd showered, shaved and headed back in.

Yesterday, five weeks after the kidnappings had started, the partially decomposed body of little Victor Morales, the second victim, had been found by municipal cleanup crews, wrapped in a tightly bound, green plastic garbage bag that had gotten itself caught in weeds in the California aqueduct, out near the desert city of Lancaster. The autopsy on the baby was scheduled for eight this morning, and the coroner's report would be faxed to the FBI's Los Angeles field office before noon.

Meantime, Dan had scheduled an eight-thirty meeting with members of his kidnap response team to review progress on the investigation. Several of his people would also be heading down to Orange County to follow up on last night's disappearance of yet another baby, a little girl this time, from South Coast Plaza. He'd be lucky to see his own daughters at all that day.

And tonight? he wondered. They'd both said they were going out, hadn't they? Dan frowned, trying to recall their exact words. Erin had tickets to a Kings game with Matt and some other friends. Okay. Matt was polite, he drove a beige Toyota Camry registered in his mother's name, and he'd never had so much as a parking ticket. Dan knew, because he'd checked the guy out.

What about Julie? She'd said she was going to—a movie? Was that it? Who with? Dan puzzled. Chrissy and Sharon? A boy? Did she even say? Damn, he should have listened more carefully. At nineteen, Erin was almost over the dangerous years, but Julie was only sixteen and still bore watching.

He should have sat down with them last night, spent some time probing what they were up to, how they were doing. The girls had been watching Letterman when he'd arrived home near midnight, the two of them sprawled on the family-room sofa, the air dripping with the scent of warm, buttered popcorn. Bubba, their huge, dopey golden retriever, had been lying on the floor beside them, his chin propped on Julie's knee, making pathetic eyes at her so she'd toss a few kernels his way. Some guard dog. Fully preoccupied with his stomach, he hadn't even stirred at Dan's arrival.

Dan had stood quietly for a while, watching them, awed at how his little girls had blossomed into these heartbreakingly pretty young women.

Wondering when it had happened. Both were dark-haired like Fiona; like Dan, too, for that matter, although he'd gone to silver a decade earlier, while still in his mid-thirties. Erin was also built small, like their mother, but Julie had inherited those long, long Sprague legs. It was a source of some kidding, the fact that the younger towered over the older. As sisters went, though, they were closer than most, it seemed to Dan. Always had been. Lucky, really.

He hadn't wanted to intrude on their camaraderie, and didn't much care for Letterman. Still, would it have killed him to sit with them and watch for a while? Then maybe they'd have talked more—during commercials, after the show was over. It was so hard to find time to talk. Hard to talk, period. Fiona was the one who'd always known what they were thinking, and when they were having problems with school, boys or whatever. And she was the one, too, who'd always seemed to know what to say and what to do about those problems.

Dan sighed. He'd call them later this morning, then try to get home at a decent time for a change. Catch up—on the girls, on chores, on sleep.

A second yawn formed deep in his throat, but caught there as he glimpsed a vision in his driver's-side mirror, coming up from behind—a woman with long, shining auburn hair fluttering in the breeze. A name slipped past his lips like an involuntary reflex, almost a sigh: "Fiona."

Then, as quickly as the image in the mirror had appeared, it vanished, and a cherry-red BMW convertible, top down, pulled alongside him. Dan looked over at the driver. Not Fiona, of course, but another woman who bore a slight resemblance to his dead wife—or rather, to the way she'd looked before the disease stole her vitality and her beautiful hair.

He turned his eyes to the road once more, determined not to stare. But his peripheral vision couldn't help noticing the woman's hand caressing her right thigh. Reluctantly, he glanced over once more. She had full, blush-painted lips, and was biting the lower one distractedly, as if lost in erotic reverie—although, he reflected dryly, she could just as easily be thinking about picking up the dry cleaning or balancing her checkbook. His forlorn fantasies were fully capable of playing tricks with his perception.

As if sensing his gaze, the woman shot a look in his direction. Her hand abandoned the thigh and moved to the steering wheel, and the Beemer sped ahead, leaving Dan to suck exhaust. He grimaced. Obviously, a middle-aged guy in a white Chevy Caprice, police edition, didn't bear a second look.

One of the radios crackled again, and the female dispatcher's calm, tinny monotone issued a call to arms.

"All units—459-A, Bank of California, Slauson and Hooper."

Dan turned up the volume on the LAPD receiver as the first bank heist of the day unfolded. There'd be more before the day ended. Los Angeles wasn't designated Bank Robbery Capital of the World for nothing. It had gotten worse since branches had begun extending hours and opening in supermarkets and malls, "freeway close" for the convenience of customers and crooks alike.

Local police forces were the first line of defense, with Dan's own bank squad concentrating on repeat offenders, whose surveillance-camera images covered one entire wall of the FBI field office. With the Christmas-shopping season in full swing, the urge to splurge would only boost the rate of unauthorized withdrawals in the days ahead.

As mobile units responded to the LAPD dispatcher, Dan approached the corner of Wilshire and Veteran, site of the heavily bunkered Federal

Building. The traffic light changed from green to yellow, and he pulled into the turn lane, slowing the Caprice to a stop. A blond, ponytailed girl started through the crosswalk on Rollerblades, her well-toned body leaning into each thrust of her long, tanned legs. Wearing a fluorescent-green bikini top and denim shorts too brief to be legal, she was somewhere between sixteen and twenty-six. It was hard to be certain. In this city, where little girls grew up fast and cheating the calendar was an advanced art, Dan always felt confused and awkward around women he didn't know. More than once, he'd caught his lonely eye straying toward females who, on closer examination, turned out to be nearer his daughters' ages than his own. It was embarrassing.

And while he was on the subject, he'd better not catch Erin or Julie going out in public like that.

The light changed and he turned, then made a quick right into the Federal Building lot, feeling another guilty twinge for taking off before they were up. He'd left an inadequate note on the kitchen table, when what he really wanted to do was padlock the doors behind him and erect barricades to shield them from unseen dangers—as if he could protect them any more than he'd been able to save Fiona. Twenty-eight years as a Kansas City cop turned FBI special agent had counted for precisely nothing in the battle against the sinister forces that had struck his wife. He'd been forced to stand by, helpless, while a virulent lymphoma brought her down so fast she was dead within three months of the initial diagnosis, leaving them all stunned and bereft.

This would be their second Christmas without her, Dan realized with a start as he pulled into the employee parking tower and the space reserved for the SAC—Special Agent in Charge of Criminal Investigations. Erin was already through her first semester as a freshman at UCLA. Julie was learning to drive. Fiona should have been there to see them so grown-up.

He snapped off the radios and got out of the car, reaching instinctively to straighten a tie that wasn't there this morning. His concession to the weekend had been to put on a navy golf shirt, as sort of a subliminal reminder to himself that downtime was a useful concept, and that his family responsibilities warranted taking some once in a while.

He grabbed his sport coat and briefcase from the back seat, worry over his motherless children bringing him back full circle to thoughts of childless mothers, two of whom he'd met in one hellish day yesterday: Flora Morales, mother of little Victor, and Marcia Goodsell, whose year-old baby daughter had vanished last night from South Coast Plaza. The kidnapper's first victim, ten-month-old Byron Jefferson, was still missing and unaccounted for. In all three cases, the only apparent common denominators were the young ages of the children and the fact that they'd happened to be in the wrong place at the wrong time when the kidnapper struck. None of the cases had produced ransom notes—an ominous predictor, born out by yesterday's grisly discovery in the aqueduct.

As in most missing child cases, the FBI had been called in from the first disappearance. The Bureau's role had been stepped up dramatically once it had become apparent they were dealing with a serial predator.

Whatever his personal problems, Dan thought, there could be no slacking off until this predator was located and taken down.

His office was on the seventeenth floor, but on the elevator, Dan swiped his ID card through the security scanner and pressed nine instead.

Entering the bank-squad area, he immediately

spotted the shiny, bald head of Doug Zellerbach, the squad leader, bent over his desk in his glassed-in corner office. In the outer bull pen, half a dozen weekend-duty agents were manning phones, files and incident reports. Glancing up, Zellerbach spotted Dan and waved him over.

Only as he came through the door did Dan realize the squad leader was on the phone. "Hi, Z," he murmured.

The burly agent leaned back in his seat and crooked the receiver against his shoulder. "Hey, boss. I'm just talking to the LAPD, South Central Division. We got some action going down over there—Bank of California, Slauson and Hooper."

"Heard the call as I was pulling in the parking lot. What's happening?"

Zellerbach punched a button on the phone base, switching it over to speaker. "This is the LAPD watch commander I've got on the horn—Lieutenant Flatley." He raised his voice a notch. "Special Agent in Charge Dan Sprague just walked into my office, Lieutenant. He heads up criminal investigations here. Any idea what you're dealing with yet?"

The watch commander's voice croaked from the speakerphone. *"First car arrived on the scene just a minute ago. So far, all's we know is, somebody was tryin' to boost the ATM. Hold on…''*

The voice became muffled as he spoke to someone else. Meanwhile, the speakerphone and Zellerbach's own police scanner crackled a report in stereo of the dispatcher exchanging information with what sounded like several cruisers arriving on the scene. Then, Flatley was back on the line.

''Okay, don't know whether you caught that, but looks like our units are giving chase on foot. Suspect's an African-American male, early twenties, five-ten or thereabouts. Took a crowbar to the machine, but we don't know yet whether he got any cash or whether our guys interrupted him before he had a chance.''

''You need assistance?''

''Naw, think it's under control. I'll keep you posted.''

''We've been investigating a series of vandalized ATMs, Lieutenant,'' Dan said. ''Could you send us over a copy of the security video when you retrieve it?''

''Sure, no problem.'' The radio crackled again as a patrol car reported an arrest. *''Okay, looks like they collared the guy.''*

''Good work,'' Zellerbach said. ''Hey, send me over the booking shot, too, would you? We'll run 'em both by our wall of fame up here, see if we can spot him in any other heists."

"You got it. Talk to you later."

"Yeah, 'tis the season, you probably will," Zellerbach said wearily. He stabbed the End-Call button, then leaned back in his chair, clasping his hands behind his shining head. "I gotta be in here today, Dan-o, Santa's elves being the busy, thieving little buggers they are, but what brings you in at this hour on a Saturday morning?"

"The TOTNAP case. What's that blight on your chin?"

Zellerbach grinned and gave the stubble a thoughtful rub. "Thought I'd grow me a little goatee. What do you think? Make me look deep and intellectual?"

Dan snorted. "Makes you look like a bald goat. J. Edgar's rolling over in his grave."

"So roll over, J. Edgar. Kristie says it's sexy."

"Yeah, well, she married you, so that says a lot about her taste." Dan pulled himself out of the chair. "I'll be in my office, anything major goes down."

"What's the consensus on those kidnappings? Same guy, you think?"

"Could be. Too soon to tell. M.O. looks similar, but there are some victim variations. If it *is* the same guy, though, he sure as hell's moving around. Doesn't make things any easier. I've put another half-dozen people on it until we get some answers.''

''The first baby still hasn't shown up?''

''Nope.''

''Great. Another serial wacko. Welcome to L.A.''

''No kidding,'' Dan muttered, heading for the door.

''The Blue Angel's in,'' Zellerbach called after him.

Dan stopped and turned back to the section chief, frowning. ''I don't want to hear anybody calling her that, Z, least of all a squad leader. Guys hear you doing it, they think it's okay. Right away it gets out of control. Next thing you know, I've got a sexual-harassment suit on my desk.''

Zellerbach raised his hands, palms out. ''Sorry—Agent Madden.''

''That's better. How do you know she's in?''

''Rode up in the elevator with her. That is one awesomely gorgeous woman, but frosty? Man! All I did was invite her out to lunch, but she brushed me off like I'd asked her to a motel room instead.''

Dan watched the bald head give a regretful

shake. No, Z certainly wouldn't have suggested anything untoward. Not yet, anyway. A motel might have been his *second* date proposal, though, had Madden taken him up on the first.

"She making any progress on this baby-nap case?" Zellerbach asked.

"She's still working up a profile of the UNSUB." Assuming they were only dealing with *one* unidentified suspect, Dan thought. You never knew when a copycat would decide to surface.

Zellerbach rolled his eyes. "Another graduate of Bull Shit U. Terrific."

BSU, the Behavioral Sciences Unit—sometimes referred to as Investigative Support to get around the unfortunate acronym—was housed in a warren of offices deep below the FBI academy in Quantico, Virginia. Its profilers were, depending on your point of view, either a useless bunch of vague, glory-seeking eggheads, or experts engaged in the most exciting advance in forensic research since fingerprinting and DNA typing.

"She comes highly recommended from headquarters," Dan said.

"Oh, yeah, real high-profile. Darling of the press after the Beltway Ripper case. So hated by her own colleagues the brass had to get her out of town before they had an internal revolt on their hands. Practically tarred, feathered and shipped her out on a rail, from what I hear. Quite the piece of work.''

Dan exhaled wearily. ''Look, Z, I'm only gonna say this once—Laurel Madden gets the same chance here as anyone else. She does her job, toes the line, I got no problem with her. In the meantime, I don't want to hear anyone repeating watercooler gossip or making unfounded allegations against a fellow agent. Can I count on you to enforce that policy in your squad?''

''Absolutely,'' Zellerbach said. Then he leaned forward, glanced around and lowered his voice. ''But just between you and me, Dan-o—think there's any truth to the rumor she whacked her husband?''

3

"You are taller on phone."

Ivan Ivankov scowled, as if irritated to have been duped, but his words were so weighted by his thick Russian accent that Claire thought she'd misunderstood.

"Taller? On the phone?"

"*Da.* Much." Ivankov leaned back in his ancient oak desk chair, its dry springs creaking in protest as he gave her a critical once-over. The air in the office of his Brooklyn garage was stuffy and close, with fumy, metallic undertones of gasoline and motor oil.

Did he recall her face from that day in the café? Claire wondered nervously.

It had been a blustery morning that past March when she'd walked into a *borscht* bistro one of her frightened sources had grimly nicknamed Killer Café, hoping to spot the Russian crime boss who reputedly held court there. It had been a one-in-a-million fluke running into Michael Kazarian there as well. They were both far from their home turf—at least, she was. In the four years she'd been working in *Newsworld*'s New York bureau, this was her first foray into Brooklyn, and her first time delving into the Russian syndicate said to be entrenched there.

When she'd discovered Kazarian, however, drinking and laughing with Ivankov, a reputed racketeer, loan shark and murderer, Claire had realized she had no idea what *his* usual beat was. When she'd met him a couple of years earlier at the FBI academy, he'd been a senior staff member there. But if Kazarian was working undercover in Brighton Beach now, she knew she'd stumbled onto a major story.

As soon as she'd walked into the café, Kazarian had spotted her, too. Shock had flickered across his features, the emotion registering and disappearing so quickly that Claire was certain no one else in the room had picked up on it. But in that instant of mutual recognition, a chilling understanding had passed between them—if she gave him away, they were both dead. She'd slipped out as soon as possible, passing on the chance to approach the Russian crime boss that day. Would it have made a difference if she'd dropped the whole project then and there? she'd agonized ever since. If she and Michael had never met again? If they hadn't become lovers? Would he still be alive today?

Ivankov shifted in his chair, and its rusty springs creaked once more. "You have voice of formidable woman, but—" He waved a dismissive hand, smirking at his three colleagues, who were appraising her from their own vantage point, slouched against office walls adorned with Penzoil and Valvoline advertisements and a calendar displaying Miss April 1987 in all her glory—an erotic golden oldie, apparently. The flunkies snickered.

Claire ignored them and focused on Ivankov, confident now that he had no memory of her coming into the restaurant that day. Nor did he appear to deem her much of a threat. In the face of such arrogance, Claire regretted not wearing the stacked-heel power boots that gave her three added inches and a feeling of invincibility. In this sleety weather, though, it was hard enough to find a cab and browbeat the driver into making the trip out to Brooklyn without the added humiliation of slipping and sliding on impractical footwear. A pratfall in front of the alleged boss of the largest Russian crime syndicate on the East Coast wouldn't have done much for her credibility. Better to have gone with the lug-soled Timberland specials she'd worn instead.

"Can I sit down?" she asked.

Ivankov nodded and pointed to a chair beside the cluttered steel desk. A stack of tumbling, yellowed tabloids printed in Cyrillic script covered the seat—one of the neighborhood weeklies aimed at Brighton Beach's large Russian immigrant population, Claire guessed. She hooked her leather tote bag over her shoulder, transferred the papers to the grimy, vinyl-covered floor and sat down. Pulling a cassette recorder from her bag, she set it on the desk between them, then withdrew her notebook.

"Do you mind if I record our conversation?"

He barely gave the machine a glance. "I am busy man, Miss—uh—"

"Gillespie. Claire Gillespie."

"Yes, of course. I should know. You are leaving messages for weeks. Perhaps you tell me now what is so important."

Ivankov propped his brown boots on the desk—soft leather, looked Italian—and laced his hands across a barrel chest. He wore a navy crewneck sweater whose polo-pony logo cantered across the spot where his heart would have been, if he'd had one. The dove suede jacket he wore open over that seemed custom-fit to the Russian's chunky frame. Heavy gold rings adorned both square-tipped pinkies. If he were part of La Cosa Nostra, Claire reflected, he'd be called Don Ivankov. In Brighton Beach, people referred to the forty-four-year-old Odessa native as "*pakhan.*" It amounted to the same thing. His immigration records said Ivan Ivankov was an auto mechanic, but his soft, white hands and designer clothes spoke of rackets, not ratchets. Michael had nicknamed him Ivan the Terrible.

Ivankov's thick lips spread in a banal smile, but there was no warmth in the slate-colored eyes. "You are writing about auto-repair shops, yes? We do excellent work here. Everyone will tell you so."

Claire glanced out at the garage beyond the office window. An old Ford was suspended on the nearest hoist, but the remaining three bays stood empty. Ivankov was reputed to own a string of chop shops that serviced the auto-theft ring he controlled, but if this was one of them, he'd obviously had the place cleared out before admitting a reporter. A burly man in blue overalls puttered around the hoist in a halfhearted show of industry, but even from where she sat, Claire could see that his hands, like Ivankov's, were clean, that his overalls bulged near his left armpit, and that he was keeping close watch on both the office and the gas pumps outside.

She turned back to meet the *pakhan's* insolent stare head-on and depressed the record button on her machine.

"Actually, Mr. Ivankov, I want to talk to you about some other matters. You haven't been in this country long, I understand."

"Nine years."

"You've done very well for yourself. You own three houses. One here in Brooklyn, and two in the Hamptons. The house you bought in Southampton last year listed for—" Claire consulted her notes "—1.8 million dollars. You paid cash."

If he was surprised by her research, Ivankov hid it well. Neither did he make any attempt to deny the facts. "I work hard. Am frugal man."

"Must be," Claire said dryly. She nodded at the pumps outside. "Let's talk about your gas bar. I noticed on the way in that your pump prices are well below anyone else's."

"Competition is good for consumer, no?"

"Looks like you've eliminated the competition. There are no other gas stations anywhere near yours."

He shrugged. ‘‘They are not good businessmen, like me.’’

‘‘People say you can sell at these prices because you mix cheaper fuels with the gasoline. Also, that you’ve created a vast trail of paper businesses whose sole purpose is to defraud the government of excise taxes on the gasoline you sell.’’

‘‘Who tells you this?’’

It was Claire’s turn to shrug. ‘‘Just something I picked up.’’

‘‘Is lies.’’

‘‘I see. What about Oleg Okrynyk?’’

‘‘Who?’’

‘‘Okrynyk, sixty-two years old? Owned a small grocery story over on Twenty-fourth? You loaned him money when his wife needed bypass surgery.’’

‘‘This is a problem?’’

‘‘It is when they paid you nearly eighty thousand dollars over a four-year period and barely touched the principal on the loan. Works out to an interest rate of around thirty-six percent, by my calculations—a little too steep for the Okrynyks, so they finally defaulted.’’

‘‘Okrynyk told you this?’’

‘‘That would be difficult, since he’s dead. It

took a while for police to identify what was left of his body in his bombed-out car, but his wife was able to identify his clothes and his wedding ring. Tell me, was what happened to Okrynyk a warning to other loan clients who might also be tempted to default?''

''I don't know who tells you these things. I never met this man.''

''I find that difficult to accept. Moreover, I have reports that men who work for you visited him every week.''

A shrug of incomprehension was Ivankov's only reaction.

''I gather,'' Claire went on, ''that you also offer 'protection' to other businesses around here?''

Ivankov merely lifted his hands.

Claire sighed wearily. ''Okay, let's try another name—Misha Kurelek.'' It was the name Michael Kazarian had used during his fifteen months working undercover in Brighton Beach. ''You knew him, I believe.''

''Many people bring their cars here. As I say, I run famous establishment.''

''Kurelek wasn't a customer of yours. I understand you were his, though.''

''I do not think—''

''Do you own a cellular phone, Mr. Ivankov?''

''Many people do.''

''I've been doing some checking. Kurelek supplied cellular phones to you and your—'' Claire glanced at the broad-faced goons around the room ''—your colleagues. He had set up an encrypted cellular communications network.''

''Encrypted? This means...?''

''Means any calls you make are sent in code, so no one can listen in to conversations that might prove...um...embarrassing, let's say.''

''I see.'' Ivankov's lower lip jutted and he nodded appreciatively, as if this was the first time he'd ever heard of the concept.

''So? Did you buy your cell phones from him?''

''Is not crime in this country to own such a telephone, I think?''

Claire suppressed an urge to hit the smug bastard. She had no doubt Ivankov knew precisely what was and what wasn't a crime here, but after operating under the invasive scrutiny of an oppressive Soviet bureaucracy for half his life, he obviously found this country's oversight systems laughably easy to circumvent.

''Kurelek was an illegal distributor of those cellular phones,'' she said evenly. ''He kept no sales records and didn't ask his customers for awkward personal information.''

Ivankov feigned shock. ''He was breaking law? Really? I had no idea.''

In a pig's eye, she thought. That was exactly what had drawn him to ''Misha Kurelek,'' who'd made a name for himself by offering safe communications to a shady circle of extortionists, drug dealers, pimps and racketeers who operated inside an immigrant community too conditioned to fear the state to turn the preying scum over to police. Unbeknownst to ''Kurelek's'' clients, however, the phone network was part of a sting.

J. Edgar Hoover, in his day, had turned a blind eye to the Mafia, but recent FBI directors were not prepared to grant Russian organized crime the same courtesy. No fewer than twenty agents in the Bureau's New York field office were tasked to investigate the East Coast arm of what was fast becoming a nationwide ring. Michael Kazarian, who'd learned to speak Russian at his grandmother's knee, had been their ace in the hole. The brilliance of his undercover operation, for as long as it had lasted, was that every word, every deal, every boast, every threat these creeps uttered over their supposedly encoded network was captured through state-of-the-art microphones and long-range transmitters embedded in the phones, and transmitted straight back to the Bureau's field office.

Now, with Michael gone, Claire had no idea where the investigation stood. Since Ivankov remained on the streets, she had to presume the Bureau was still collecting the evidence it needed to put him away. That meant she had to walk a tight line here.

"I'm investigating Misha Kurelek's activities for my magazine. At least, I was, until he was murdered." Her stomach fluttered, sick at having to talk about Michael as if he'd belonged to the same scummy world these guys inhabited.

Ivankov frowned. "I heard something about this. An ugly thing. But if he was a criminal, as you say—"

"He died in much the same way as Oleg Okrynyk. Do you know who killed him?"

"Me? Why would I know?"

"Maybe you decided Kurelek was untrustworthy?"

"*I* decided? He was telephone salesman. I am auto mechanic."

Claire waved a hand at the empty garage bays. "Business seems a little slow, Mr. Ivankov. And pardon me for saying so, but you live awfully well for a grease monkey.''

''Is only bad weather brings slow business. And I work hard, am boss now. My workers fix cars. I look after investments.''

Time to go for broke. ''Maybe somebody thought Misha Kurelek was an informer—or worse.''

''Worse?''

''I don't know… Maybe somebody was worried he was a policeman himself? Something like that?''

''He was?''

''No, not that *I* know of,'' Claire said, ''but maybe somebody else got such an idea. Could that be why he died?''

Ivankov scrutinized her, his expression no longer smug. Suddenly, his feet crashed to the floor, and he leaned across the desk, smashing his fist down on her tape recorder. The machine sputtered and died.

''Girlie, you think I am stupid? You think I am ignorant peasant does not know what happens to people who kill police in this country?'' His eyes narrowed. He glanced at the smashed machine, then examined her more closely, as if weighing his options. ''I tell you something else,'' he said.

"What's that?"

His fist pounded his chest. "Maybe *I* want to know who killed Kurelek more than anyone else. Maybe I take care of son of bitch myself."

"Why not leave it to the authorities?"

"Who? Police? I think police are thieves."

"Thieves?" Claire shook her head, confused. "I don't understand."

He sat back in his chair and waved a hand disgustedly. "No, girlie, you don't understand, because police don't tell whole story. They say they find Kurelek's body in car, yes?"

She nodded.

"Find bullets, find melted phones. But police don't say they find money, do they?"

"What money?"

Ivankov's voice rose to an angry pitch. "Nearly five hundred thousand dollars Kurelek is on way to deliver to Ivankov. Money killer stole, bloody thief!"

Claire had asked the taxi driver to wait for her, but when Ivankov's goons frog-marched her out of his garage a few minutes later, the yellow cab had driven—or been scared—off. After a quick glance around to confirm that the car was really gone, she flipped up the collar of her coat and headed quickly in what she hoped was the direction of the subway station, counting herself lucky to have been merely left on the sidewalk in the freezing rain. After dropping the bombshell about the missing money, Ivan the Terrible had handed Claire the ruined tape recorder and put her out on the street with her remaining questions unanswered and her confusion total.

Her mind raced as she hurried down the road. If the Russian was telling the truth, it opened up a whole new angle on Michael's murder—the possibility that he was killed, not on Ivankov's orders, but by someone else who knew he'd be carrying money that day.

One of the Russian's cronies? Surely Ivankov would have considered the possibility, but if he was still this angry, then obviously he hadn't identified the guilty party, much less recovered his cash.

Could the money have been burned up in the car fire that followed the explosion? she wondered. Even in one-hundred-dollar denominations, you were looking at five thousand banknotes, tightly wrapped and packed. And it was far more probable, in fact, that the money would have been in the smaller denominations favored by organized criminals. Very unlikely a bundle that huge would have been consumed without a trace—not in a fire that had left enough of a man's body and his personal effects to allow forensic identification.

Shivering, maybe from the damp cold, more likely from nervousness, Claire slowed at an intersection and glanced behind to see if she was being followed. Except for a few parked cars, the streets were oddly deserted for a mid-Saturday. The only movement she perceived was vaporous, malodorous steam rising from the sewers. Obviously, no one else was idiot enough to venture out on foot in such foul weather. Or maybe it was just the neighborhood. Ivankov's garage was blocks from residential Brooklyn, with its arching trees, weathered brownstones, inviting stoops and lively, polyglot, working-class population. Inland, too, from the boardwalk and Brighton Beach Avenue, and its Russian cafés, fortune-tellers and cheesy trinket shops. This was the part of Brooklyn that urban renewal hadn't found—dozens of square blocks of warehouses with smashed windows, and scrubby vacant lots cluttered with rusted-out car frames, rotting garbage and discarded hypodermic needles.

Hunkered down in her coat, wind and freezing rain biting her cheeks, Claire sprinted across the intersection, doubly thankful now for her sure-footed hiking boots. Praying for a cab, she kept a nervous eye on every car that skidded by, dreading Ivankov's goons even more than gangbangers. No one stopped, or even slowed to check her out. Not at first.

But when she paused a couple of blocks later to try again to orient herself, her back suddenly prickled with the distinct awareness of being followed. She spun around, scanning up and down the block, taking in grimy buildings and shot-out windows. Nothing.

Then, just as she began to turn away, she spotted him—a shadowy figure in a dirty, dark sedan idling at the curb half a block behind her. Waiting. Watching.

She started walking again, faster now, wincing at the sound of the car's tires spinning on the pavement, accelerating out of the parking space. She hurried on, but sensed it moving close behind now, keeping pace with her.

Suddenly, it sped up and pulled alongside her. Out of the corner of her eye, Claire saw the passenger-side window drop. Reluctantly, she glanced over. The driver ducked his head to see her through the window. He looked vaguely familiar, with close-shorn, peppered hair and penetrating black eyes. Under sharply defined cheekbones, he had a face rendered even more angular by a shadow of stubble that appeared not to have met a razor in a day or two. There was a rip on the sleeve of his army-surplus parka, and a strand of kapok stuck out the hole.

"Can I offer you a lift?" he called, wearing what Claire guessed was meant to be a reassuring smile.

She did not feel reassured. One of Ivankov's mob? she wondered. She'd heard no trace of a Russian accent, but still…

"No thanks," she said, walking on. Cringing internally as the car pulled alongside her once more, she brought her clenched fists from her pockets, getting ready to fight or flee.

"Terrible weather for walking. I really think y'all should let me drive you."

Claire ignored him. Tried to disregard her rising panic, too, as she scanned the deserted street, looking for a subway entrance. It was a bad day all around when the New York subway system presented itself as the safest haven available. Approaching the next intersection, she launched into a sprint, hoping to find an entrance around the corner. But the car sped up, as well, and swerved into the empty cross street. Slamming on its breaks, it swerved and skidded to a halt directly in her path. Claire froze.

The driver leaned over and opened the mud-spattered passenger door. The grin was gone now, and his impatient voice left no doubt he wouldn't take another no for an answer.

''Get in the car, Ms. Gillespie. Now!''

4

A mop-haired toddler in denim overalls and ruffled blouse stared up at Dan from the photograph in his hand. It was a professional five-by-seven, shot against a backdrop of puffy clouds, taken at Sears or some other studio that specialized in cute-kid shots. Under her blond curls, the little girl's velvet eyes were sober, her rosebud lips unsmiling and slightly parted. A tiny, upraised thumb sparkled wetly, as if it had been pulled from her mouth only a split second before the picture was snapped.

Dan could almost hear the photographer's plea: "Come on, sweetie, let's take that thumb out, okay?" Her cooperation had been reluctant, he thought. Little Erica Goodsell looked like some preternaturally gifted infant clairvoyant, who'd gazed into her own future and foreseen only disaster.

"It was taken just three weeks ago," Oz Paterson said. He was squad leader in the Violent Crimes Unit, one of a dozen agents meeting with Dan in the Emergency Response Center conference room that morning to review the TOTNAP case. Paterson's deeply lined face and the pouches under his watery, bespectacled eyes spoke of years of round-the-clock manhunts for the worst of the worst.

Also seated at the table were a couple of evidence technicians, a polygraph specialist, a media relations agent from the press office and representatives of the Rapid Start team, who'd arrived from FBI headquarters soon after the first kidnapping to automate the investigation, plugging clues and leads into a centralized computer database that would sift and analyze them, looking for common denominators and potential links to other kidnap cases nationwide. Glancing at the faces around the table, Dan found himself racking his brain for a couple of names. With more than six hundred agents in the office, it was hard to know them all individually, but if they worked with him, he made the effort.

One other newcomer rounded out the group, but even without the whispers of notoriety that swirled around her like a miasma, Dan would have had no difficulty remembering Special Agent

Laurel Madden. She was, as Doug Zellerbach had said, a beautiful woman, with long, honey-blond hair that she kept clipped back at the nape of her neck, high cheekbones and clear, almost translucent skin. Her uniform of conservative blouses and muted trouser suits was no doubt meant to strike a professional, low-profile note. Didn't do much good. Since Madden's arrival in the field office, Dan had noticed how conversations sputtered and died whenever she entered a room. If the woman were ever to put on a dress, she'd probably be declared a national emergency.

He turned to Oz Paterson, tapping the photo in his hand. "The Goodsell baby's a year old?"

"Just turned."

"The other two victims were a little younger, no?"

"Victor Morales was ten months old, Byron Jefferson eight months. But she was small for her age."

Dan handed the photo back to Paterson. "Up to now, I thought we were dealing with a pedophile with a taste for very young, male victims."

"The mother said she was wearing these overalls at the mall last night," said Paterson. "Maybe the suspect mistook her for a boy. It's an easy mistake to make with babies."

''I don't know. Curls like that, she seems all girl to me.'' Reminded him of Erin and Julie at that age, Dan thought with a shudder.

Ron Younger, the polygraph specialist, leaned forward. ''Maybe we're dealing with a different UNSUB on the Goodsell snatch? A copycat?''

''I don't think so,'' Laurel Madden said.

The photo had made its way back along the table, and she was paper-clipping it into a manila folder, her hand trembling a little, Dan noted. Was she nervous? Anxious to prove herself? But then, something else flashed through his mind—lose a child, lose your heart—and it suddenly occurred to him that Laurel Madden might not be the best agent to work a case like this.

As if reading his mind and his doubts, she leaned back in her chair and turned emerald-hard, pure-business eyes on him. ''Serial molesters who prey on very young children tend not to be overly choosy about gender.''

''Do we know for sure we're dealing with a sexual predator, Laurel?'' Alice Wentzl asked. An unflappable sixteen-year veteran, she represented the press office. Like Madden, she was a recent transfer from headquarters.

''The autopsy on the Morales baby should give us a better idea,'' Madden said, ''unless fluid evidence was washed away by the aqueduct. The bag wasn't watertight. The suspect might have counted on that to help cover his tracks, which would make him both intelligent and organized."

"Finding one of the victims dead kind of puts paid to the baby-market theory, though, doesn't it?"

"Probably," Madden agreed.

"Have we definitely ruled out the parents as suspects on the first two cases?" Dan asked. Nine out of ten child-murder cases involved a parent, so it was always the obvious place to start an investigation.

"Them, the grandparents, baby-sitters, pretty much everyone who had easy access to those babies," Paterson said. "Their alibis all checked out, and they're about as devastated and angry as you'd expect people to be who'd had a child stolen. We're still looking into the Goodsells."

"The father was away in Chicago on business, and the mother was under heavy sedation by the time we spoke to her last night," Dan told the others. He'd been working late when the call came about the mall kidnapping, so he'd run down to Orange County with Paterson to scope out the situation. They hadn't been able to exchange more than a few words with the baby's distraught mother. ''Did Mr. Goodsell finally get in, Oz?''

''Arrived at John Wayne Airport a little after midnight. One of our people met him. I've contacted the Chicago field office, asked them to confirm he was actually out there for the past three days like he said he was.''

''Good. Let's make sure the marriage is solid and nobody's playing child-custody games here.''

''That's an angle we're checking out today,'' Paterson said. ''I've also got people heading back down there as we speak to reinterview witnesses from the mall. Meantime, Quinn and I are going to go over the security videos again.''

John Quinn, an evidence technician, nodded from his perch at the end of the table.

''We've done polygraph tests on the Jeffersons and on Victor Morales's parents,'' Younger added. ''No sign of deception in their responses. I'm heading out in a while to see if the Goodsells will consent to be fluttered.''

A derisive noise came from the end of the table and all eyes shot Madden's way once more. ''You've got a problem, Agent Madden?'' Dan asked.

''With polygraph results? No more than with a Ouija board.''

Younger bristled. "Some people would say the same about that profiling mumbo jumbo."

Madden shrugged. "It's an art and an investigative tool. We don't make claims of scientific infallibility. You, on the other hand, want people to believe that machine can't be beat. That's bunk."

"This isn't the place to debate methodology. We'll go with everything we've got," Dan said abruptly. In proposing Agent Madden's transfer, Personnel had briefed Dan on her history. They'd asked him to give her the benefit of the doubt, and he had. He hoped he wasn't going to regret it.

"Speaking of which," Paterson said, "we've had a couple of psychics call in and offer their services."

Dan rolled his eyes. "Oh, joy."

"Some investigators swear by 'em."

"Yeah, so I see on the psychic-hot-line infomercials." He sighed. "Tell them politely we'll be happy to hear whatever they're picking up through the ether and give it due consideration."

"Roger."

Dan turned back to Madden. "Assuming there's only one snatcher here, are you getting anywhere on a profile?"

"Until the Morales boy's body turned up yesterday, I didn't have a whole lot to go on beyond the crime sites. I do think we're dealing with only one UNSUB, but the fact that these crime scenes are so scattered puts a wrinkle in the profile."

"In what way?" Wentzl asked.

"Serial offenders usually start committing crimes close to home. As far as we know, the Jefferson baby was the first TOTNAP abduction, but he was taken at Universal Studios. I've checked our own and the LAPD and county databases for pedophiles or molesters who might have been reported operating there or in surrounding neighborhoods, but nothing much turned up. Of course, a theme park like Universal attracts people from all over the country, so our guy could have dropped in from anywhere."

"Then the second victim, the Morales baby, disappeared in Lancaster," Dan noted. "That's what? Sixty miles away? Any chance that's our guy's real home base?"

"Maybe," Madden said. "It's a much smaller population profile, so theoretically, any previous offenses of a similar or related nature should jump out at us. I've been wading through reports of incidents involving children out there. So far, though, I've come up with zip."

''Then, last night, our guy, if it is the same guy, moves south to Orange County to nab the Goodsell baby.''

''It's like he's jumping around just to keep us off guard,'' Paterson said.

''Which tends to reconfirm my suspicion that he's highly intelligent and organized,'' Madden said. ''Maybe even a police buff—someone who knows about different police jurisdictions and is deliberately moving between them to keep us off base. We've been feeding that possibility into Rapid Start system. Maybe this isn't the first time he's played this game.''

''Okay, good,'' Dan said. ''Anything else?''

''Well, all three babies were spirited away from crowded locations.''

Dan nodded. The Jefferson baby's parents had been at an outdoor concession stand at Universal Studios, buying lunch, while little Byron slept in his stroller at a nearby table area, his six- and ten-year-old brothers watching over him. The Morales boy had been left in his car seat for a few minutes in a strip-mall parking lot while his mother ran to an ATM. A security camera had confirmed her visit to the bank machine, but the car itself had been out of the camera's visual range.

''I think our UNSUB is an opportunist,'' Madden went on. ''I doubt very much that he knows his victims or selects them very far in advance. He'd have had no way of knowing that the Morales baby would be left in the car while his mother ran to the ATM that morning, any more than he could have predicted that the Jeffersons' oldest boy would have had to chase down the middle kid, leaving the baby alone for a minute. So our guy probably lurks in crowded places, waiting and watching for an unattended baby, then makes his grab.''

''Sounds like a thrill junkie,'' Paterson said. ''Nerves of steel.''

''Yeah, real big hero,'' Alice Wentzl said, ''targeting young mothers and their babies. More likely some young punk skinhead, trying to make himself feel like a tough guy.''

''No, I don't think so,'' Madden said. ''As I said, he's intelligent and organized, plans his getaway carefully, despite the apparently random nature of the snatches.''

''Just the same, he's got to be psycho.''

''Definitely not a well-balanced individual,'' Madden agreed, ''but I'm thinking we're looking for someone in his mid-twenties, minimum, to have developed this level of shrewdness and, for whatever psychosis he's suffering from, to have reached such an advanced state. He might even be a little older, although obviously, he has to be fit enough to move fast once he selects his target at these busy sites.''

''What about his choice of victims?'' Dan asked.

''I've been focusing on common denominators there.''

''Byron Jefferson is black. That's a problem, no?''

''Yes, it is. Even more bothersome than the fact that the first two victims were boys and the third was a girl. Cross-racial preying is rare.''

''We're not talking crazies like the KKK or Aryan Nations.''

''Doubt it. Not their M.O. at all. Racially motivated killers generally go after bigger targets. Look at the Atlanta child murders. The African-American community was convinced a racist fanatic was stalking their neighborhoods.''

Dan nodded. The killer had turned out to be Wayne Williams, an African-American—which, in retrospect, made sense, since a white guy wandering around all-black neighborhoods looking for victims would stand out like a sore thumb.

''But you're convinced the Jefferson kidnapper is the same guy as in the Morales and Goodsell cases? Why?''

"I'm thinking our guy makes an effort to blend," Madden said. "That teenage witness in the Morales case said he thought he'd seen a dark-haired man with a mustache carrying off little Victor. This was at an Inland Empire shopping center, remember, a working-class neighborhood with a large Hispanic population."

The witness had also said the man he saw was wearing a ball cap, Dan recalled, and could have been Anglo or Latino. He hadn't been close enough to be certain. "So the guy camouflages himself. You think he dyed his skin when he snatched the Jefferson boy?"

Madden opened the file marked Jefferson, Byron and withdrew the little boy's picture. "Maybe he didn't have to," she said, passing it along the table. "Byron's quite light-skinned. If the UNSUB was tanned, dark-haired, maybe wearing sunglasses and a baseball cap, he might have passed unnoticed through that noisy mob—with a baby who, don't forget, was covered up and asleep in his stroller."

Dan turned to the squad leader. "There were twelve thousand people at Universal Studios that day. Not one witness has come forward?"

Paterson shook his head. "And, of course, the security system in the picnic area would be on the fritz. Murphy's Law."

''Or not,'' Dan mused. ''Anybody look into the possibility the camera had been tampered with? If our guy's as clever as Agent Madden here suggests—''

''We're checking out park personnel,'' Paterson said. ''So far, it's a wash, but we could still find something there. Obviously, the guy would have had to know the layout of the park to have made such a quick getaway.''

''So we're talking someone who works there, or someone who does his homework very, very well,'' Alice Wentzl said.

''Right,'' Dan said. ''Okay, people, let's follow up closely on the Goodsell case while the trail is fresh. The longer she's missing, the less chance she'll show up alive. Agent Madden, you stay on the San Bernardino coroner's office about that autopsy on the Morales baby. If we know how he died, we're that much further ahead on establishing method and motive.''

She nodded.

''I'm going to need a press line,'' Wentzl said.

''It might be better to hold off until we have a little more information to offer.''

''I've got yellow slips a foot deep covering my desk, Dan. And in case you haven't noticed, TV crews have started staking out the front of this building.''

"They have?" Dan rolled his chair back to the window and craned his neck to see past the building's entrance arcade. He counted three satellite vans in the parking lot and at least half a dozen people milling about on the front sidewalk. He slumped back down. "Great. Just bloody great."

"We need to think about making a statement," Wentzl told him.

"The Goodsell baby's photo was released last night," Dan said. "That's the most important thing in case someone spotted her with the kidnapper. Let's make sure it and a description of what she was wearing are blanketed across the state—and the country, for that matter. The longer she's missing, the less likely our chances of finding her. Let's get all the help we can up front."

"The story's already getting national coverage," Wentzl said, pressing her point. "Every parent in the state's terrified their baby's next. That makes for a lot of angry sound bites. I know we're giving the case top priority, but that point needs to be made absolutely obvious."

He sighed. "All right. Draft me a press line and bring it to my office. The rest of you," he added, "let's blanket the territory and nail this bastard."

5

Heart pounding in her ears, poised to bolt, Claire kept a wary watch on the sinister character behind the wheel of the battered black sedan.

She was trapped between it and a gray cinder-block wall that ran the full-length of a street unbroken by a friendly doorway or an alley refuge. Through the car's open passenger door, the driver stared back at her, unsmiling mouth and anthracite eyes demanding she submit to the inevitable.

I don't think so, fella.

At the same time, she asked herself how she'd come to this pretty pickle. When Ivankov had agreed to an interview, she'd taken the precaution of insisting on a daylight meeting in a visible location. For added insurance, she'd given Serge Scolari the details of the rendezvous and had also coaxed the cabdriver with promises of an outsize tip if he'd wait.

But then, the weather had kept witnesses out of

the streets; the cabbie had been sufficiently intimidated to abandon his post, tipless, and Ivankov's disdain had shifted to anger with the fluid capriciousness only a true sociopath can muster. By the time Scolari figured out she was missing, Claire realized, she could be eel food in Lower Bay. So much for insurance.

She sized up the driver, estimating her chances in a struggle, *mano a mano.* It was hard to guess the guy's height, sitting behind the wheel, but as goons went, he didn't look overly brawny inside that padded jacket. Still, it was a sure bet he was bigger than she was—most everyone past puberty was—and those bare hands of his were big and powerful-looking.

But she wasn't helpless, either, Claire reminded herself. She hadn't been raised in a cop's family without acquiring some defensive skills, and five years of living in New York had only reinforced those early lessons Sean Gillespie had drilled into his daughters. Her mind tipped into overdrive, racing to recall the basic precepts of what her dad had called *Gillespie's Guide to Getting Out in One Piece.*

"Avoid tight spaces" was high on the list, she recalled. That seemed to preclude getting into the car.

''When in doubt, run like hell first, ask questions later.'' Nice in theory, but not too feasible in this case. She couldn't outrun a car at the best of times, much less under these icy conditions.

''Scream bloody murder.'' Right. A lot of good that would do. The street was deserted, with nary a shop or gas station in sight, only dingy brick warehouses with padlocked doors. A graffiti-scrawled phone booth with one cracked window leaned drunkenly at the next corner, but even if she could reach it—and the thing was working—she'd never get the 911 punched in before he was on her.

''Stay calm, use your head, distract your attacker, discourage his interest.'' But how? Claire wondered. What *was* his interest—and who was he? He knew her name and looked vaguely familiar, with those piercing black eyes and that close-clipped, peppered hair. Was this the shadow she'd sensed trailing her ever since Michael's murder? One of the enforcers who skulked in the *pakhan's* bloody wake? He definitely had no Russian accent, but still…

''Did Ivankov send you after me?'' she asked.

His scowl deepened, and panic clamped onto Claire's heart as his right hand slipped inside the army-surplus jacket.

Jesus, Mary and Joseph, he's going to shoot me down right here, like a dog in the street!

Crouching lower, she backed away from the car and pressed herself, terrified, against the gritty cinder-block wall. But as the bulge of his hand inside the jacket closed on the gun, something in Claire's brain disengaged with an almost audible click, and a warm tide of fatalism washed over her. At least the ache would stop, she thought wearily, watching now with sharpened but detached slo-mo perception as his hand inched out of the jacket.

She debated idly if it would be prudent to cross herself. Except for weddings and funerals, she hadn't been inside a church in years; had lost both faith and interest about the time of her father's senseless death. But if Sister Paul Ignatius, the scourge of her youth, turned out to be right, after all, she'd check out here with a hefty debt of unconfessed guilt on her tab and a one-way ticket to the inferno. Too bad Rome had decided to cancel purgatory, that convenient halfway house for middling sinners and doubting Thomases.

The goon's hand reappeared, but instead of a gun, it held a leather folder, which he flipped open to reveal a familiar brass shield and photo-ID card. Michael had had one just like it.

Claire's weary resignation was swept away on a wave of irritation. ''Oh, for the love of—! You're FBI?''

''Special Agent Doucet,'' he said, glancing around. ''Now, would you *please* get in the car before somebody spots us?''

New York might be the city that never sleeps, but it seemed to be skidding to a halt that Saturday. Doucet made slow progress on Brooklyn's sleet-slickened roads, heading, near as Claire could tell, toward Battery Tunnel and back into Manhattan. The streets were eerily quiet, and a soporific gray stillness hung in the air. Inside the old beater, only the swish of the wiper blades and the hum of the overworked heater fan broke a silence that was near complete.

Claire examined the car's frayed upholstery, so grimy it was difficult to tell what color it might originally have been. Fast-food wrappers cluttered the floor, emitting a distinctly greasy odor, and she had to keep pushing them aside with the toe of her boot as they tumbled and rolled over her feet. A hole yawned from the center of the cracked vinyl dashboard, dripping wires from where the car radio had evidently been boosted. No police band radios, either, she noted.

"Has the Bureau fallen on hard times, or are you working undercover?"

Doucet said nothing. Claire sighed. He'd brushed off every attempt at conversation since the moment she'd gotten into the car. His big, rawboned hands gripped the steering wheel tightly at the ten- and two-o'clock positions as he negotiated the slick roads, veering cautiously around a couple of fender benders. From time to time, his clenched, stubbled jaw muscles flicked nervously.

Prairie-born and -bred herself, Claire was never fazed by winter storms. But New Yorkers, she'd noticed, never seemed to grasp the required driving technique—not that this Doucet character struck her as the Big Apple type. "Where were you raised?"

He shot her a startled look, then fixed his frown on the road once more. "Louisiana."

She snorted. "Figures."

"Why?"

"No reason."

The frown deepened, but he fell back into a silence broken only by the *fwap-fwap* of the wiper blades smearing ice and muck across a windshield that the car's defroster seemed incapable of clearing. From time to time, Doucet unlocked one hand from the wheel just long enough to give the brume inside the glass a hasty swipe. The car slipped and slid on the frozen pavement, but he wasn't driving fast enough, Claire decided, to risk a serious accident. The air grew closer by the minute, until she became so antsy she thought she'd scream.

She ventured another stab at conversation instead. "Were you the one who scared off my taxi?"

"Nope. Think he just didn't like the neighborhood."

Aha! Garbo talks! Multisyllables, too.

"And what about you? Were you spying on Ivankov or on me?"

"What were you doing there?"

"I asked you first."

He shook his head grimly. "You think this is a game? It's not, you know. You want to watch your step."

"Is that a threat?"

"What's your relationship with Ivankov?"

"Relationship? With that thug? You've got to be kidding."

"So what were you doing there?"

She shrugged. "Asking questions."

"About what?"

"Michael Kazarian."

That got a reaction. Doucet slammed on the brakes, and the car fishtailed, narrowly avoiding an oncoming UPS truck that seemed to have appeared out of nowhere. The big brown van swerved, then sailed by them, horn blaring. The car continued to careen. Claire grabbed the armrest on the door, but it came off in her hand, and sideways momentum sent her skidding across the bench seat into Doucet's musty parka. His left hand reached across his right arm to hold her off, awkwardly grabbing a fistful of her coat while his other hand wrestled with the steering wheel. They lurched and tumbled as the tires bounced against the curb, then rebounded. The car skidded sideways for a few more feet. Finally, with one last shudder, it shimmied to a stop.

Claire gave him a mighty shove to push herself upright, determined to reestablish both her equilibrium and her dignity. "You idiot! Are you trying to get us killed? Why did you hit the brakes like that?"

He wrenched off the ignition and pivoted to face her, his own expression equally furious. "You discussed Agent Kazarian with a major organized crime figure? Are you out of your mind?"

"Oh, for the love of—! How dumb do I seem

to you? Of course I didn't use his real name! I asked Ivankov about Misha Kurelek, Michael's alter ego. It's not like you people are doing much to find his killers,'' she added angrily.

''Kazarian, Kurelek—how do you even *know* any of this?''

''I knew Michael.''

''What do you mean, you knew him? How?''

Claire hesitated—what to say?

That I started out as Michael's headache, and ended up his port in the storm? That he spent the last night of his life in my bed?

But as she struggled to decide how much to tell this Doucet, Claire experienced a vision, like a blurry camera shot suddenly pulled into sharp focus. In her mind's eye an image appeared of Doucet comforting a beautiful, grieving woman. *Now* she remembered where she'd seen him before.

''You were at Michael's funeral,'' she said.

For the first time since he'd stopped her in the street, Doucet seemed unsure of himself. ''You were there?''

''At the back of the church. After Michael died, I contacted Fred Baker in the Bureau's New York field office. There didn't seem to be much point in playing dumb about the undercover operation anymore. I'd dealt with Baker on other organized crime stories I'd done and I figured he'd know what was happening about the funeral. He was the one who told me about the service. I saw you there, with..." Claire hesitated once more.

"With Laurel, Michael's wife."

She nodded slowly, recalling how uncomfortable she'd felt, slipping into the pew at the back of the church, grieving alone for Michael among his family and friends, all strangers to her—most of them FBI agents, by the clean-cut, regulated look of them. Recalled, too, her stunned reaction when the priest had reached out a hand to the shoulder of a woman in the front row, exuding sympathy for a widow Claire hadn't even known existed. At that moment, a cavern had opened around her, and she'd slipped into the black maw of pain and confusion that had overwhelmed her ever since.

"Was Michael...was he a friend of yours?" she asked.

Doucet nodded. "We went through the academy together. What about you? How did you know him?"

Claire retreated to the corner formed by the seat and the door. Her cheeks, warm now with self-consciousness, puffed up as she exhaled slowly. "I'm a journalist. I was working on a *Newsworld* piece on recent developments on the organized crime front. My dad was a cop, so the beat comes naturally to me,'' she added, stalling. It was something she often found worthwhile explaining to her law enforcement sources. Most of them saw journalists as muckraking scum, but she, at least, was muckraking scum with a pedigree. It helped when they knew where her natural sympathies lay.

Doucet nodded again; obviously he'd already checked her out. Why was she not surprised?

''Anyway, I'd put together, piece by piece, a fairly complete organization chart for the Russian mob down here, and come to the conclusion that Ivan Ivankov was the *capo de tutti capi,* or at least the Russian equivalent. I was hanging around Brooklyn, asking questions, trying to see what I could find out about him, when I stopped into this Russian café in Brighton Beach one day last March. Who should I see there but Ivankov himself, having lunch with a bunch of his cronies—one of whom I recognized as Michael Kazarian.''

''You already knew him?''

''Slightly. I met him a couple of years ago at Hogan's Alley.''

Doucet frowned. ''What were you doing in Hogan's Alley?'' It was a mock town site on the grounds of the FBI academy in Quantico, Virginia, used to train agents in the arts of surveillance, SWAT ops and arrests.

"I was a guest participant in a recruit training exercise, something the Office of Public Affairs set up to try to improve the Bureau's image after the schmozzles at Waco and Ruby Ridge. I was doing a feature for *Newsworld* on how the Bureau trains its junior G-men. Michael was head of the SWAT training unit at the time."

Doucet nodded once more.

"They wouldn't let us use his picture for the story, though. Afterward, I realized it was because he was on the undercover reserve list. So that's how we first met. I didn't let on I knew him that day in Brighton Beach, though."

"Did he recognize you?"

"Apparently so. A few days later, he showed up at my apartment in Chelsea, and that's when we struck the deal."

"Deal?"

Claire shrugged. "It didn't take a rocket scientist to figure out what he was doing there, and I certainly didn't want to get in the way of a murderous creep like Ivankov being put out of commission. So I said I'd back off my story for a while if Michael would keep me up to date on the investigation and give me an exclusive once it wrapped.''

''He agreed to that?''

''He wasn't happy about it, but I guess he put it to the Bureau brass and they agreed. After that, we met from time to time. More frequently, near the end.'' Claire frowned. ''But you should already know all this.''

''No.''

''Nobody briefed you on our deal?''

''No, because nobody in the Bureau ever authorized such a deal. What's more, I don't believe a word of it. I knew Mike Kazarian, Ms. Gillespie, and he would never have discussed an undercover operation with an outsider—especially a reporter. He had absolutely no use for the press. So, how about you start again? And this time, I think you should give serious consideration to telling me the truth about what went down here.''

In the clammy front seat of that rundown Pontiac, which might have been new in the era of disco and polyester leisure suits, Special Agent Doucet grilled Claire with a laserlike focus that belied his grungy dress and eccentric transport. But eventually, he eased back a little, and as he did, faint traces of Cajun drawl began popping up in his speech, like dandelions in a manicured lawn. Claire tried to decide whether he was deliberately feigning this good ol' boy routine to throw her off guard, since the Spanish-inquisitor bit obviously hadn't produced whatever result he was after. If so, she wasn't fooled for a second.

"Now, why don't y'all just start once more? And tell me the truth this time about how you knew Agent Kazarian and why you're still dogging his trail."

She threw up her hands in exasperation. "I told you three times already—our paths crossed accidentally. Call the FBI academy. They'll confirm I was at Hogan's Alley two years ago this past August, and that I met him there. I had no idea he was working undercover when I started looking into the Russian mob here."

"Quite a coincidence, your paths crossing again like that, wouldn't you say?"

"Yes, it was. And frankly, from a professional point of view, it was a big pain in the butt on both sides."

"Why's that?"

"Because I had to put my research on hold, and Agent Kazarian was worried his operation was compromised."

"Rightly so, I expect."

"No, not rightly so at all. I'm a cop's kid, Doucet. I don't necessarily like every law enforcement officer I meet—present company included—but I like racketeers, extortionists and killers even less. I wanted my story, sure, but not at the price of messing up an investigation that might have gotten Ivankov off the streets."

"Very commendable, I'm sure. We'll have to nominate you for citizen of the year."

She ignored the sarcasm. "And I certainly wouldn't have done anything to put Michael in harm's way."

"So you keep saying."

"Yes, I do, and frankly, I don't give a hoot whether you believe me or not."

"But you didn't walk away, did you? Not then, not now. Why is that?" When she said nothing, Doucet's panther gaze narrowed. "You fall in love with him, Claire? Is that it?"

She looked away, and he assumed a sympathetic tone.

"I can understand how it could happen. Y'all don't have to be embarrassed. Mike was a big, good-looking guy. Plenty of women had crushes on him."

"You're disgusting."

"Why does that upset you? Because you

weren't the only one it happened to? Or because he was married?''

''I didn't know he was married.''

''Uh-oh! Led you on, did he? I see.''

''You see what? What are you driving at?''

''Only this—maybe he turned on the charm here. You know, to get you to do what he asked? Back off your own work while he went about his? And then, if you were to find out he was just playing you along—that he was married and all? Well, I think you'd have a perfect right to be upset, wouldn't you?''

Claire reared back. ''What are you saying? That I betrayed him? Told Ivankov he was a fed?''

''Is that what happened? Maybe not on purpose, mind. Maybe it just slipped out. I can understand how it could happen. Anyone would—''

''No!'' Claire cried, fighting the lump in her throat. This was so damned unreasonable. Why was he doing this to her? ''I never even met Ivankov before today. And as for Agent Kazarian being married—''

Come on, girl, pull it off.

''—why would that make any difference to me? We were cooperating on a professional level, nothing more.''

Doucet snorted his disbelief. ''A professional level? Then why these crocodile tears? Way I see it, girl, you're either nursing a broken heart here, or this is cover for a guilty conscience.''

''You go to hell.''

''I've checked you out, you know. You been covering the crime beat for nigh onto twelve years. Interviewed the worst of the worst, from what I hear—rapists, pedophiles, homicidal maniacs. Seen more murder scenes than your average midsize city cop, and listened to some real blood-curdling evidence along the way. But it never gets to you, by all accounts. You just cover each story and move on to the next. So, what I'm wondering is, what's got you so obsessed that you're still hanging around here? It's a mystery, you see.''

''I want to know what happened! Don't you? Don't any of you? My father was murdered, Doucet, and they never found his killers, either. I don't want Michael's death going unpunished.'' Claire drove the heels of her hands into her eyes.

Don't cry in front of him!

She took a slow, deep breath, and when she thought she could muster a firmer voice, added, ''Besides which, I'm not even sure anymore it was Ivankov who had Michael killed.''

Doucet frowned. ''How's that?''

"Ivankov hinted just now that 'Kurelek' was carrying money that day. A lot of money. Money he was supposed to deliver to the *pakhan* himself. Ivankov intimated that it's missing, and that he wants to know as badly as anyone who took him down."

"He said this to you? You can prove it?"

Claire grimaced. "No. I taped the first part of the interview, but then he lost his temper and smashed my machine. That's when he suggested the possibility that somebody else did Michael in and ripped him off in the bargain. Afterward, he pretended he was just speaking hypothetically. But he meant it, Doucet, I know he did. I think Ivankov really is as confused and furious as anyone about the murder, and I think he'd give a lot to get his hands on whoever's responsible."

Agent Doucet said nothing for a very long moment. When he finally did speak, the Cajun-hick routine had vanished, and with it, all pretense at empathy. "You want a piece of advice, Ms. Gillespie?"

"No, but I have a feeling I'm going to get one, anyway."

"Leave this alone. Walk away from it right now, while you still can."

"And if I don't?"

"If you continue to compromise an official investigation, the Bureau will be forced to take legal action against you for obstruction of justice. That's federal time you're looking at. For your own good, do what I'm telling you. Drop this, right here and now, and get on with your life."

6

After winding up his meeting with the TOTNAP team, Dan glanced at his watch, then picked up the phone to call home. As he listened to the ring on the other end of the line, he straightened the framed photographs on his credenza, which the cleaning staff seemed to delight in rearranging every night: Erin's high-school graduation portrait; Julie dressed as Annie Oakley for her last school play; Fiona with both girls on the Santa Monica pier, the photo taken about a year before she died; an older Christmas picture of them all, Dan included, taken when they were still a complete family.

He leaned back in his chair, spinning his wedding band with his left thumb as he stared at the grainy image of Fiona smiling into the sun. Her face was fading in his mind, he'd lately realized, its lively fluidity settling into the static forms of this and other photographs he kept of her. He could hardly recall the sound of her voice, except in quiet moments just before he fell asleep at night, when he sometimes thought he heard an echo of her warm laughter. Her absent touch had left a dull, permanent ache deep inside him.

Dan closed his eyes. ''Please,'' he murmured under his breath, without thinking. He opened his eyes once more. Please what? Give back lost time and words left unsaid? He'd had his chance at happiness. If he'd squandered too much of it, not suspecting how soon it would disappear, he had no one to blame but himself. He'd still had more than most.

On the fourth ring, Erin picked up the phone. In the background, Dan heard loud music, Julie's bubbly giggle and Bubba's goofy, bass-baritone *woofs.* He frowned. ''Are you guys having a wild party there, or what?''

His elder daughter laughed. ''No, we're watching Lexie. Bridget's gone grocery shopping and Chris is on call this morning. Julie's giving Lexie a ride on Bubba.'' On cue, a toddler's high-pitched squeal of delight cut through the background brouhaha.

Dan leaned back in his chair and swiveled it to face the window, propping his feet on the sill.

"You guys be careful. Bubba outweighs her by a good eighty pounds."

"Oh, he's so gentle with her, Dad. He slows right down when she's around. Doesn't even mind when she holds on to his ears."

Dan's frown relaxed to a grin. "Dopey dog."

Bubba and the two-year-old were in the thrall of a mutual love affair that had been going on almost since Alexis was born. The big retriever was so smitten that, if Lexie happened to fall asleep on him while watching "Sesame Street" during one of her frequent visits to the house, Bubba would lie motionless for hours—gazing up with sad, resigned eyes at anyone who passed by, but never abandoning his watch.

Lexie lived with her parents, Chris and Bridget McCabe, in the small apartment over the Spragues' garage. Chris McCabe was an intern at UCLA Medical Center. His wife was the daughter of Sean Gillespie, Dan's former Kansas City police partner—one of five Gillespie girls, in fact. With seven daughters and no sons between them, Dan and Sean had decided something in the department's water supply must be responsible for their apparent inability to pass on a Y chromosome.

The young couple had just learned Bridget was

pregnant when they'd arrived in L.A. for Chris to start med school—not brilliant timing, they'd admitted sheepishly. Dan had fixed up the empty apartment and rented it to them for next to nothing—a small enough gesture, he felt, to honor the memory of a partner who'd watched his back and seen him safely through more than a few tight spots in the years they rode together. Since Fiona's death, Dan had the eerie feeling Sean Gillespie's spirit was still hovering nearby, watching his vulnerable zone and arranging for the McCabes to be close at hand for his girls during the long hours the job kept him away from home.

"You working all day today?" Erin asked.

"Probably a few more hours."

"That Southland Snatcher thing?"

"Yeah."

"I heard they found one of the babies."

He sighed. "Yes, they did. It's a pretty sad case."

In general, he resisted taking the ugliness home, or worrying his family with details of intractable investigations, but Erin was talking about majoring in criminology and heading for law or police work—maybe even a career in the Bureau. The family disease, Dan thought resignedly. His father had been a cop, too. Julie, however, was set on a career in show business. He wasn't sure which daughter's ambition worried him more.

"What time are you and Matt leaving for the hockey game?" he asked.

"He's picking me up at five-thirty. We're going to grab something to eat beforehand."

"What about Julie? Who's she going to the movies with?"

"Julie," Erin called. "Dad wants a license-plate number to run on that biker you're seeing tonight."

Dan heard his younger daughter's groan in the background. "Tell him not to sweat it," she called back. "Spike's parole officer says he's gotta be back at the halfway house by midnight, so we won't be late."

"Wise guys," Dan grumbled.

"She's going with Chrissy and Sharon, Dad." Erin laughed.

He heard Julie's mischievous voice once more. "Tell him Mrs. Tate's going to come by for me at five!"

Dan grimaced. Chrissy Tate's parents were divorced, and no matter how much he insisted he was capable of managing his own social life, Julie and her giggly friends seemed determined to play matchmaker between him and the girl's mother—*their* idea, not the mother's, he was sure.

"I can take them home afterward," he told Erin, ignoring the hint. "Just let me know where and when."

"I'll tell her."

"I have to go now, but I'll check in with you later, okay?"

"We'll be here. Bye, Dad. Love you."

"I love you, too, honey."

Dan dropped his feet back to the floor and swiveled his chair around to hang up the phone. But then, startled, he dropped the receiver. It clattered into the cradle.

Laurel Madden was standing in his open doorway, a cool, vaguely bemused expression on her face.

"Sorry," Dan said, flustered. "Didn't see you there. I was just calling home. I left before anyone was awake this morning. What's up?" he added briskly. Why was he explaining himself to her?

"The coroner's report on the Morales baby just came in."

"They made a firm ID?" After meeting the family yesterday, Dan had held out a vague, irrational hope that some mistake had been made, and that the tiny, moldering corpse from the bag in the aqueduct wouldn't be their missing infant. But, of course, the clothing had been a match, and if it wasn't little Victor Morales, then it only meant tragedy for another family.

"They managed to lift a partial footprint," Madden said. "It matched the Morales baby's neonatal record."

"Was he drowned?"

She shook her head. "No water in the lungs. The baby was dead before he was put in the aqueduct."

"Cause of death?"

"Medical examiner's calling it suffocation."

"He certain?"

She nodded, consulting her notes. "Victim presented broken capillaries on the conjunctiva and thymus. That's an indicator of oxygen deprivation..." Her voice trailed off, and she looked up with an odd expression on her face, like a deer caught in headlights.

As her gaze dropped again to the sheaf in her hand, Dan flashed on a case he'd handled a few years earlier in Florida, where a few broken capillaries had been the only postmortem finding in another baby's death—a symptom that often presented in both SIDS and suffocation deaths. In the Florida case, the cause of death was ruled Sudden

Infant Death Syndrome until the nanny was discovered to have lost another child to SIDS a couple of years earlier. After a failed polygraph, the unstable baby-sitter had confessed to smothering the two infants. Since then, a forensic pall had fallen over many SIDS diagnoses—a trap that had apparently ensnared even Agent Madden and her husband when their own baby died two years ago. What must it be like, Dan wondered, to endure suspicious whispers on top of the insufferable pain of a child's loss?

"Ligature marks?" he asked, anxious to help her out here.

Madden looked up, head shaking. "No, it looks like the child was suffocated in the same plastic bag in which the body was found. There was a torn fragment of it clenched in his fist, as though he'd struggled a little before losing consciousness. They found no other evidence of trauma. None of sexual abuse, either."

"What about time of death?"

Whatever momentary unease he'd perceived had passed, and Madden was detached and businesslike once more. "Hard to be certain, under the circumstances, but given the level of decomposition, prevailing water temperature and environmental conditions, the M.E. figured it at twelve to fourteen days ago, give or take.''

''Which means there's a good chance he was killed right after the kidnapping. Definitely eliminates the baby-market theory, doesn't it?'' Dan leaned back in his chair and rubbed his face wearily. ''So what does it mean? Guy steals babies, smothers, then dumps them? Why? Does that fit any serial-offender profile you've ever seen?''

Madden indicated a chair. ''May I sit down?''

''Yes, go ahead—sorry.'' Had it been anyone else, Dan realized, he would have invited them in right off the bat, but Madden's demeanor was like razor wire strung around her. It neither invited nor appeared to welcome easy approaches.

She sat down, her silk blouse settling into shimmering folds as she propped her elbows on the chair's arms and crossed her tan-trousered legs. When the air stirred between them, Dan was conscious of its utter neutrality. If she was wearing perfume, it was too subtle to be noticed. Her only jewelry was a pair of tiny gold earrings. Everything about her was deliberately understated, he realized, as if to avoid drawing attention to herself. Fat chance. He noticed something else: she was a nail-biter, a curious thing in someone so self-contained and seemingly self-assured. Perhaps she wasn't as confident as she seemed. For a naturally shy person, traffic-stopping looks might be more curse than blessing. Maybe that was her problem.

"I've been meaning to ask how you're getting on here," he said.

"Why? Is there a problem?"

"No, no problem. I just wondered if you'd gotten oriented, found a place to live, that sort of thing."

"I bought a condo in Brentwood."

"Close by. Smart." And expensive, Dan thought. With west end L.A. real estate out of the price range of any government employee without private resources, most of his people lived in the distant suburbs. His own place was in neighboring Santa Monica, but only because he and Fiona had inherited the house from her parents when they'd retired to Palm Springs. Fiona's desire to be near them in their final years had been the main reason Dan had taken this job—only it had turned out to be *her* final years, instead.

"I think Alice Wentzl rented an apartment nearby, too—in Westwood, wasn't it?" he asked. The media rep had transferred in from headquarters only a few months ahead of Madden, and Dan had the impression they'd dealt with one another back there.

Madden had been examining the framed letters of commendation on his wall, but she turned back to him now and shrugged. "I don't know."

"Oh. Well, I think that's where she is. And the office? You've got the lay of the land, more or less?"

She nodded.

"I hear you've met some of the other squad leaders."

"Have there been complaints?"

"Complaints? No, not that I'm aware of."

"Rumblings, then."

"Should there be?"

Madden exhaled sharply. "Look, sir, I'm not stupid. I'm sure you know about the allegations made against me back at headquarters." Dan must have flinched, because she grimaced. "Of course—they'd have had to warn you, wouldn't they?" She leaned farther back in the chair. "I know about the names people call me behind my back, too, you know. Which one's the favorite these days? The Ice Queen? Mommie Dearest? The Black Widow, maybe? That one was very popular about the time I left Quantico."

Dan felt an uneasy twinge, thinking of Doug

Zellerbach's "Blue Angel" crack earlier. Sometimes the Bureau felt too much like a small town, he thought wearily. No need to encourage paranoia, however. "Aren't you being a little defensive? Maybe you should give this place a chance."

"Is the place prepared to give *me* a chance?"

"I am."

Madden's head dropped and she shuffled the pages in her hand once more, as Dan watched her uneasily. She was far too volatile for his liking—but then, she'd been through a lot, he reminded himself, starting with the Beltway Ripper and going downhill from there.

A couple of years back, over a six-month period, an elusive psycho with a knife and a grudge had murdered four federal employees in the D.C. area. In the course of an all-out FBI manhunt, the telegenic Agent Madden had caught both the media's and the Ripper's attention. Driving home from Quantico late one evening, she almost became his fifth victim, but her academy training prevailed. Before the night was over, the Ripper was dead, Madden was injured but alive, and the press and made-for-TV movies were left to scream the sensational details.

More recently, events from her personal life

had put her back in the spotlight: the death of her infant son and subsequent battle with an over-eager pathologist out to make a name for himself. Talk of marital strife. Then, more suspicion when her husband, also a federal agent, was cut down in his prime. Each new development had fed a rumor mill hungry for salacious gossip—and maybe too eager, Dan suspected, to condemn an attractive, competent female agent who had looked, up until then, to be on a promotional fast track.

Madden raised her head, and her green eyes bore through him once more. ''We were discussing the Snatcher.''

''Right. I was wondering what you think about his psychological makeup.''

''I'm still trying to get a fix on whether we're dealing with a spree or serial killer here,'' she said. ''It's difficult to tell. Serial killers tend to act out of some bizarre fantasy, but so far, it's not clear that these are the kind of ritualized crimes that fit that mold. Spree killers, on the other hand, generally act out of rage, after some kind of stressor pushes them beyond their personal Rubicon. But without knowing a little more about why our guy's choosing these particular targets, it's hard to say which model he fits. I will say this, though—it takes a very particular set of psychological misfirings for someone to go after children, especially ones as young as this.''

''Is there any—'' The phone pealed, and Dan shot it an irritated glance. On the second ring, he held up a forefinger and lifted the receiver. ''Sprague.''

''This is Agent Soroka, the duty officer, sir. I've got a call here from a Lieutenant Delgado of the Orange County Sheriff's Department. He wants to talk to somebody about TOTNAP.''

''Put him through.'' The line clicked. ''Lieutenant Delgado? This is Dan Sprague.''

''Yes, sir. I understand you're working the missing-baby case?''

''I head up criminal investigations here. What can I do for you?''

''We had a call-out to the county fairgrounds about twenty minutes ago that I thought you'd better know about. Looks like we've got another kidnapping on our hands. It's another baby.''

7

Agent Doucet dumped Claire unceremoniously at the DeKalb Avenue subway station—still in Brooklyn, unfortunately—with a blunt admonition to forget Kazarian, Ivankov and anything to do with the Brighton Beach mob. "This is the last warning you'll get. The next time I come after you, it'll be with a warrant for your arrest."

On that final note, tires spinning, kicking up a mucky mess, the car skidded away. Claire had to leap aside to avoid being spattered. Fuming, she watched until it had disappeared, then turned toward the subway entrance and trudged down the concrete steps to the platform, sidestepping a sprawled wino doing a gargled, off-key performance of "Stranger in Paradise." The least Doucet could have done was drive her back into the city, she fumed. On the other hand, his winter driving skills being what they were, the subway was probably a safer bet.

When the train came, she sank into a corner seat, trembling, now that it was over, at his skepticism and threats, and at the emotions the whole episode had stirred up. But underneath the churning in her mind, a realization dawned. Doucet had pulled a classic cop maneuver, demanding information but answering none of her own questions. Did he know about the allegation that Michael was carrying money that last day? About Ivankov's claim the money had been stolen? That the *pakhan,* if he were to be believed, had half a million reasons of his own to find the killer?

So many unanswered questions. But was Doucet right? Was she obsessed? Serge Scolari had suggested much the same. What if there was no rational explanation for Michael's death? What if what happened to him was nothing more than a random act of violence, perpetrated in a rough area by some petty thug who happened upon Michael and the cash he was allegedly carrying? Claire sighed wearily. Could she live with another meaningless death of someone she deeply cared about?

She studied the closed, frowning faces around her, a dozen or so desultory Saturday commuters hunched in varying degrees of personal gloom under garish, graffiti-resistant ads for bank loans, tropical vacations and TV sitcoms. In a city this size, any one of them could become the next victim of haphazard violence.

How was it that she'd ended up here? she asked herself yet again. Moving to New York had been Alan's idea, not hers, just as all the major decisions of their marriage had flowed from his needs and desires, leaving her in the perennial position of playing catch-up.

She'd been a junior police-beat reporter at the *Kansas City Star* when she'd met Alan Toole, freelance theater critic and book reviewer. ''Just a part-time gig until I finish my play and get together the financial backing I need to produce it.'' Lean, intense, bearded and handsome, he was alternately cocky and massively insecure. After much prodding on her part, he finally showed Claire a draft of his unfinished play. She was blown away. She was a decent wordsmith herself, but this went far beyond mere competence. Visions of Eugene O'Neill and Thornton Wilder danced in her head as she found herself falling for the brilliant young dramatist who agonized over every line and withdrew into deep depression at the mildest critique. All he needed was someone to believe in him, she decided.

And, oh, how she believed! Alan fairly

bloomed in her unstinting praise and encouragement. When they married a few months later, Claire encouraged him to take a year off and devote himself full-time to finishing the play. Alan was eager to take her up on the offer, but decided Kansas wasn't the place to develop the literary connections he needed. The University of Iowa's world-renowned writers' program had launched several prominent American men of letters; that was where he belonged. So Claire quit her job at the *Star* and found another stringing for Associated Press in Iowa City, supporting him through what turned into an extended stay at the writers' workshop—a period that yielded a second unfinished play, an incomplete master's thesis and a brief affair between Alan and a ditsy, wanna-be actress, whose signature silver bracelet Claire found caught in their mattress pad when she returned from covering a lengthy murder trial in Des Moines.

Tunnel lights swam past the subway-car window as she recalled her sense of devastation at that first infidelity. At that point, though, she'd still loved him enough to let herself be convinced by Alan's pleas of creative stress—and to feel guilty when he'd reproached her for her absence during the murder trial. ''She was nothing. It's you I need, babe, but you weren't here for me,'' he'd added, sulking.

The subway car rocked and swayed as it hurtled under the East River, metal wheels kicking up acrid odors and shrieking in protest at each curve in the rail. Claire stared out at cavernous black walls, wondering at his slick ability to turn a situation on its head so that she always ended up feeling like the guilty party. Wondering, too, at her own capacity for martyrdom. Where had that come from? Instead of walking away as she should have if she'd had any brains or self-respect at all, she'd stuck it out. Alan got a job teaching English at a local community college, and for a few months, they seemed almost happy. But then, he developed a restless certainty that only New York offered the proper milieu to foster a talent such as his.

''What about a child?'' Claire had argued. ''We agreed we were ready, Alan. You want to raise a child in New York?''

''For God's sake, you're only twenty-nine! I just turned thirty. There's plenty of time for kids. This is my career, my *life* we're talking about. I'd think you'd be a little more supportive.''

She'd resisted until his sulking got to be too much to bear, then given in.

Should have gotten out then and there, you idiot, before he could pull the same stunt again. And again. Should've realized he wanted groupies, not an adult relationship. Should've bolted before Nicky showed up and Alan fixed his sights on her.

Still, at the thought of Alan and her youngest sister, Claire couldn't resist a smile. There was a certain sweet irony to his fate, after all. Unlike the others, Nicky really did seem to have captured Alan's heart. Had he discovered yet the steely will that lay beneath her wide-eyed winsomeness? That she was a flower, not a gardener—and a fairly high-maintenance flower at that?

Nicky's refusal to stay in New York had forced Alan to choose. In the end, after waffling for weeks, he'd followed her back to Kansas. Or maybe it was just a convenient out for him, Claire thought, since the theater community here had largely ignored him, anyway. Now he was teaching again, Nicky was expecting his child, while Claire, the reluctant transplant, was still here—thriving, if outward appearances were to be believed. After all, she had a stimulating career, a couple of national press awards and good friends. So what if it wasn't exactly the life she'd planned? Whatever those dreams once might have been, they'd long since been torpedoed and lay sunk now beyond an unreachable horizon.

Nestling deeper into the corner of the seat, resting her aching head against the cool window, Claire closed her eyes, letting herself feel held and rocked by the motion of the train. Maybe Agent Doucet was right. Maybe it *was* time to put what was lost behind her and move on.

When she finally arrived back at her Chelsea condominium building, Claire found Zeke, the gregarious doorman, standing watch for her. As soon as she came through the wrought-iron entry gate, he stepped outside his office, took her elbow and steered her to the far side of the sheltered archway that led to the building's central courtyard.

"Glad you're back. She's taken over my chair. I didn't know what I was going to do with her if you didn't show up soon."

Zeke's habit of launching into conversations at midpoint aggravated some tenants, but Claire approached it as a kind of daily intellectual puzzle—quicker than the *New York Times* crossword, and with the added advantage of being interactive. He had lost most of the 1970s to a drug habit that had left his hard-wiring a little fried and his face lined and weathered as a satellite survey of Mars. He could easily have ended up one of the nameless corpses that washed up every day from the hidden refuges of the homeless, but his innate affability had earned him the attention of a proselytizing ex-junkie who'd led him to twelve-step salvation. Now Zeke was the most reliable of watchmen. If some condominium board members regretted his tendency to engage every passerby in lengthy conversation, at least they knew he was on the job.

"What you were going to do with *who,* Zeke?"

"The old lady. She arrived about an hour after you left this morning. Said it was urgent."

Claire looked back at his office. In the window, between reflected shadows of the overcast afternoon sky, now turned drizzly, she could just make out the back of a snow-white head—a Q-Tip, in the irreverent parlance of traffic cops tailing slow-moving vehicles driven by senior citizens. "Who is she?"

Zeke shrugged. "She wrote it down in the book, but long names defeat me, you know. I'll show it to you. I said I didn't know when you'd be back. Told her she should leave a number and you'd call, but the old girl came in from the boonies on an early-morning bus. Said she's planning to leave again, soon as she talks to you. She's pretty wiped.''

''I know the feeling,'' Claire said ruefully. All she wanted was a couple of aspirin and her bed. ''Okay, let's see what this is all about.''

She followed Zeke to his little office. Inside, chin on her chest, an elderly woman dozed in a large, seedy armchair cast off by some long-ago tenant. Claire's stomach flipped when she got a closer look at her visitor, and she didn't need the doorman's log to tell her the woman's name.

''Zeke,'' she whispered, ''could you give me a few minutes alone here?''

''Sure, no problem.'' He shambled out and closed the door behind him.

Claire watched him go, then turned back to her visitor. The older woman's rotund body strained the buttons of her worn blue tweed coat. Her gnarled fingers intertwined atop a black leather purse that perched on her chest, rising and falling in a steady rhythm as she dozed. She wore thick woolen stockings, and her stubby feet, crossed at the ankles, were clad in short, salt-stained boots that dangled a couple of inches off the floor. She did, indeed, look exhausted.

Claire crouched in front of her, placed one hand

on the woman's and shook gently. "Mrs. Kazarian?"

Startled awake, the older woman glanced around, confused. Her eyes were a bright Delft blue, just like Michael's. Finally, they settled on Claire and seemed to focus.

"I'm Claire Gillespie, Mrs. Kazarian."

"Oh, Miss Gillespie, yes! Sorry, I must have dozed off. I'm so glad you're here. The doorman told you who I am?"

Claire nodded, but in fact, she'd seen Michael's mother at his funeral, sitting in the same pew as his wife. She, too, had been singled out by the priest for special mention. Claire hadn't approached her that day—hadn't been able to bring herself to talk to anyone there, after the shock of discovering Michael was married.

"I'm sorry to drop in on you unexpectedly like this," Mrs. Kazarian said. "Michael gave me your phone number, but when I tried to call, the operator said the number was no longer in service, and they didn't have another listing for you."

"Oh, yes, that's true. I got a new number a couple of months ago, after—" Claire hesitated. It was when she'd gotten fed up with taking calls for Alan, especially calls from querulous, anonymous females who wouldn't take no for an answer. "I had some problems with that old number, so I had it changed and left it unlisted."

"I decided to take a chance on coming here. I thought if you'd moved, maybe I could get a forwarding address for you."

"No, I'm still here." Not much choice, Claire thought. She might have considered moving after Alan took off with Nicky, except that affordable apartments in the city were few and far between—certainly ones as convenient and attractive as this renovated Chelsea prewar building, several of whose elderly residents puttered and planted the summer away in the pretty center courtyard garden, with its benches, birds and flowering trees.

"I'm a little confused, Mrs. Kazarian. Why did Michael give you my address and phone number?"

"He said you were a reporter."

"That's right."

"You were a friend of his?"

"I hadn't known him long, but—" Claire hesitated.

Don't go there. There's nothing you can say that isn't going to sound like a hollow lie.

She shifted gears. "He was a fine man, Mrs. Kazarian. My father was a police officer, and he died in the line of duty, too, so I know how difficult this is. I'm terribly sorry for your loss. It must have been a shock.''

The older woman nodded, teary-eyed. ''A mother shouldn't have to bury her children. He was my only child, you know.''

Yes, Claire did know. She knew quite a bit about her and about Michael's steelworker father. Also about his grandmother, this lady's mother, who'd lived with them in the small Pennsylvania town he'd grown up in—the *baba* who'd spoken only Russian and called him Misha, so that, when he'd adopted that name for his undercover identity, answering to it had been second nature. She knew, too, by Michael's blushed confessions of treats and small sacrifices, how mother and grandmother alike had doted on him. How the family had scrimped on a steelworker's wages so that he could attend private Catholic schools and colleges. About their pride in his sports trophies, and the pro-football offers he'd turned down to study criminology. In his FBI career. Michael had told Claire a lot about himself, neglecting only the minor detail of his marriage.

Mrs. Kazarian shook out a tissue from her pocket and blew her nose, then twisted it into a knot. ''Michael said if anything happened to him,

I should talk to you. Said he trusted you, and you'd know what to do.''

Claire was curious to know what else Michael had said about her, but this wasn't the time or place to ask. ''I'm not sure what you mean, Mrs. Kazarian. Do about what?''

''Michael had a feeling he was in danger. He said they might try to make it look like something else, but at first, after he died, I thought, no, this was about his work. Now—'' Her voice catching again, the old woman paused, then shook her head and sat up straighter, the blue eyes glinting angrily. ''Now, from things people have said to me, I think he was right. I don't think my son died in the line of duty like your father, Miss Gillespie. That's why I had to see you. I think they're covering up what really happened.''

''Who?''

''The FBI.''

Claire rocked back on her heels, frowning. ''From what I understand, he was working on a sensitive case. There may be details the Bureau won't release in order to protect the operation he was involved in, but—''

''They're not protecting any operation. They're protecting her.''

''Her? Who?''

''Laurel, Michael's wife. Her and that Gar Doucet.''

Claire felt her blood freeze. ''Doucet?''

Mrs. Kazarian nodded, eyes flashing. ''He was Michael's best friend—until *she* got her hooks into him. The two of them—that's who killed my boy.''

8

There was no pit deep enough, no fire hot enough, no judgment terrifying enough for predators of children, Dan fumed. He hung up the phone after his conversation with Delgado of the Orange County Sheriff's Department, sickened by the report of yet another baby's disappearance. This shouldn't happen in a civilized society. A species that preyed on its own young was contemptible. If there was a single, universal human imperative, surely it was that the youngest were inviolate, to be protected at all cost? Yet someone was systematically turning that obligation on its head, targeting the most vulnerable, least resistant of victims for no obvious reason except to strike terror and satisfy some sick inner craving.

Back-to-back kidnappings—what did it mean? There'd been a three-week gap and a sixty-mile spread between the disappearances of the Jefferson and Morales babies. Fifteen days and another sixty miles or so between the Morales case and last night's snatch of little Erica Goodsell. Now, eighteen hours later, another baby had vanished less than five miles from the site of the Goodsell kidnapping.

It was an investigative nightmare, spreading scarce resources too thin. But it was an opportunity, too, Dan tried to tell himself. Moving this fast, the kidnapper was going to start making careless mistakes, leaving clues.

Determined to hit the Orange County fairgrounds while the trail was hot and potential witnesses were still at the scene, Dan hoped he could slip past the media contingent camped outside the Federal Building. He'd left Alice Wentzl working on her revised press release after giving her a heads-up on the latest Orange County report. It was a thankless job she had. There were no glib words to calm the fear these kidnappings had stirred up; no easy answers, short of an arrest, to the justifiable demand that the bastard be stopped.

But when he and Laurel Madden hurried through the sliding front doors onto the building's sun-streamed arcade, a cry arose from the sidewalk beyond. "It's Sprague!"

"Hell," he muttered, watching with dismay as the pack scrambled up the steps toward them.

Laurel took on her caught-in-the-headlights look again. "I'll handle this," he said quietly, "keep it short and simple."

She gave him an uneasy nod, and slipped a pair of sunglasses from the pocket of the jacket she'd grabbed on the way out. "Your show. I won't say a word."

Dan buttoned his sport coat, regretting the golf shirt now. His daughters said he always dressed as if he was on his way to court or a funeral, and kept pushing him toward trendy styles—and available women, Dan thought, wincing at the image of Chrissy Tate's mother. But he was a creature of habit in all things, social and sartorial. He didn't do blind dates, and he didn't like deviating from the dress standard. After yesterday's twin tragedies—the discovery of little Victor Morales's body and the disappearance of the Goodsell baby—he should have known a media scrum was inevitable and dressed more soberly.

"Has the Morales family been given the autopsy results?" he asked quietly.

"Yes," Madden murmured. "The coroner's office said the parents waited outside with their priest until the results were known."

Dan nodded.

The phalanx of reporters closed around them.

Recognizing several faces, he studied them, trying to decide whether or not they'd picked up on the latest report from Orange County. Lieutenant Delgado had said they wanted to keep a lid on the situation at the fairgrounds until they had more information, but there was no telling when some helpful citizen might decide to phone in a press tip. Microphone booms swung toward them, while video-camera operators jostled for a clear shot. Several men threw furtive glances in Madden's direction, Dan noted, though the questions were directed at him.

"Can we get your comments on the Southland Snatcher case, Agent Sprague? Any new developments?"

"Has the baby in the aqueduct been identified?"

"What about the kidnapping at South Coast Plaza last night? Is it connected?"

Dan held up his hands. "Slow down, people. One at a time. We'll have to make this brief, but let me say this—the body discovered in a Los Angeles aqueduct yesterday has been positively identified as Victor Emanuel Morales, ten months old, of Lancaster."

"Was he drowned?"

"No. The coroner's office has ruled that the

cause of death was most likely suffocation. The body was left in the aqueduct postmortem.''

''Any idea when he was killed?''

''It's difficult to be precise when a body's been in water a long time, but probably soon after his disappearance.''

After consultation between the Bureau and the local authorities, it had been decided not to reveal certain details on exactly how the body had been wrapped and taped. The physical evidence had already been shipped to the FBI lab for analysis, and if there was any chance that a clue could be gleaned from that source, Dan didn't want to tip their hand.

''Does the discovery of the body mean you've ruled out the theory that this is some kind of rogue adoption ring?''

''It does look less likely.''

''What about abuse—sexual, satanic ritual, anything of that nature?''

''The medical examiner found no evidence of physical abuse beyond the immediate cause of death. Nor was there any indication of sexual abuse. Other than that, I can't say more right now, since the case is obviously under active investigation.''

''What about the Jefferson and Goodsell babies? Can you confirm now that you're dealing with one perp in all three cases?''

No mention of the fairgrounds incident, Dan noted. The reprieve wouldn't last long, though. ''I'd say there's a good chance we're looking for a single suspect in all three cases, but we have to examine each incident carefully and allow for the possibility this isn't the case. I'm hopeful that whoever is responsible for the disappearance last night of little Erica Goodsell will realize that this baby belongs with her mother and return her safely.''

While Dan spoke, he noticed that Jeff Greene from Channel 2 News was keeping a curious eye on Madden. Finally, the reporter pushed to the front of the group. ''Aren't you the profiler who broke the Beltway Ripper case in Washington a couple of years back,'' he asked. ''The one they made the movie about? Agent Madden, right?'' He held out his microphone and camera lenses swiveled in her direction.

Madden's expression behind the sunglasses was blank as she gave an almost imperceptible nod.

''Were you brought in specially to profile the Southland Snatcher, Agent Madden?''

She clasped her hands in front of her and

dropped her gaze to somewhere in the vicinity of her feet, her body language as much as telling Dan, "You said you'd handle things. Handle this."

"Agent Madden was assigned to the Los Angeles field office in a routine rotation well before these kidnappings began," Dan said. Camera lenses shifted back to him. "More than two dozen agents from this office are working the case. We're also drawing on the Child Abduction Unit and other resources at FBI headquarters. There should be no mistake about this, people—finding the missing children is our top, I repeat, top priority. We *will* identify, apprehend, indict and convict whoever is responsible for these outrages."

"Are you looking for help from the public?"

"Good question. Absolutely. As you know, we have a twenty-four-hour tip line in place—1-800-555-0101. Anyone who might have seen anything, however insignificant, or with any information to offer on these disappearances, is asked to call in."

"Has the tip line been active?"

"Very, and along with a strong contingent of investigators, we've deployed the Bureau's Rapid Start computer system to sort and analyze all the information that's coming in. We're going to stay on the job until the other children are found and the suspects are in custody.'' Dan took a step back. ''And that's all I have to say for now, folks. If you'll excuse us, we have work to do.''

He sidestepped the clamor and headed down the walk, resisting the impulse to take Madden's elbow and rescue her from the reporters' clutches—hoping, nonetheless, that she'd keep up with him. He reached the steps in a few rapid strides. When he started down, she was right alongside him, taller than he'd realized, easily matching his pace as he loped toward the employee parking structure.

That fragile appearance was deceiving, Dan decided. But this was, after all, the iron lady who'd outwitted the Beltway Ripper, bringing down that murderous psychopath single-handedly—not to mention weathering a string of subsequent personal disasters and a nasty whispering campaign that would have crushed a lesser mortal. Obviously, Agent Madden required no antiquated chivalry from him.

With the light bar spinning and siren screaming to open the roadway ahead, Dan pushed the speedometer into the eighties and held it there for most of the drive down the 405 freeway to Orange County. He covered the distance from the Wilshire Boulevard field office to the Orange County fairgrounds in a scant thirty-nine minutes—a zip around the block, by sprawling L.A. standards. In that time, he and Madden exchanged no more than a few words. There was a kind of nervous anticipation that took hold of him, Dan found, whenever he was about to enter a fresh crime scene, as if his brain was focusing all its effort on preparing for the intense analytic effort to come. Agent Madden, thankfully, didn't seem to mind his silence.

When they pulled up to the fairgrounds entrance, the site was in the process of being evacuated, the crowd herded out between parallel lines of yellow police tape like cattle moving through a chute at auction, while a veritable army of law enforcement scrutinized every man, woman, child, shopping bag, cart and stroller.

Dan squinted up in the bright midday sun at a police helicopter circling overhead, the thump of its blades reverberating deep in his chest. Hearing someone call his name, he glanced over at a police barricade off to the side, where several reporters were being held at bay like hyenas at the fringes of a kill. Obviously, in the time it had taken him to get down there, the cat had slipped out of the bag.

''What's going on here?'' Madden asked, ignoring the press as she studied the departing crowd casually dressed in shorts and T-shirts, lugging bulky packages. ''These people look like they've been shopping.''

''Weekend swap meet.''

''They trade things?''

''No, it's a misnomer. Come on, let's find the on-site commander, and you can see for yourself.''

They withdrew their badges and flashed them at the nearest sheriff's deputy, who directed them toward a giant, inflated rubber gorilla floating above the center of the fairgrounds. Moving against the human current like salmon swimming upstream, Dan and Madden entered the fairgrounds and aimed for the flying ape.

For three weeks every summer, Orange County pretended it was still a rural, agricultural community. At its annual county fair, farmers displayed prize fruits, vegetables and livestock. By tacit agreement, fair visitors and the media alike conveniently ignored the fact that a dwindling supply of leased military land grew the county's few remaining vegetable crops and provided grazing for a couple of vastly reduced cattle herds. As for the ''orange'' in Orange County, the last large citrus groves had long since been bulldozed for development projects to house a burgeoning population. Oblivious to the irony, county-fair patrons rode the Ferris wheel, strolled the fair munching hot dogs and cotton candy, two-stepped to country music and admired 4-H projects harkening back to simpler times.

For the remaining forty-nine weeks of the year, however, modern commerce reasserted itself. Nestled between Costa Mesa and upscale Newport Beach, the fairgrounds played host every Saturday and Sunday to a swap meet, where nothing was swapped but plenty was sold at prices rivaling any commercial emporium. Thousands of customers a day—more now, with the Christmas-shopping season under way—strolled aisle after aisle of stalls hawking every product imaginable, from socks and T-shirts to hot tubs, sporting goods and Chinese-made knockoffs of Tag Heuer watches and Dooney & Bourke handbags. Navigating toward the center of the grounds, Dan noted the dour expressions of merchants in their overstocked, patronless booths. Obviously, kidnapping was bad for business.

Suddenly, a scrabbling sound bore down on them from behind. Dan glanced back, then pulled up short, grabbing Madden's arm. He yanked her aside just in time to avoid being bowled over by a large black-and-tan bloodhound. The dog barreled past, mammoth ears flapping, a shower of slobber flying in his wake, leaving a droplet trail on the pavement. Sprinting after the dog, with the business end of a leash in one hand and a duffel bag in the other, a gray-haired, khaki-uniformed handler threw a quick nod in their direction as he passed. A terry-cloth towel dangled from his back hip pocket, bearing a red-embroidered warning: SPIT HAPPENS.

''No kidding,'' Madden said wryly.

Dan glanced over at her. She was wiping her spattered pants with her free hand, but smiling. Well, well, he thought, miracles do happen.

''Thanks,'' she added as he released her arm.

''No problem. That's a handful of dog.''

''Hope he locates his quarry.''

He nodded. ''Come on, looks like they've got a command post set up ahead.''

The flying rubber gorilla marked a centralized food-concession area, where uniformed cops and plainclothes detectives were hovering near picnic tables, taking witness statements. Dan felt his stomach growl at the rich scents of cinnamon churros, fried onions and yeasty, fresh-baked bread. He'd had a glass of juice before leaving the house that morning, and a cup of bad office coffee later. He was starving.

''There's a sergeant talking to the dog handler over there,'' Laurel said.

They walked over and flashed their IDs once more. ''I'm Dan Sprague from the FBI field office in Los Angeles,'' he told the sergeant. ''This is Special Agent Madden. We had a call from Lieutenant Delgado.''

The stocky cop held out his hand to each in turn. ''Don Guzman. The lieutenant told me you were on the way. I hear your people are talking today to the parents of the baby snatched at South Coast last night?''

''That's right. You working that one, too?''

''I got called out on it last night. Looks like we're all gonna be pulling double shift again today, hey?'' Guzman said wearily.

''Looks like.''

The sergeant nodded to the dog handler. ''This is Hal Hamblin from the sheriff's Search & Rescue bloodhound team. And this here's Duke.''

As Dan and Hamblin shook hands, Madden reached down to the bloodhound and ruffled his baggy neck. He wriggled excitedly, gazing up with eager, slightly crossed eyes, jowls flapping.

''He's real happy when he knows he's going to

work,'' the handler said, watching her. ''’Course, it's just a big game of hide-and-seek to him. Here, better use this. He's a mite drooly.''

One of life's great understatements, Dan thought as Madden straightened, still smiling, and took Hamblin's towel to wipe her hands. A woman who appreciated big, ugly dogs couldn't be all bad, he decided, no matter what they said about her.

He turned back to Guzman. ''Can you bring us up to date, Sergeant?''

''Call came in from fairground security just before noon reporting a missing child. We've got the mother in the office behind the burrito stand over there—Jennifer Lynn Kirkendall, nineteen. She's a single mom, waitresses at Planet Hollywood.''

''What about the father?''

He consulted his notebook. ''Name's John Renquist. Girl says he lives in Arizona.''

Madden had slipped out her own notepad and was looking over the sergeant's shoulder, copying down the name.

''We'll check him out just the same,'' Dan said. ''And the child?''

''Ryan John Kirkendall, twenty-two months old. Mother had a picture with her. Here.'' He handed Dan a wallet-size photo, another Sears special, by the look of it. It was a head shot of a blond toddler wearing a striped knit shirt and a mischievous grin. Old enough to have had his first haircut.

Dan passed the picture over to Madden. "Twenty-two months?" she repeated, tucking her sunglasses away as she peered at it.

Dan shared her puzzlement. This child was older than the other three victims, more toddler than baby. Another twist in the victimology.

"So what does she say happened?" he asked Guzman.

"Apparently she got here about eleven, had the baby in his stroller, asleep. She says she was right beside it, but turned her back for a moment to examine some merchandise. When she went to move on, baby and stroller were both gone."

"Did she see who took it?"

"No. The swap meet was mobbed and it's full of side alleys, as you can see. Place is pickpocket heaven, I can tell you. We get a lot of theft reports out of here."

"Anything useful from witnesses?"

Guzman shrugged. "Not really. Like I say, place was pretty busy, what with Christmas shoppers and all. The merchant where Ms. Kirkendall was shopping and a few others reported they heard her screaming. A bunch of people ran to help. They fanned out and hunted in the vicinity for a couple minutes before somebody called security, but nobody saw a thing.''

Dan glanced around. ''Any surveillance cameras?''

''Nope. Security's a couple of rent-a-cops, that's about it.''

The bloodhound yelped plaintively, straining at his leash. ''You said you had a personal item from the child for the dog to scent on?'' the handler said.

''Yeah, the mother had the baby's jacket in her bag.'' The sergeant retrieved a Ziploc plastic bag from a nearby table and passed it over. He cocked a thumb in the direction of the helicopter hovering above. ''We got a bird standing by, case you pick up the trail. Hopefully, the creep isn't too far away yet.''

''I'll need the mother,'' Hamblin said.

''Excuse me?''

''The mother's scent will be on the jacket, too. We need her out here so Duke knows not to hunt for her. It's called the missing-member method. He'll follow the scent of the person who's not here, long as everyone else is where they should be.''

''Okay, we'll get her.'' Guzman called to a sheriff's deputy near the burrito stand to bring her out.

Madden, Dan noted, was barely listening to the others, her gaze sweeping up and down the aisles of the swap meet. She was frowning, looking as preoccupied as the dog waiting to begin his hunt. Dan recognized that expression, having seen it before on the faces of many good investigators. She was struggling to get inside the kidnapper's mind—trying to visualize what he'd seen and what he'd been thinking in the moments immediately preceding and following the snatch.

The dog handler, meantime, set the plastic evidence bag aside on a table and withdrew a leather harness from his duffel bag. Switching harness for leash was obviously a signal that the game was about to begin, because once he'd been wrestled into it, Duke grew as skittish as a Thoroughbred at the post.

Another sheriff's deputy emerged from a nearby building trailing a young woman in jeans and a purple Calvin Klein sweatshirt. With dark eyes and frizzled fair hair clipped high with a plastic comb, she was passably pretty, Dan thought, despite the fact that her nose was red and her eyes swollen from crying. Madden also turned and watched her approach.

Guzman explained to the girl about the bloodhound, and she nodded. The handler then withdrew the missing child's jacket and held it out to the dog. Duke's wrinkled nose took one brief sniff, another of the mother, then bounded away with Hamblin in hot pursuit, holding tight to the harness.

Dan turned back to Guzman. ''We'd like to talk to Ms. Kirkendall, Sergeant, if you have no objections.''

''None at all. I'll let you know if the dog finds anything.'' The sergeant turned to the girl. ''These people are from the FBI, Ms. Kirkendall. They have some questions for you. Meantime, I'm going to follow up with some of my people here, okay?''

The girl nodded once more, then looked nervously from Dan to Laurel and back again. ''FBI?'' Her eyes suddenly grew wide. ''Oh, God! You think it's that Southland Snatcher guy? Is that why you're here?'' Her face crumpled and she sank onto the nearest picnic bench, rocking and crying. ''Oh, no, God, please, no!''

Dan cocked his head at Madden, then walked

around and sat on the other side of the table. In the next aisle over, he could see the bloodhound running back and forth and around in circles, nose to the ground, tail flipping excitedly.

Madden settled beside the mother. "Can you tell us what happened?" she asked gently.

"It's like I told the others, I was shopping for a couple of Christmas presents. I stopped to look at some Tupperware. Ryan was asleep in his stroller. I just turned my back for a minute, you know? It wasn't long at all, I swear. And when I looked back, he was gone."

"Had you noticed anyone following you?"

The girl shook her head.

"Or watching you? Anyone show an interest in Ryan?"

"Not really. I mean, sometimes you see people looking at the baby, you know, smiling or, like, waving or stuff? He was really cute. And I always dressed him—" Her voice broke again.

Madden put a comforting hand on the girl's arm. "It's okay, Jenny. We know how hard this is for you."

Dan found himself watching Madden, fascinated. Her behavior was perfectly professional, but her expression was gentler, more unguarded than he'd seen it. But then, she knew what it was to lose a child, didn't she? Who better to empathize with a distraught young mother? As difficult as this must be for her, he was glad she was here.

When the girl was a little calmer, Madden continued, "Ryan was asleep, you said?"

Jenny nodded.

"Had he eaten?" Dan asked.

"Eaten?"

"Yes. It was around lunchtime, after all, and little kids can get cranky when they're hungry."

"I'll say. He had a real good appetite, too." A wan smile played at the corner of the girl's lips. "'Course, he's an active little guy—terrible twos and all, always on the go."

Madden returned her smile. "A real handful?"

"All boy," Jenny said, rolling her damp eyes.

"So you fed him beforehand?" Dan pressed.

"Yeah, just before we left. He fell asleep in the car."

"Didn't stir when you put him in the stroller?" Dan asked. The girl shook her head. "You're lucky he sleeps so soundly."

"Guess so." She began to rock back and forth again. "How could somebody steal my baby?"

From the next aisle over, the bloodhound howled in apparent sympathy.

"We're going to do everything possible to find

him,'' Dan assured her. ''Can you tell us about Ryan's father?''

She sniffed. ''Not much to tell. He took off when he found out I was pregnant. He's never even seen the baby, except for maybe one picture. I sent it to him after Ryan was born, but he never even called.''

''He's shown no interest in his son since then?''

''Never. Said he was too young to be tied down. I thought he might change his mind after he saw the baby, but when he didn't, I just decided to forget him, you know?''

''And you're sure he's not in town?''

''No, and who wants a guy like that, anyway? We were better off without him.''

Dan nodded sympathetically. ''Must have been tough, just the same. Do you have any help? Your parents, maybe?''

The girl shook her head. ''My parents divorced when I was nine. My dad's remarried, lives back East. I haven't seen him in ages. And my mom—well, she's got health problems, so I couldn't really count on her much. But it was okay. I love my baby, and I'd do anything for him.''

The dog bayed again. Startled, Jenny looked up, her expression terrified. Then she looked at

Madden. ‘‘You probably think I’m awful, losing my baby from right under my nose.’’

‘‘No, nobody thinks that.’’

‘‘I’ve been a good mother, I really have.’’ The girl resumed rocking back and forth, holding herself. ‘‘Oh, God, I want my baby back!’’

Madden patted her arm. ‘‘We’re going to do everything we possibly can to find Ryan.’’

Behind them, the bloodhound howled again, a deep, painful wail.

The young mother’s swollen eyes grew wide with terror. ‘‘What’s happening? Why does he keep doing that?’’

Dan glanced over to the next aisle, then rose and cocked an eyebrow at Madden.

‘‘Just sit tight for a second, Jenny, while we go see what’s up,’’ she told the girl.

She got up and followed Dan to the next aisle. As they turned the corner, they saw the bloodhound sitting back on his haunches, head to the sky, baying steadily now, his mournful wail growing louder and louder.

‘‘This doesn’t look good,’’ Dan said quietly.

9

Like some nervous candidate for daughter-in-law fearing the white-glove treatment, Claire was too embarrassed to have Michael's mother see her messy apartment. But even if he had still been alive, the daughter-in-law position was already filled, she reminded herself, grimly amused by her own neurotic insecurities. Alma Kazarian's only interest here was to spark a public inquiry into her son's death. Nevertheless, Claire opted to take her to her favorite neighborhood eatery rather than up to her apartment.

The Saturday lunch crowd had pretty much thinned out by the time they arrived at the Café Chanteclair, which occupied the ground floor of a weathered brownstone down Eighth Avenue a couple of blocks from Claire's apartment building. Casual and pseudo-French, with Paris newspapers and magazines hung over racks near the door and posters of Deneuve, Delon and Depardieu adorning its wood-paneled walls, the bistro fairly dripped with transplanted atmosphere, the air luscious with the smell of fresh baguette, the chef's *potage du jour* and other daily specials scrawled on a blackboard near the kitchen. In true French fashion, service tended to be unhurried and faintly disdainful. But at the same time, no one cared if you lingered for hours over your *café au lait,* which made the place a favorite hangout for the struggling writers, artists and sundry other loft-dwellers who called Chelsea home.

At Claire's request, the kohl-eyed waitress led them through closely spaced tables to a far corner booth, where they could carry on a discreet conversation with little risk of being heard over the clanking of dishes and the hum of other voices. After they had removed their sleet-spattered coats and settled into the banquettes, Mrs. Kazarian fished reading glasses out of her battered leather handbag to study the fare.

Over the top of her own menu, Claire studied the woman once more. A little older than her own mother, she estimated—mid-sixties, with a tightly curled helmet of rust-colored hair that could not have come from nature's palette. Under the blue tweed coat, laid carefully now on the bench beside her, she wore a black cardigan over a bright print blouse and black skirt, all of them wrinkled after her long bus rides from Pottsdown to Philadelphia, and from there to the nearby Port Authority Bus Terminal. The hands gripping the menu were blunt-fingered and slightly arthritic-looking. Those hands, Claire knew, had spent a lifetime at physical labor, caring for her own family and cleaning other people's houses so her son could have the little extras a steelworker's salary couldn't manage. A string of artificial pearls puddled on the shelf of Mrs. Kazarian's ample bosom, and her ears were adorned with screw-on pearl studs, as if she had dressed carefully for their meeting.

Claire felt touched, flattered and perturbed at the same time. What could she possibly do for this poor, grieving woman?

When the waitress appeared to take their order, there was none of the chirpy ''Hi!-I'm-Brandy-and-I'll-be-your-server-today'' blather that always drove Claire slightly nuts; she felt no need to become close personal friends with a stranger just to fill her stomach. Rather, they got an abrupt ''What'll you have?'' Fine. The Chanteclair's food was more than adequate compensation for the staff's surliness.

Nervously, Michael's mother pointed to her

choice: soup and a *croque-monsieur* sandwich. She folded her glasses carefully and put them away. Claire picked a Nicoise salad, having no desire to eat it or anything else, then passed her own menu back. When the waitress had slouched off, Claire leaned forward, crossing her forearms on the table.

"I have to tell you, Mrs. Kazarian, I'm pleased to meet you, but I'm confused about why you made this long trip."

"I owed it to my son. It's not right, what they did to him. I tried talking to his supervisors. So have some of his colleagues in the Bureau, I know. But nobody's doing anything. I didn't know where else to turn. Then, I remembered Michael telling me about you, and how I should contact you if anything went wrong."

Amazed that Michael would have mentioned her to his mother, Claire was also struck by the accuracy of his premonition of danger—but then, undercover work did carry certain life-expectancy risks. She was sorely tempted to ask exactly what Michael had said about her and how he'd described their relationship, but somehow, it didn't seem appropriate.

"They can't get away with it, Miss Gillespie."

''Call me Claire, please. Do you mean Michael's wife and this Doucet character?''

''Laurel and Gar, yes.'' Opening her pocketbook once more, Mrs. Kazarian withdrew a photograph and handed it across the table. ''This was taken at Michael and Laurel's wedding five years ago. That's Gar in the picture with them. He was Michael's best man.''

Claire took the photo, heart thumping at the sight of Michael, looking younger here, his shock of wheat-colored hair a little thicker, no lines of worry or weariness in his face. Those large, Delft-blue eyes were just as arresting, though, as was his commanding physique. She had nothing to remember him by, Claire realized sadly—no photos, no personal effects. Only a set of gaily painted Russian nesting dolls that Michael had given her a few days before he died. ''Because you're a puzzle master,'' he'd said, sprawled out on her open sofa bed, his muscular upper body propped on one elbow. His free hand had gently brushed a dark curl out of her eyes as he watched her open one doll after another, working her way down to the smallest. ''My feisty little Claire, who never gives up till she gets to the truth at the core.''

Michael had never said he loved her, Claire had to admit, but there'd been real warmth and affection in his voice and his touch. Whatever distractions and delusions she may have been under during their brief affair, she knew she hadn't been mistaken about that.

In the wedding-day picture, he and Doucet stood on either side of his bride, who was blond, statuesque and stunning by anyone's standards. The men wore boisterously wide smiles, their faces flushed with celebration; hers was more restrained.

Studying Laurel's face, Claire had the vague sense, as she had at Michael's funeral, that she'd seen this woman before, but she couldn't put her finger on where. Hadn't actually met her, she didn't think, but recognized that cool, Pfeifferesque image. How?

Laurel and Michael had made an exceptionally handsome couple. Staring at the two of them together, Claire felt voyeuristic and inadequate. Since his death, she'd foolishly tortured herself from time to time with idle speculation on what might have happened if they'd had a little more time. But that relationship had risen out of unique circumstances, at a time when they'd both been under intense personal and professional strain. She knew it now; she'd known it then. It was folly to imagine it could have developed into anything more.

"Michael said he and Gar were both after Laurel at first," Mrs. Kazarian was saying, "but she chose my son. Gar seemed to take it fine when they decided to get married, though, and the three of them stayed good friends."

Claire shifted her focus to the best man, whose hand cupped Laurel's slender waist. He was as dark as she and Michael were fair—more so in this photo than the pepper-haired agent she'd encountered in Brooklyn that morning. With Doucet, too, the intervening years seemed to have taken their toll. Those black eyes, which had fixed on Claire with a look of cold, frank calculation, glinted with devilry here. Claire tried to picture him and Laurel as an item, but Beauty and the Best Man struck her as an awkward contrast.

"Laurel's with the FBI, too?" she asked.

Mrs. Kazarian nodded. "She's a…what do you call it? Not a psychiatrist—"

"A psychologist?"

"That's it. She studies how criminals think. When the FBI is looking for, say, a killer or something, and they don't know who he is, her job is to figure out what his habits are, how old he is, what he does for a living, that sort of thing."

''A profiler.''

''I guess that's what they call it, yes.''

''So the three of them were friends, but somewhere along the way, you suspect Laurel and this Doucet character became involved and began plotting against Michael, is that it?''

The other woman nodded again.

''Why do you think that?''

''Michael as much as told me. I knew he and Laurel had been having problems ever since the baby died. Michael was trying to work things out. Laurel, though—'' Mrs. Kazarian shook her head. ''She was a strange girl, you know? I don't think she ever really wanted a child. And then, after Theo died, there was talk—''

Claire was barely listening. At the first mention of the word *baby,* a deep, dizzy buzz had begun to resonate in her brain.

You never told me this *either, Michael! Why not? You told me about your first dog. About stealing the communion wine when you were an altar boy. You even confided in me about the strain of working undercover, pretending day after day to live in someone else's skin. But you never said anything about a wife, or a child, or problems in a marriage. Why not? It wasn't as if*

I wouldn't have understood. I'd been there myself. You knew that.

"Claire?"

Snapping out of her bitter reverie, she met Mrs. Kazarian's puzzled look. "I'm sorry. I just—I never knew he had a child."

"A little boy. Theo would have been two in February. The most beautiful baby you've ever seen." The older woman's eyes glistened.

Claire took her hand and gave it a gentle squeeze. "What happened to him?"

The heartbroken grandmother fished in her sweater pocket for a tissue and wiped her eyes and nose. "He was just five months old, poor lamb. Michael was away working. He'd already started that undercover assignment here in New York. Anyway, Laurel said she nursed Theo and put him to bed about midnight. He'd been fussy, she said, but generally he was sleeping through the night by then. Laurel was glad about that, because she'd gone back to work part-time. Michael didn't think she should have. Neither did I, to be honest, but I would never interfere. It was too much for her, though. She was exhausted. That night, she said she went to bed herself after putting the baby down and slept until six the next morning. When she got up to check on Theo, he was lying peacefully in his crib. It was only when she touched him,'' Mrs. Kazarian added, her voice catching, ''that she realized he was cold and not breathing.''

''Was there an autopsy?''

Mrs. Kazarian nodded. ''The baby was perfectly healthy. They thought it must be a case of crib death, though one doctor suspected Theo had been smothered. Michael was furious with the man. Laurel was the only one in the house that night, and he was certain she would never harm the baby. He stood by her all the way. Since they couldn't prove anything, in the end they did put Theo's death down to SIDS.''

Claire nodded; this was a familiar story. There had been several SIDS-related scandals in recent years, generally involving multiple cases of infant mortality within single families, where the Sudden Infant Death diagnosis collapsed under the weight of repeated incidents. In single cases, however, medical examiners were understandably reluctant to accuse grief-stricken parents of murdering their own child.

''You said Michael supported Laurel at the time. Did he change his mind?''

''I'm not sure. I know *I* didn't want to think it

was possible. Who could believe that a mother would kill her own helpless baby?''

Who indeed? Claire thought, but it happened more often than people realized. ''So he and Laurel began having problems after the baby died? That's not surprising, is it? They say the strain of a child's death often destroys marriages.''

Mrs. Kazarian nodded and began to say something, but at that moment, the waitress returned with their orders.

''Go ahead and eat,'' Claire said.

The older woman hesitated, but then, obviously as hungry as she was travel-weary, launched into her soup and *croque-monsieur.* Claire picked at her salad, thinking. She felt like a police artist, trying to piece together an image of people and their complex relationships based on an outside observer's sketchy, overwrought and possibly biased memories.

''What about Laurel and this Doucet?'' she asked finally, when Mrs. Kazarian had made her way through much of her meal. ''What makes you think they had anything to do with Michael's death?''

''I saw Michael a couple of weeks before he died. I'd sold my house,'' Mrs. Kazarian explained. ''My husband died four years ago, and it was becoming too much for me to keep up. Michael came to help me move into an apartment, and I asked him how Laurel was. I knew she'd been upset about him taking an undercover assignment. She *insisted,* by the way,'' Mrs. Kazarian added, her painted-on eyebrows rising pointedly, ''that Michael take out additional life insurance before he started that assignment.''

''Life insurance?''

''A one-million-dollar policy, would you believe? Like she wasn't already well enough provided for?''

''You're sure about that?''

''One of Michael's friends told me after he died that he'd heard the same thing.''

''I see. So, when you saw Michael that time, when he came to help you move—?''

''He was reluctant to say much at first, but I could see he was unhappy. Finally, he told me he'd found out Laurel and Gar were having an affair. And later, just before he gave me your name, Michael said something else. It seemed crazy at the time, but now I'm not so sure.''

''What?''

The old woman shuddered, as if shaking off a bad dream. ''Michael said Gar Doucet was stalking him.''

* * *

It was nearly dark when Claire finally returned to her apartment after accompanying Mrs. Kazarian back to the Port Authority Bus Terminal. She'd tried to convince her to stay in the city overnight—said she'd get her a hotel room so she could rest up and head home the next morning—but Mrs. Kazarian was determined to return to her own turf now that she'd fulfilled her duty to her son. Claire had put her on a bus back to Pittsburgh with a promise to keep in touch, to look into her allegations about Laurel and Doucet, and to let her know if she uncovered anything.

Standing at her apartment door, fitting her key in the lock, she pondered her next move. A call to Fred Baker, her usual contact in the FBI's New York field office, seemed in order. Saturday evening or not, if she told the weekend duty officer it was about the Kazarian murder, she knew Baker would call her back when he got the message.

Gruff but media-savvy, Fred Baker was Special Agent in Charge of the New York field office criminal investigation unit. In the five years Claire had been covering the crime beat for *Newsworld*, they'd developed a good working relationship. Baker was straightforward and reasonably forthcoming with her, and she never blindsided him.

If she had to report something negative about the Bureau, she always warned him ahead of time, giving him a chance to refute her information if he could, or to prepare damage control if he couldn't. Baker repaid the favor with background briefings on significant cases and the occasional tip-off when a major bust was about to come down.

Unlocking her door, she debated how best to frame her inquiry about Gar Doucet and Laurel Madden. It was a little tricky, accusing two FBI agents of conspiring to murder another. On the other hand, if there was one thing she knew after being raised by a cop and her own years on the crime beat, it was that lust was powerful motivation. Moreover, if anyone could get away with murder, deflecting attention from themselves and onto another, more obvious suspect like the mobster Ivankov, who better than two top criminalists?

Claire opened the door and flipped on the lights, then froze. Someone had been in the apartment. She felt the cold certainty of it like an ice-pick stab in the chest, although, as she glanced around, the place was in no more than its usual disarray. She surveyed the room, but, clearly, there was no one concealed in its eccentric nooks and angles. The door to the bathroom stood open. She tiptoed across the hardwood floors, peering cautiously around it. Empty. Turning to the main living area once more, Claire's gaze landed on the cigar-ruined red silk blouse, flipped over the arm of the chair next to her desk. When she'd left for her meeting with Ivankov, the blouse had still been draped over the computer where she'd tossed it after Serge Scolari's Christmas party. Her heart plummeted when she spotted a toppled file of manila folders next to the monitor.

"No!" she cried, rushing to the desk.

The files had been neatly stacked, as always, when she left. Whatever her deficiencies as a housekeeper, her work area was always meticulous. It wasn't so much their disarray that disturbed her as the fact that the folders appeared to be empty.

She sank onto the chair and pulled the shrunken pile toward her, opening the folders rapidly, one after another, only to have her worst fears confirmed. All her research on the Brighton Beach crime syndicate was missing—copies of birth, death and immigration records; DMV printouts; county clerks' records; police blotters; tax assessment files; trial transcripts—ten months' worth of tedious digging, gone. All that remained were a few useless newspaper clippings. Whoever had done this had taken his time and been selective.

From the lower corner of her vision, Claire registered another irregularity. She glanced down at the desk drawer on her right and let out a groan. It stood about a quarter of an inch ajar. This was where she kept her interview tapes. She knew that she'd locked it the previous evening before leaving for Scolari's party, because she'd been replaying an interview with the widow of one of Ivan Ivankov's extortion victims in anticipation of her interview with him that day.

Claire opened the drawer wide, knowing she should call the police and stop mucking up possible fingerprint evidence, but unable to stop herself. She had to see what had been taken. In any event, she had a sneaking suspicion the Crime Scene Unit would draw a blank when they dusted the place. This job was too professional for the perp to have left behind a digital calling card.

She rummaged through a clutter of plastic cassette boxes containing several years' worth of carefully labeled interviews with various subjects. The intruder had been no less selective here. As far as she could tell, only four cassettes were missing—all related to the Brighton Beach project.

Sickened at the loss and at having her personal space invaded and pawed over, Claire was almost afraid to check her computer files, but she forced herself to flick on the laptop. It took a moment for the monitor to come to life, and when it did—

"Oh, please, no!" she groaned.

Next to the flashing cursor, a heart-stopping message burned itself into the screen: *"Drive C unreadable."*

The bastard had crashed her system.

Slumped onto her bay-window seat, Claire watched the fingerprint technician pack up his supplies. Gray powder smudged the computer, the desk, the files, the door and doorjamb. But, as she'd predicted, the only fingerprints the tech had located were her own.

A detective from the local NYPD robbery unit clicked his pen and closed his notebook. "You're sure no one else had a key to the apartment besides the building super?"

Only a dead man, Claire was tempted to say—except she knew from Fred Baker that Michael's key case with her spare apartment key had been found on his body. Alan had turned over his when he'd moved out. "No, no one."

''This looks like a pretty professional job. Although,'' the detective added, ''getting past that doorman couldn't have been much of a challenge. Don't know whether you've noticed, but that guy's a couple of sandwiches short of a picnic. We'll be takin' a closer look at him, case it was an inside job.''

''Don't bother. Zeke's all right. It wasn't him, I can assure you.''

''Yeah, well, we'll check out that Brighton Beach thug you mentioned, too, Miss Gillespie, but frankly, a job this slick—'' He shrugged.

''I know. I won't hold my breath waiting for my files to turn up.''

''Nobody else took an interest in this story you were workin' on? Like, maybe some rival reporter hired somebody to steal your information?''

''I doubt it.''

She *could* give the detective the name of the person she really suspected, Claire reasoned, but she'd only get herself pegged as some paranoid conspiracy theorist if she accused Agent Doucet. Besides which, although there was no love lost between the NYPD and the FBI, she doubted the detective's brass would let him pursue a stalking allegation against a federal agent that seemed, on the surface, to be so far-fetched. Better she tackle the Doucet angle herself.

Fred Baker returned her call to the FBI weekend duty officer reasonably promptly, as she'd guessed he would. While waiting, Claire wiped up after the fingerprint technician. Then, in a flurry of purposeful energy generated by anger, she went on to tidy the entire apartment.

"Doucet?" the SAC repeated when Claire told him about her encounter in Brooklyn that morning.

"Special Agent Gar Doucet."

"Never heard of him."

"He may be based in Washington, but he's been hanging around New York off and on for several months now, near as I can tell."

"Uh-uh. If he were operating on my turf, I'd know about it."

"He's one of yours, Fred. He showed me his ID."

Baker exhaled sharply. "Okay, let me do some checking."

"I really appreciate it."

"I sure as hell hope you do. The Rangers are in overtime against Montreal."

"I owe you one."

"Call you back," he grumbled, then hung up.

Claire set the phone back in the cradle and stretched out on the sofa, drained and exhausted after too many hours spent running on little more than nervous energy. She reached for the television remote and started channel-surfing, looking for the hockey game. The least she could do was watch the end of it, in case Baker missed the winning goal while he was phoning around for her.

She'd already flipped past CNN when the realization dawned that there'd been a familiar face on that channel. She switched back in time to catch a close-up of her father's former KCPD partner being interviewed about the Southland Snatcher case in California. At the bottom of the screen, a line of text appeared under a red bar: *"FBI Agent Daniel Sprague. Recorded earlier in Los Angeles."*

Claire smiled at the sight of him. She'd had a huge crush on Dan back when he was a rookie cop riding with her dad. After the Spragues' first daughter, Erin, was born, Claire had been their baby-sitter. She remembered her cheeks growing warm whenever Dan's car pulled into the driveway to pick her up, and the agony of her four younger sisters, who never failed to notice her blush, giggling hysterically, until Claire was forced to threaten dire physical retaliation if they didn't can it.

She studied the face on the screen. Dan was still an attractive man, though a far cry from the young green cop she'd fallen in love with at sixteen. Fiona's death had been particularly hard on him. Claire recalled his look of quiet devastation during the funeral, which she'd flown out to California with her mother to attend a couple of years earlier. According to her sister Bridget, who lived with her family in the apartment above Dan's garage, he still seemed to be in a state of shock half the time.

She turned up the volume on his familiar voice.

"*...hopeful that whoever is responsible for the disappearance last night of little Erica Goodsell will realize that this baby belongs with her mother and return her safely.*"

One of the reporters pushed forward, his attention focused off to one side of Dan. "*Aren't you the profiler who broke the Beltway Ripper case in Washington a few years back? Agent Madden, right?*"

The CNN camera panned left, and Claire found herself staring at the downturned face of Michael's wife, hiding uselessly behind sunglasses.

Laurel nodded her response, saying nothing, but Claire wasn't listening, anyway.

"The Beltway Ripper—of course!" she breathed, amazed that the penny had taken so long to drop.

She'd wanted to cover the story of the D.C. serial killer, but the national editors had given it to their Washington correspondents instead. The killer's fatal tangling with the photogenic female FBI agent had eventually generated a full-page article in the magazine, not to mention a couple of weeks' worth of tabloid copy and, as the reporter in Los Angeles pointed out, a made-for-TV movie. And now, there was Laurel Madden, working with Dan Sprague out of the FBI's Los Angeles office.

The phone rang, and Claire muted the television's sound as the cameras shifted back to Dan. "Hello?"

It was Fred Baker. "Okay, here's your answer—there is no FBI agent by the name of Gar Doucet."

"Impossible."

"You want an on-the-record answer, that's it."

"Ah, I see. What about off the record?"

Baker's hesitation was palpable. "I don't know..."

"Come on, Fred, just between you and me. I won't do anything with it unless I get independent confirmation from somewhere else, in which case, I'll use that attribution. Your name will never be mentioned, I promise."

"All right. Off the record, Doucet was employed by the Bureau until mid-October."

"What happened then?"

"He was fired. You're sure you saw his ID, Claire? He shouldn't have been in possession of it anymore."

"Saw it up close—badge and photo ID. Looked legit, but maybe they were faked. Who knows? Why was he fired?"

"Unprofessional conduct. He had an affair with another agent's wife, for starters."

Claire glanced back at the television, but Dan and Laurel were gone, and the CNN anchor had reappeared on the screen and gone on to another story. "Had an affair with Laurel Madden, who was Michael Kazarian's wife, right?"

"You didn't hear that from me."

"Gotcha. You said 'for starters.' What else?"

Baker sighed. "Some other allegations. There seems to be an investigation under way. Very hush-hush, nobody saying much about it. Serious stuff, though."

"Like what?"

"I can't say."

"Can't, or won't? Come on, guy, give me a break."

"Can't *and* won't. Sorry, Claire, but I've told you all I can."

It was her turn to sigh. "Fair enough. But if anything breaks, you'll let me know?"

"I'll do my best, but no promises."

"Okay, I understand. I appreciate this, Fred, more than you know. Thanks." The only answer she got was a grunt, then the buzz of the dial tone.

Claire hung up the phone and sat for a while, pondering her next move. Then she punched another number into the handset.

Serge Scolari picked up on the third ring. As an editor used to dealing with temperamental creative types, he had the grace not to ask why when she told him she'd changed her mind and would go out to Los Angeles to cover the Southland Snatcher case, after all.

Part II

Black Widow

10

Standing on the observation side of a one-way mirror, Dan felt his attention split between the frightened girl being strapped to the machine in the next room and the tense, angry woman beside him.

Jennifer Kirkendall, the young mother from the Orange County fairgrounds, was about to undergo a polygraph exam to rule her out as a suspect in her son's disappearance. Laurel Madden, case-hardened professional that she was, had accepted in principle the necessity of the test, but it seemed to provoke in her a resentment whose source Dan could only guess at.

"How can we put her through this?" she fumed. The question was directed more at herself than him, it seemed. Dan gave her a puzzled look. She was shaking her head in…what? Disgust? Dismay?

For a rare change, she'd worn her hair down

this morning, tucked loosely behind her ears. When she moved, a clean citrus scent wafted between them, as if she'd showered en route to the office—working, like him, through another weekend. The mental image of her in the shower sent a small flip through his solar plexus, springing from urges Dan didn't even want to think about.

They'd spent the entire previous day together, from the early-morning meeting of the kidnap response team to the frustrating trip to Orange County to follow up on the Kirkendall and Goodsell cases. Then, when there was nothing more to accomplish until the field agents doing background investigations reported in, and realizing they were both hungry, they'd gone for what turned into a protracted late lunch/early dinner, reviewing over and over what few facts they had on each of the four babies' disappearances.

Dan had listened to Laurel systematically suggest, analyze and discard a dozen possible motives, means and profiles for their UNSUB, working the puzzle with single-minded intensity—oblivious to the mesmerizing effect she was beginning to have on him, despite his best efforts to resist it. Last night, in restless sleep, he'd dreamed about her. This morning, he'd awoken early and dressed hurriedly, knowing they'd be back at it today. So much for spending more time with his girls, Dan thought guiltily.

"If she's lying about taking the baby to the fairgrounds yesterday, I want to know now," he said brusquely, nodding at the Kirkendall girl in the next room. "I'm not wasting valuable time when we should be working TOTNAP."

"You don't know she's lying. Just because the bloodhounds couldn't find the trail—"

He cut her off. "There was no trail to find."

Handler and hound had repeatedly circled the area where the toddler had allegedly disappeared. But after scenting off the child's jacket and frantically searching, Duke had finally plunked himself down and bayed in frustration at his failure to find matching scurf, the cast-off skin cells that launch a bloodhound on the game it's bred and trained to love—protesting indignantly at being cheated out of his fun. Hamblin had eventually taken him back to his truck and brought out a second dog. But Sherlock, a nut-colored eight-year-old who'd tracked lost children, hikers and fugitives over every conceivable type of terrain, had had no more luck than Duke in picking up the scent of little Ryan Kirkendall.

"The scent was there," Laurel insisted. "It had to be. It would have been on the mother's car, at the very least, from the jacket she'd carried in. If those dogs were so good, why didn't they alert on that and trail it back to the parking lot?''

Dan shook his head. ''That's not how it works. If a fox crosses the trail of a rabbit in the woods, you don't think it runs backward to where the rabbit's *been,* do you? It doesn't. Nobody quite understands how it works, but dogs only move forward on a scent. Except in this case, the child's scent didn't go anywhere, because his jacket was the only part of him that was ever at that swap meet, and the jacket never left the area. That's why the dogs were so frustrated.''

Laurel continued to look skeptical.

''There's not one witness who can confirm they saw Jenny there with a stroller or her son,'' Dan told her.

''The place was crowded. No one came forward at Universal Studios to confirm that the Jeffersons had had their baby with them, either.''

''That's true. But the dogs did pick up a trail in that case, one they followed right to the freeway on-ramp, obviously the kidnapper's escape route. Didn't it strike you as odd,'' Dan added, ''that every time the girl spoke of her son, it was in the past tense? He *was* an active little boy? She *was* a good mother? Like she'd already written him off for dead? You, of all people, should know she's lying.''

Laurel spun to face him. ''What does that mean, *me* of all people?''

He was taken aback, until it dawned on him that she thought he was referring to the controversy surrounding her own baby's death. He raised his hands. ''All I meant is that as a criminal psychologist, you know language often gives people away.''

Her glare was unabated.

Dan sighed. ''Look, I know what you went through when you lost your son—''

''No, you don't. You have no idea. Have you ever lost a child? Been accused of murdering your own baby? Known what it's like to die inside from grief and guilt, only to have people look at you like you're some kind of unnatural monster? Whispering and whispering—'' Her voice broke, and she turned back to the glass.

Laurel watched Jenny. Dan watched Laurel, sensing her anger and her agony. Was tempted to say the hell with it, and touch her—at least put an understanding hand on her shoulder. Knowing he couldn't do that.

''I'm sorry,'' he said. ''I wasn't suggesting anything personal.''

She pressed her lips together.

"But as long as the subject's come up, I have to tell you I've been wondering whether it's fair to ask you to work this case. Maybe it strikes a little too close to home?"

Her green eyes laser-locked on him once more. "Is my professional competence in question now, too?"

"No. It's got to be stressful, that's all—"

She laughed bitterly. "I can handle stress, believe me. This—" She waved at the glass and the young girl in the next room, who sat with her back to the polygraph machine, staring nervously at the gray walls. "This is nothing—a walk in the park."

"You don't think there's a chance your judgment might be colored by your personal experience? That maybe you want to believe Jenny because of what happened to you?"

Her expression hardened again. "What are you saying? That I'm not allowed to express an opinion that differs from yours?"

"Of course I'm not saying that."

"Well, excuse me, but that's what it sounds like to me. And frankly, that's unacceptable. I can't do my job if I'm not free to explore every possible angle, including the possibility that a suspect just might be innocent. I certainly can't do it if every time I turn around, someone's second-guessing my motivation or my ability to work certain kinds of cases. So if you're having concerns along those lines, sir, maybe you should think about having me reassigned somewhere else."

Nice going, Sprague. So much for promising to give her a chance.

At the same time, Dan wondered what on earth had possessed him to accept the transfer of an agent with such a troubled past. But he had. Now he'd deal with the consequences. "There's no need for reassignment," he said. "You're on this team and on this case. If you say it's not a problem, that's good enough for me. And one more thing—people around here usually call me Dan, not 'sir.' Do we understand each other?"

She studied him for a moment, then nodded and turned back to the glass.

In the next room, the tester was aligning ink needles on graph paper behind the girl. Special Agent Ron Younger was chief polygraph examiner in the field office. Determined to get to the bottom of the Kirkendall child's disappearance sooner rather than later, Dan had pulled him in for weekend duty rather than Ron's fully qualified, but less experienced junior partner.

Stepping around the desk, Younger looped corrugated rubber hoses around the girl's chest and abdomen—always an awkward step, especially with female subjects. But Younger's sad, weathered face and apologetic tone seemed custom-designed to put them as much at ease as possible, under the circumstances. Through the one-way sound system, Dan and Laurel heard his careful explanations.

"These are called pneumograph tubes, Jenny. They register respiration rate and depth. Just breathe normally and try not to hold your breath when we start the questions, okay?"

The girl nodded.

Next, he attached electrodes to the index and ring fingertips of her trembling left hand to record fluctuations in the galvanic skin reflex. "Comfortable?"

"Yes," the girl said, not looking comfortable in the least.

"These measure electronic changes in your skin caused by perspiration."

"I'm real nervous. Won't that mess up the readings? Make it look like I'm lying when I'm not?"

Younger paused, a worried crease wrinkling his broad forehead. "Are you planning to tell any lies here, Jenny? Because if you are, we really shouldn't do this. You can leave, you know. You're not obliged to take this test.''

On the other side of the glass, Dan smiled to himself, in spite of the tension. There was as much psychology as science in a good polygraph exam, and this was a classic gambit. The test was always voluntary; but what suspect would back out at the last minute, when it would seem such an obvious admission of guilt?

It reminded him of the yarn about the ancient Arab lie detector: suspects were put in a tent with a donkey and told the animal would bray if a guilty man pulled its tail. What they weren't told was that the tail had been greased. Any man who emerged from the tent with clean hands was presumed to have a guilty conscience.

''No, it's okay,'' Jenny said quickly. ''I just wondered whether I'd mess things up, being so nervous, is all.''

''Don't worry, everybody's nervous, even seasoned FBI agents who take the test every couple of years. The machine takes that into account.''

''It does?''

''Sure. Remember how we went over the questions I'm going to ask you?'' She nodded. ''Well, the first couple, about your name and your son's name and so on, establish what we call the baseline reading. The machine doesn't care if your hands are sweating or if your heart's beating fast. All it registers is changes in physical response from one question to another. Those changes happen when a person knowingly tells a lie. I won't pull any tricks or ask any surprise questions, I promise. Just tell the truth and there'll be no problem."

Standing next to Dan, Laurel muttered, "Yeah, right," so low that Dan doubted he'd heard correctly.

"Pardon?"

"Nothing."

"You don't seem to be a big fan of the polygraph." She'd also made disparaging remarks about the procedure at yesterday's meeting of the kidnap response team, he recalled.

"Let's just say I've seen results interpreted in ways that erred in both directions."

"That's always a risk, but Younger's one of the best in the business. Look, Laurel, nobody's going to hang Jenny Kirkendall out to dry on the basis of one polygraph. But if this gets us a step closer to finding her child, it'll be worth it, right?"

She nodded. "I agree."

Younger slipped a blood pressure cuff around the girl's right upper arm. "This measures your pulse rate and blood pressure. It's a little uncomfortable—kind of like when a doctor takes your blood pressure, except I have to keep it inflated for the whole ten minutes or so it takes to run the test. You going to be okay with that?"

Jenny nodded.

"Attagirl. Okay, just sit quietly now and look straight ahead at the wall there, and we'll get started." The test room was soundproofed and unadorned to eliminate distractions that might render the test results inconclusive.

Younger inflated the blood pressure cuff, then moved behind the girl once more, started the graph paper rolling through the machine and pulled a pencil out of his shirt pocket. As he worked his way slowly through the prepared set of ten questions—all of them discussed ahead of time to ensure, as he'd promised, that there were no surprises to compromise the readings—he marked Jenny's responses on the graph paper: a plus sign for "yes," a minus sign for "no." Some questions were banal control items; others went to the heart of the investigation.

"Is your name Jennifer Lynn Kirkendall?"

''Yes.'' The pens zigged along the rolling graph paper in a steady, regular rhythm.

''Do you have a son?''

''Yes.''

''Are you nineteen years old?''

''Yes.''

''Do you know where your son is at this moment?''

''No,'' Jenny answered without hesitation.

Dan craned his neck for a better look at the lines on the graph. Had they jumped, or was it his imagination?

''Is your son's name Ryan John Kirkendall?''

''Yes.''

''Did you take Ryan to the Orange County swap meet yesterday?''

''Yes,'' she said firmly.

This time, there was no doubt about it. The pens made a frenzied leap, like a seismograph registering a sudden, devastating shift in the earth's tectonic plates. Dan looked over at Laurel. She stared at the girl for a moment, then closed her eyes, sighed and dropped her chin to her chest.

Dan, Laurel and Ron Younger were in a conference room down the hall from the polygraph unit when Oz Paterson rapped on the door.

"Got a second, Dan? It's about the Kirkendall case."

"Come on in. We were just going over her polygraph results."

The squad leader dropped wearily into a chair. "You fluttered her already? Has she left?"

Dan shook his head. "She's down the hall. Ron still has to do the post-test interview. We're just deciding on a strategy here."

"She flunk?"

Dan deferred to the examiner.

"When I asked her if she knew where her son was, the response was inconclusive," Younger said, showing the place on the graph where she'd responded to question number four. The lines registered a slight fluctuation in her heart and respiration rates. Then he moved along the graph to the place he'd marked "Q 6" next to a plus sign. Here, the needles had gone mad. "When I asked her if she'd taken him to the swap meet yesterday, she said yes, but there are clear indications of deception. I repeated the test three times, and the results were identical each time. In my opinion, she's lying about taking the kid. She may or may not know where he is, but I don't think he was anywhere near that swap meet yesterday.''

Paterson nodded. ''Doesn't surprise me.''

''Why?'' Dan asked.

''OC Sheriff's deputies found an abandoned stroller in a dump bin behind a Ralph's supermarket about a mile from the girl's apartment. Her mother was at her apartment when they took it over there a while ago. Ten in the morning, she's drunk as a skunk, but coherent enough to confirm that the stroller's her grandson's.''

''The kidnapper could have put it there,'' Laurel said.

''That's true,'' Dan said, ''except her place is, what, Oz? Eight, ten miles from the swap meet?''

Paterson nodded. ''And not only that.''

''What else?''

''We interviewed people she worked with at Planet Hollywood. Turns out Ms. Kirkendall's latest boyfriend dumped her last week. Bartender there said he'd dated her himself a few times, but stopped seeing her after she got too anxious for a commitment. Guy wasn't interested in acquiring an instant family. I think 'Why buy the cow when you can get the milk for free?' was the very witty and original phrase he used.''

''Jerk,'' Laurel muttered.

''What about the baby's father?'' Dan asked, letting the comment pass. Jenny's innocence was looking more doubtful by the minute, but there was no point in rubbing Laurel's nose in her misplaced faith.

''Phoenix checked him out. Found him in hospital in traction with a broken hip. Fell off a scaffold last Tuesday.''

''So no way he had anything to do with this,'' Dan said. ''Okay, Oz, that's helpful. We'll have to go back at her. Anything new on the Goodsell case?''

''Better news there. We retraced Mrs. Goodsell's steps in the mall Friday night and found a security camera record of her at FAO Schwarz earlier in the evening with little Erica in the stroller. Also, a lady called the tip line after seeing the baby's picture on the eleven o'clock news last night. She says she saw a man carrying a baby who maybe looked like Erica. He was leaving the mall through the Macy's parking lot exit. She said she noticed the baby crying and fussing. She figured it was just another harried dad watching the kid while mom shopped. Feels pretty crummy about it now, obviously.''

''She get a good look at the guy?''

''Not certain, but the sheriff's department is

hooking her up with a sketch artist as we speak. Meantime, we got Macy's pulling their security videos for us.''

''All right, good work. Keep on it, Oz, and let me know what happens.''

Paterson's joints cracked as he lifted himself out of the chair. ''You bet.''

After he'd left, Dan turned back to the others. ''Okay, let's get this follow-up interview done and out of the way. Tell Ms. Kirkendall she failed the test, Ron. See if you can break her story so we can get back to TOTNAP.''

''Let me talk to her,'' Laurel said.

Dan shook his head. ''It's the examiner's job.''

''But I think we've developed a rapport and she trusts me. Nothing personal,'' she added to Younger. ''You were great, but I think she'll open up more easily to another woman. Another mother,'' she added quietly.

Younger shrugged and looked to Dan for a decision.

Laurel clasped her hands together and leaned toward him. ''Please. I think I understand what happened here. Let me try to get through to her.''

Dan glanced over at Younger. ''You okay with that, Ron?''

"I've got no problem."

"All right," he said. "See what you can do."

"I failed?" Jenny Kirkendall's hands closed around raw, bitten fingernails. "That's impossible! There must be some mistake. Those machines aren't always right, are they? You can't think I—"

Dan watched Laurel settle across from the girl and put a soft drink in front of her.

"I don't think anything, Jenny. The others—my boss and the agent who gave you the test—well, naturally, they're a little concerned about this result. They're down the hall, getting ready for the follow-up interrogation, but I decided you'd been sitting here by yourself long enough."

Such a nasty word, "interrogation," Dan thought. But as the girl squirmed on her chair, he saw that it had hit home. He and Younger had obviously been cast as the bad cops in this little scenario Laurel had decided to play out, with herself cast as the sympathetic good cop. Fair enough. It was a hoary old technique, but still surprisingly effective.

"The other agents should be here shortly, but I thought maybe you could use a cold drink in the meantime."

"Why would I lie about losing my baby?" Jenny asked.

"Well, exactly. That's what I said. I mean, why would any mother lie about a thing like that. And to say you'd taken Ryan to the swap meet, of all places!"

"I did."

"I know that."

Dan watched Laurel's perfect forehead wrinkle in a puzzled frown. Don't push it, he thought. This dumb-blonde routine was a bit of a stretch.

"You know what the problem is?" she said. "They're having trouble figuring out how the Snatcher got to that Ralph's grocery store so fast."

The girl's head shot up. "Ralph's? What do you mean?"

"Didn't they tell you?" Laurel asked, looking puzzled.

"Tell me what?"

"That they found Ryan's stroller in a Dumpster behind the Ralph's near your apartment."

"And Ryan—?" The girl's voice wavered.

Laurel put a hand on her arm. "No, I'm sorry, Jenny, they haven't found Ryan yet."

"Well—how'd they know it's my stroller?"

"I guess the sheriff's deputies took it to your

apartment, not realizing you were here with us. Your mother was there. Apparently, she was a little…under the weather, but she was able to identify it."

"Was she drunk when the police got there? Oh, great, Mom! Thanks a bunch. I called her last night to tell her what happened and she came right over. I figured maybe, just this once, she'd stay sober for a day or so. Obviously not."

Laurel nodded sympathetically. "I know how it is. My father was a drinker, too. You can never really count on them in a pinch, can you?"

"That's for sure."

"Your dad's back East, you said?"

"Haven't seen him in years."

"And Ryan's father flew the coop, too. Everyone kind of left you stuck high and dry, didn't they?"

"What do you mean?"

"Well, with a young child. They can be a handful, I know, especially when you've got to hold down a job, too."

The girl peered at her. "You got kids?"

Dan expected Laurel to flinch, but she bluffed right through with a nod. "I know how it is," she said. "You work hard to be a good mother, but it's exhausting, holding down a job and taking care of a baby."

"I'll say. I mean, my mother baby-sat once in a blue moon, but—" The girl shrugged. "Mostly it was just me and Ryan."

"Was your mother taking care of Ryan this weekend before he disappeared, by any chance?"

"No. Like you said, she was never much help in a pinch."

"Were you in a pinch?"

"What do you mean?"

"Have you been having any special problems lately? Work, boyfriends, anything like that?"

Dan watched as the girl sat up straight in her chair. The lights had finally turned on in Jenny Kirkendall's brain, he thought, and she'd figured out that this lady FBI agent was not, after all, her best girlfriend.

"No. And what's that got to do with anything? Look, are you people going to find my baby or not? How many more kids does this Snatcher guy have to steal before you do your job?" She shoved back her chair and stood up. "Why are you wasting time asking me all these questions? I told you, I got up yesterday morning and took Ryan to the swap meet, and that's where it happened. What more do you need to know?"

"Jenny, I know how upsetting this is. Anyone can see how hard you've been struggling to be a good mother to Ryan. It's just—"

"What?"

"When the examiner asked whether you knew where Ryan was, it looked like you weren't sure. Like, maybe you had an idea."

"How would I know where this Snatcher guy took my baby?"

On the other side of the glass, Dan threw up his hands. "This is going nowhere. She's obviously determined to stick with her story. You'd better go in there and give it a try, Ron."

Younger was leaning against the corner of the window, arms crossed, also watching. "Hold on for a minute. I think I see where's she's heading."

"Who?"

"Agent Madden—Laurel. She's a crafty one."

"You think there's some method here?"

He smiled. "Oh, yeah. I do."

"Well, would you care to enlighten me?"

"Watch. She knows what she's doing, all right."

Laurel, meantime, had also risen and moved around to Jenny's side of the table. She perched herself on the edge. "Well, that's the problem I've been having, too, Jenny. Where would a guy like that go?'' She glanced around, then leaned forward, lowering her voice. ''I'm not supposed to talk about other cases, but I get the idea you've been giving this a lot of thought. And rightly so. I know if someone had taken *my* child, I'd be racking my brain to think where he could be.''

''Well—yeah,'' the girl said cautiously. ''So, like, maybe that's what threw off the machine?''

''Could be. But I'll tell you something—I've been working the Southland Snatcher case from the start, and it's really confusing. He moves around, takes kids at random. Anyone, anywhere could be the next victim, right?''

''Like me and Ryan.''

''Exactly. And to be honest? This moving around of his? It's a major problem for me, because I just relocated here a couple of months ago. I hardly know my way around L.A., and as for Orange County? Forget it. And now there are two kids missing down there.''

Jenny nodded, eyes wide.

''I haven't got a clue where the Snatcher could go in that area. I know there's the ocean, but would he use a beach? I have no idea.''

The girl shook her head slowly. ''I don't know. Beaches are pretty public, even at night. Somebody would spot him.''

''Someplace else, then? Can you think of *anywhere* down there we should be looking that we might not have thought of? Because it really bothers me,'' Laurel added, when the girl started to back away, ''the idea of those kids not ever being found, except maybe by animals.''

Jenny hesitated. ''Animals?''

''This guy's got me so upset, doing what he does. Because even if something terrible's happened, a child's body deserves to be treated with dignity, don't you think?''

''Well...'' Jenny started to cry softly. ''Maybe he'd go someplace where not many people go? At night, say? With lots of, like, weeds and stuff for cover?''

Laurel nodded. ''That would be his style. But where's there a place like that in Orange County? I haven't seen much of it, but what I have seen is developers' heaven, built up and busy. Seems to me there's not a lot of wild space.''

''Not much, except maybe around Newport Bay. It's pretty isolated. When I was in high school, we used to go down there sometimes for, like, drinking parties and stuff? It's real quiet at night. You could slip down there, hide a body, and it'd be weeks—months, maybe—before anybody found it.''

In the next room, Dan felt his blood turn cold. He turned to Younger. ''You think we should get the bloodhounds out to search Newport Bay?''

Younger nodded grimly. ''I think it'd be a good idea.''

11

''Annie-Care! Annie-Care!'' The joyous, high-pitched cry ripped through the Sunday-morning tranquillity of residential Santa Monica.

Claire climbed out of the rented red Mustang convertible she'd parked in front of the Spragues' garage, next to their Jeep and her sister's Toyota, and grinned up at her niece. Lexie was coming down from the apartment above as fast as her chubby legs and tiny red Weebok sneakers could negotiate the steps. Luckily, Bridget was holding tight to one of her hands, because Lexie looked ready to pitch herself, airborne, into Claire's arms. They reached the bottom of the staircase at the same time, and Claire swooped her up.

''Who's this?'' She laughed as Lexie planted a sloppy, wet kiss on her chin—wispy blond hair caught up in pigtails over her ears, blue bobbles and yellow poodle barrettes holding it in place. Bright blue-and-yellow-striped knickers peeked out from under a matching knit dress. She was diaperless, Claire noted; there'd obviously been some changes in the couple of months since she'd last seen her. "What happened to the baby girl who used to live here?"

"I a big girl!"

"You sure are." Snuggling her neck, Claire inhaled soft, baby-soap warmth.

Bridget joined them in a group hug. "Annie-Care made it—hooray!"

Lexie had bestowed the nickname during Claire's last visit, when the mouthful of consonants in "Auntie Claire" proved too much for even a precocious chatterbox like herself. Claire felt honored. With no domestic obligations since Alan's defection and a job that often brought her to the West Coast, she was the only family member Lexie knew well enough to miss. Even Grandma Gillespie was a rare visitor, her sole grandchild not quite enough to overcome her reluctance to face Dan Sprague and the memories of happier days he represented. But thanks to Alan and Nicky, Claire recalled grimly, her mother would soon have another grandchild close to home to stoke her grand-maternal urges.

"Sorry it was such short notice."

"Doesn't matter," Bridget said. "You're here, that's all that matters."

Claire swayed with Lexie on her hip, closing her eyes and lifting her face to the warm sun. "I left sleet and leafless trees in New York. This is gorgeous."

"Not very Christmassy, though."

Claire looked back at her sister, reaching out to stroke her sandy-red hair. Bridget was the only Gillespie girl those wild, black Celtic curls had bypassed—all the excuse her sisters had needed for endless childhood teasing about Britty being left in a basket on the doorstep. "You feeling homesick?"

"Not really. It's just a little hard at this time of year, with Chris working so much."

"Are you on your own today?"

Bridget rolled her eyes. "As always. He's doing thirty-six-hour rotating shifts at the hospital. When he's home, he sleeps most of the time."

"Must be exhausted."

"Total basket case. We keep reminding ourselves that this won't last forever, but some days..." Bridget shook her head.

"You guys needed company like you need a hole in the head, Britty. Maybe I should stay at a hotel?"

''No way.''

''It's not a problem—*Newsworld*'s tab, you know. I like to remind my editor from time to time that I deserve a little pampering.''

''Remind him some other time. I need some adult conversation or I'm going to commit a desperate act of Barneycide.''

Claire laughed and turned to Lexie. ''Barneycide? We can't have that, can we?''

''Barney purple,'' Lexie informed her solemnly.

''He is that, isn't he? More than sufficient grounds for murder. Guess I'd better stand guard. Can I share your room again?''

''I got a big bed!''

Claire gave her a look of incredulity. ''What? No crib?''

''Nope. A big bed.''

''It's a trundle bed. You get the roll-out, I'm afraid,'' Bridget said, wincing. ''It's really tight in there. You probably would be more comfortable in a hotel, but…''

''Hotels don't have hot-and-cold-running nieces, do they?'' Claire tickled Lexie once more.

''Annie-Care sleep in *my* room,'' Lexie said firmly.

''You bet. I'm used to cozy, Britty. It'll be like old times.''

''That's for sure.''

Five daughters and two parents in a three-bedroom, one-bath prairie bungalow had never been anything less than cozy. Claire was the eldest. Two years behind her came Heather and Hannah, identical twins who'd grown up in a busy, secret-language world of their own. Bridget, quiet and sweet-tempered, was born when the twins were three, Nicolette following a scant eleven months later. Also called Afterthought, Gillespie's Folly or, simply, the Holy Terror, Nicky had roared into the household with a bellowed notice that ''last in'' was *not* to be interpreted as ''least noticed.'' She'd been such a handful from the start—colicky, wakeful, with a subsequent childhood stream of minor but attention-grabbing ailments—that watching over Britty had fallen to Claire more often than not. Caught outside the twins' closed club, their mother's preoccupation with Nicky, and Nicky's preoccupation with herself, the two of them had become lifelong allies.

Claire studied the anxious lines in Bridget's face and her damp brown eyes, regretting that she'd even hesitated to come. ''Why don't we lug my stuff up?'' she suggested.

Bridget nodded.

Carrying her niece to the back of the car, Claire fished in her pocket for the keys, and she set Lexie on the ground to open the trunk. Just as she did, the Spragues' back door opened and their massive golden retriever erupted from the house with an exuberant *woof!* Behind him came Erin and Julie Sprague, smiling and waving. Erin pulled the door shut, checked the lock, then followed her younger sister down the walk.

''Bubba!'' Lexie cried, running toward him. ''Bubba-Bubba-Bubba!''

The huge dog bounded across the drive. Claire's heart stopped, certain Lexie was about to be knocked for a loop, but at the last second, he pulled up short, only his tail still flapping like a great, feathered banner as he gave her several ''I've-missed-you-so-much!'' licks on the face. Leaping to Claire next, he slobbered a welcome over her hands, ran a couple of celebratory circles around them all, and plopped down once more next to the primary object of his adoration. Lexie threw her arms around his neck. Exhaling a deep sigh, Bubba gazed at the others with an expression of pure bliss. They burst out laughing.

Erin and Julie approached, Erin dangling car keys—looking more and more like her mother, Claire thought, with those warm eyes and soft smile. Julie had Fiona's coloring, too, but she was tall, towering above her older sister, with a lithe dancer's body and that intense, sparkly sixteen-year-old energy that can be exhausting to be around. Watching the two of them, Claire suddenly felt very old.

Julie gave her a big hug. ''Hi! Bridget just told us this morning you were coming. It's so good to see you again!''

''You, too. I got a sudden assignment out here. Hi, Erin,'' Claire added, turning to embrace her, as well. ''I swear, you guys make me feel ancient. Erin, I remember when you were Lexie's age.''

''Isn't she a doll?''

''She is that.'' Claire cocked her thumb at the Jeep. ''How's your dad? He home?''

Erin shook her head. ''At work. We've hardly seen him all weekend. He drives a Bu-car most of the time.'' She added, ''Leaves me the Jeep.''

''Me, too,'' Julie said. ''I got my permit, Claire!''

''That's great.'' Claire turned back to Erin, trying to read her—remembering the added responsibilities she herself had assumed when her father died and her mother went temporarily to pieces. Did Erin resent being left in effective charge of the Sprague household? ''How are you guys getting on?''

''Okay. Dad needs to slow down, but otherwise, we're fine.''

''Work, work,'' Julie added, ''that's all he does. He even hardly plays golf or anything anymore. And he's got zero social life. We keep trying to get him to loosen up—like, maybe go on a *date* or something?'' She rolled her eyes. ''But he gets so-o-o embarrassed when you mention it! Kind of hilarious, really.''

Claire smiled at all this Valley Girl sophistication. ''He's a pretty conservative guy, but he'll get around to it when he's ready, you'll see.''

Erin nodded. ''We stick around as much as we can so he doesn't end up coming home to an empty house. He'll be back for supper. We're just heading to the mall to do a little Christmas shopping in the meantime. You're going to be in town for a while, aren't you, Claire?''

''Hard to say for sure. A few days, anyway.''

''Great! We'll see you later then.'' Erin turned to Bridget. ''Can Bubba stay with you, Britty, or should I leave him in the house?''

''Bubba come *my* house!'' Lexie said firmly.

Bridget nodded. ''He'll be fine. You and your dad want to have dinner with us tonight?''

''Sure,'' Erin said. ''I'm not sure what time to expect him, though.''

''I'm flexible. It's already made and ready whenever we are. Chris won't be home till after six, anyway.''

''Do you really want us on Claire's first night here?'' Erin asked.

''A gang would be wonderful, believe me,'' Bridget assured her.

Claire and Bridget stood at the counter in the tiny kitchen, ripping greens for the dinner salad while Lexie ate lunch. From time to time, Lexie passed a dry Cheerio down to Bubba, who lay sprawled at the base of her high chair. Despite his giant maw and canine incisors, he accepted each little oat circle with the careful delicacy of a gentleman caller taking cucumber sandwiches at high tea. Suppressing a grin, Claire pretended not to notice.

Bridget finally did, but she just rolled her eyes. ''Those two!''

''A girl and her favorite dog.'' Claire turned back to her sister. ''How about you, Britty? Are you all right?''

"Oh, sure. Suffering a little cabin fever, that's all. Toddler play groups and lunch dates at McDonald's don't quite match the excitement of a newsroom."

Before Lexie was born, Bridget had had the beginnings of her own promising career in TV news. But after falling in love with her new baby, she'd put it on hold rather than try to juggle job and child care in an unfamiliar city.

"Are you thinking about going back to work?" Claire asked.

"Not until Chris finishes his residency. Lexie'll be in preschool by then. If Chris can carry a little more weight at home, maybe I can pick up some freelance work." She sighed. "It's not his fault he's got to work these hours, I know that. He's a great guy, and I really do love being with Lexie. But sometimes, it's hard."

"And here I am, envying you. I guess nothing's ever ideal, is it?"

Bridget turned to her, stricken. "Oh, Claire! I didn't mean to sound so whiny."

"You didn't, Britty, really. I know what you mean. It's just..." She sighed. "It's always something, isn't it?"

"What about you? Are you okay?"

"Me? I'm fine."

Bridget studied her, as if looking for a crack in the facade.

Claire put on a determined smile. ''I am. Honest.''

Bridget frowned and went back to running raw spinach under the cold water.

Claire turned to Lexie, whose cup was empty. ''More juice?'' Her mouth stuffed with cheese, Lexie nodded. Claire refilled her tip-proof cup and snapped its lid. ''Have you spoken to Mom lately?'' she asked her sister.

''About a week ago. She called to see if we were coming home for Christmas.''

''Are you?''

''With the happy couple staying there? What do you think?'' Bridget wrenched the tap closed and slapped the spinach onto a tea towel. ''I gather you're not, either?''

''Not this year, I think.''

''I can't believe the nerve of those two. No way I could stomach spending the holidays with them.''

Claire sighed. ''I appreciate your loyalty, Britty, but we will have to accept this eventually. Nicky's got home-field advantage and she knows it. All she has to do is sit and wait. It's not Mom's fault, or the twins'. If we stay away, it's like punishing them, and forcing them to take sides.''

''Maybe,'' Bridget said dubiously, rolling up the greens in a damp towel. ''Fortunately, Chris is on call till noon Christmas Day, so it's not an issue this year. Anyway, we can't afford to fly out there. I tried to convince Mom to come here for the holidays, but she says she can't leave right now, Nicky's having morning sickness.'' She rolled her eyes. ''Nicky's back's bothering her. Nicky's got a varicose vein. Sheesh! My legs turned into a Rand McNally map when I was carrying Lexie, but I didn't notice Mom dropping everything to be here.''

Claire put an arm around her shoulders. ''It's not you, kiddo. You know that, don't you? Mom still has a problem seeing Dan.''

''Yes, I know. But that doesn't make it any fairer. Dan's been so great, and yet sometimes I think she blames him. Like Dad wouldn't have died if Dan had stayed on the force instead of joining the Bureau.''

Claire shrugged. ''It's illogical, but I guess she feels she has to blame someone.''

''It's been eighteen years. She needs to deal with it, already.''

''Mommy?'' Lexie asked. ''You mad?''

Bridget turned to her and growled playfully. "*Really* mad. Grrr!"

Claire shrank in mock terror. "Your mommy's ferocious, Lexie."

"You foshus, Mommy!"

Bridget kissed her, then turned to Claire. "How about you? I know you said you had a big project back in New York, but it's only ten days till Christmas. Stay?"

"Maybe so. It's not like there's anyone for me to rush back to. It depends how things go with this story."

Bridget shivered. "This Southland Snatcher is creepy. He's getting a ton of press play. CNN and everybody's been on it."

"Unfortunately, that may be what he wants."

"Dan's working the case, you know."

Claire nodded. "That's one reason I was sent. Serge, my editor, knows Dan has given me some leads in the past. He's hoping I'll be able to jump the wall the Bureau's put around the investigation."

"That's a little awkward, isn't it? Dan's practically family."

"Yes, it is, and I turned down the story at first. But then, the trail on this other project I've been working led out here, too, so I decided to kill two birds with one stone.'' Claire exhaled sharply. ''Frankly, I think I needed to get away for a while, too. Between Alan and…well…some other stuff, it's been a rough year.''

''What other stuff?''

''I'll tell you later. Right now, I should make a few phone calls. Do you mind?''

''Were you going to call Dan?''

''Probably.''

''No need.'' Bridget nodded at the window over the sink. ''He just pulled into the driveway.''

12

It struck Dan as he turned into his yard—that pit-sinking sense of things out of order, objects out of place. His pulse began to race, and memory flooded over him of another afternoon, just like this one, when he'd dropped home between meetings, only to find Fiona unconscious on the kitchen floor. It was the first indication they had that what they'd thought was lingering flu was in fact something far more serious. He'd lived ever since in dull dread of life's fickle tendency to turn itself upside down without the slightest warning.

He noted Chris and Bridget McCabe's car parked in its usual place, but an unfamiliar red Mustang convertible was parked next to the space where his own Jeep should have been, but wasn't. He told himself to relax. The girls had gone out, Bridget had company. Nothing more.

Still, leaving the Caprice near the street, he took the precautionary step as he climbed out of reaching under his jacket to flip the safety strap on his waist holster. He scanned the street and yard, then moved up his driveway. Peering at the apartment over the garage, he saw Bridget's wave at the kitchen window. Dan raised his own hand in greeting. At the same moment, the door at the top of the stairs opened and her sister stepped out onto the landing.

"Claire?"

"Hi there," she called, starting down.

"Hi yourself! I didn't know you were coming." Dan strode toward her, his sense of dread dissolving in her megawatt smile.

Once, in the 3:00 a.m. quiet of night patrol, Sean Gillespie had confessed to Dan a special affinity for his stubborn, hyperresponsible firstborn. "That one's got a hard head, but a real soft heart, Dan-o. Someone's going to break it for her one day, mark my words. Worries the heck out of me to think I might not be around to beat the dickens out of the creep when it happens."

Prophetic words, Dan thought—wondering what Sean would have done to Alan Toole if he'd been alive to see the mischief the guy had sown in his family.

Claire waited for him on the bottom step, the extra few inches bringing her almost to eye level.

They embraced with the spontaneous warmth of two people who've seen each other over the years cross the entire emotional spectrum from joy to intense grief. Holding her, Dan felt her curls against his cheek, soft as a child's. But despite that and her small stature, it was a distinctly womanly body in his arms, he realized. He withdrew shyly and busied himself resecuring his sidearm.

"Were you planning to shoot someone?" she asked.

"Busted," he confessed, returning her grin. "I saw the Mustang and thought I was going to have to chase off some young stud trying to seduce my daughters. Glad it's you, instead."

"You may not be when you find out why I'm here."

He grimaced. "Let me guess. They sent you to cover TOTNAP—what the media's calling the Southland Snatcher case."

"'Fraid so."

He shook his head slowly. "Our press office is handling media inquiries." It sounded stiff and bureaucratic, he knew, but professional conflicts aside, he had no desire to see Claire get herself mired in a case as depressing as this one. In his mind, he understood that she was a professional in her own right, who'd delved into God only knew what recesses of the criminal underworld. He'd also read enough of her stuff to know she could digest it with the analytic detachment a cop could appreciate. But in his heart, she was still the kid he'd known since she wore braces, someone for whom he, too, had a particular soft spot, maybe because of how much she'd meant to his partner and friend.

"Alice Wentzl is your media rep?" she asked.

"That's right. You know her?"

"I saw her name on yesterday's press release. She's an old friend. I dealt with her for years back at headquarters before she got transferred out here. She's the one who organized things when I did that piece on the academy a couple of years ago."

"A friend, hey? I don't know if I like the sound of that. I may have to have a word with old Alice, make sure she doesn't give away the family jewels."

Claire laughed. "You don't have to worry about her. She's very discreet."

"I can give you her number."

"I've already got it and I will give her a call, but I need to get up to speed on the details first. This just got dropped in my lap yesterday. I was working another story in New York and haven't been following the Snatcher case too closely. I read most of the press coverage on the flight out here. I was kind of hoping,'' Claire added, ''that if you had a little time, you might fill in some holes for me. Strictly background. My filing deadline's not until Wednesday, so there's plenty of time for quotables—the advantage of writing for a weekly.''

Dan sighed, then glanced around. ''Have you seen Erin and Julie?''

''When I first arrived. They're so grown-up, Dan! What great people they've turned into. You must be so proud of them.''

He nodded. ''I'd like to take the credit, but that's all Fiona's training. Do you know where they are now?''

''They went Christmas shopping. They weren't expecting you home till supper.''

''I was waiting for some field reports to come in, so I thought I'd stop by and see what they were up to. Are they gone for the afternoon, do you think?''

''I'd say so. Bridget invited everyone for dinner. You, too. She told the girls that Chris gets home from the hospital around six, so I think the plan is to eat then.''

''Sounds fine.''

Dan rocked back on his heels, thinking—torn between the weary urge to crash for a while and the itch to follow up firsthand on the lead Jenny Kirkendall had unwittingly given Laurel. And then, he thought, there was Claire here. Professional conflict or no, he was glad to see her. She was easy to talk to; always had been. "Do you want to go for a ride?" he asked.

"Sure. Let me check with Bridget, but she's got dinner under control, so I don't think she needs me. Where to?"

"Newport Beach. That's about forty minutes south of here."

"The two Orange County babies who were snatched this weekend?"

"Yeah. We got a lead on one of them. There's a chance the disappearance is unrelated to TOTNAP. A team's out now, searching. I thought I'd take a run down, see if they've found anything. On the way, I'll tell you what I can about the Snatcher. But off the record and strictly for background, okay? And when we get there, you may have to wait in the car until I see what's going on. Agreed?"

"Deal. I'll run up and tell Britty."

In the absence of any great emergency, he decided to forgo the siren. It got in the way of conversation, and drivers tended to do stupid things when sirens came screaming up behind them on the freeway. In any event, traffic was light on the 405—by L.A. standards, though no one else's, Dan thought wryly, realizing how acclimatized he'd become. The flashing light bar was enough to keep him moving without causing any accidents.

"We think we're looking for a white male suspect, mid-twenties to mid-thirties," he told Claire as he negotiated a lane change. "Intelligent, well-organized. Probably reasonably fit, given how fast he gets away. He may be a police buff."

Claire looked up from the notebook in which she was jotting notes. "Why do you say that?"

"Because of the way he's skipping around. Discounting this last incident—which, as I say, may be bogus—each snatch has occurred in a different police jurisdiction. Makes coordinating the investigation that much more difficult. He may well be counting on that."

"But the Bureau's been on the case from the start, hasn't it?"

He nodded. "True, but the UNSUB might not have expected us to get involved so soon. Kidnapping's not necessarily within our jurisdiction."

"You bend the rules where kids are involved?"

"Let's say we interpret them broadly. It *is* in our bailiwick if there's a chance the suspect's fled across state lines, or if there's sexual exploitation of minors or extortion involved. Local forces can also request our assistance. And then, if worse comes to worst, there's always federal civil rights statutes to justify our jumping in. Frankly, it's not really an issue. No one objects to the Bureau assisting when kids are at risk. Quite the contrary."

"The first child was African-American, wasn't he? You're sure your guy's white?"

"Reasonably, especially after the snatch at South Coast Plaza Friday evening. That kidnapping exactly fit the M.O. of the first two. He must have cased the mall before choosing his target and deciding on a plan. Maybe followed her for a while. That place is as white-bread as they come, but he seems to have slipped in and out virtually unobserved."

"Virtually? Does that mean you've got a witness?"

She didn't miss a thing, Dan thought ruefully. Off the record or no, he was going to have to watch his step. Making an investigation completely transparent was rarely the best way to trap a felon. Some details had to be kept under wraps. ''We're still interviewing witnesses who were there that night, trying to see if anyone remembers anything out of the ordinary. But the point is, he probably wouldn't have gone there unless he was reasonably certain of blending in.''

''The first two victims were little boys, one black, one Hispanic. But the South Coast Plaza victim was a white baby girl,'' Claire said. ''You think that's part of his effort to confuse the investigation?''

Dan nodded appreciatively. She was going through exactly the same thought processes his kidnap response team had as they tried to piece together a picture of their UNSUB, his method and his motives. Claire really should have been a cop, he thought. She would have made a good one.

''Our behavioral science people tell us gender's less of an issue with predators who target the very young.''

''I noticed you've got a profiler working with you—Laurel Madden, right?''

He glanced over, surprised. ''You know *her,* too? Sometimes I think you have better law enforcement contacts than I do.''

She smiled and shook her head. "I only know her by reputation."

"The Beltway Ripper episode, I suppose."

"Partly. Has Madden been working for you long?"

"No. She's another recent transfer."

"October?"

Dan gave her a puzzled look. "That's right. How did you know?"

"Just a reasonable deduction. That's when the agent she was having an adulterous affair with got fired."

"Now hold on a minute—that's allegation, not proven fact."

"Agent Doucet *was* fired, wasn't he?"

"I've never met Doucet, and I have no personal knowledge of what may or may not have led to his firing."

She made an exasperated sound. "Well, Agent Sprague, *that* sure sounded like a textbook non-answer. Do they hold special classes to teach you how to do that when you get promoted to SAC?"

If he hadn't been doing seventy-five miles an hour on the freeway, Dan would have been tempted to pull over, stop the car and ream her out for her smart mouth. Instead, he shot her an irritated look. "What's going on? You told me you were covering TOTNAP. What does this nonsense have to do with anything? I swear to God, Claire, if you're playing games here, digging for dirt on the Bureau, I—''

''No,'' she said hastily. ''No, sorry. I really do need background on the kidnappings. I didn't mean to get sidetracked on the other business.''

''Then what was that about?''

She said nothing.

Dan had conducted enough interviews in his time, as both cop and parent, to know a reluctant witness when he saw one. ''I expect an answer,'' he said tersely.

He got a question instead. ''Did you know her husband? Laurel Madden's, I mean?''

''A little. We worked together a couple of times. Not recently, though.''

''You know he was murdered a few months ago?''

''Yes. What's that got to do with you?''

''I knew him, too. I interviewed him at Quantico a couple of years ago, and then I ran into him by chance again in New York earlier this year, not long before he died.''

''How?''

''I was investigating the same Russian mob

he'd infiltrated. When he realized I had him made, he agreed to share some information."

"Claire! You *blackmailed* him?"

"No! Honestly," she said, slapping his arm, "what do you take me for? It was nothing like that. He asked me to back off my research in exchange for exclusive coverage when the operation wound up, and I agreed. Only then, he was killed. And nobody's been indicted for his murder," she added pointedly.

Dan stared straight ahead, regretting that he'd offered to take her along. This was why it was never a good idea to mix business and pleasure. Old friend or no, Claire was still a reporter. Obviously she'd picked up on the rumors that had driven Laurel from Quantico just one step ahead of the scandalmongers' long knives. Now he had to wonder why Claire was really here. Even if investigating Kazarian's murder and Laurel Madden weren't her main objectives, the paths of those two were pretty much bound to cross—possibly even in a few minutes, Dan realized uneasily. When he'd left the office, Laurel had also been thinking about meeting the bloodhound team at Newport Bay, once Jenny Kirkendall had been sent home pending further investigation. If Laurel *had* gone on ahead—

He exhaled heavily. Just the kind of distraction he didn't need in the middle of an already impossible case. He mulled in silence, debating whether to turn the car around. Finally, he settled on a solution—probably only delaying the inevitable, but maybe enough of a stop-gap measure to get him through the afternoon.

When they got to the bay, Claire would stay in the car. Period. After that, as far as TOTNAP was concerned, she was on her own.

13

"Way to go, Gillespie," Claire muttered to herself. Left out of the action—and, worse, in the doghouse with Dan—she slumped down in the front seat, listening to the irritating crackle of police radios and their staccato stream of clipped banter and cryptic orders.

Dan had positioned the car in a line of other cruisers and unmarked police vehicles parked on a ridge overlooking a broad estuary plain. Here, in an ecological preserve located smack in the midst of some very expensive real estate, the silted outflow of the Santa Ana and San Diego creeks mingled with briny Pacific backwash from Newport Bay. The estuary was home to cranes, herons and other endangered birds, who strutted regally across muddy islands, looking singularly unimpressed by the magnanimous human gesture that allowed their precarious survival in one of the few undeveloped niches left on California's Orange Coast.

Twenty or thirty feet beneath the ridge where Claire sat brooding, sheriff's deputies and Newport Beach PD officers were searching the bushes. The entire area had been cordoned off, including surrounding access roads, leaving the forces below to carry out their work blessedly free of the curious eyes of the press or the public. Claire was the only outside observer who'd been allowed on the site, and then, only at a distance.

It was high tide, and water covered much of the estuary. Running against the offshore wind, a pair of flat-bottomed, aluminum boats rigged with fume-free electric outboard motors slowly crisscrossed the water, each one carrying a bloodhound and its handler. Held on short leashes, the hounds lay draped across the prows like vain, baggy nymphs admiring their own reflections. In fact, Claire knew, they were sniffing, trying to detect a very particular human scent—the kind of trace scent that emanates from floating body oils or rising decomposition gases.

A line of flags and marker buoys outlined a trail running from the gravel shoulder of Backbay Drive down the bank and into the water at a point that might have been passably shallow when the tide was well out. It was on that gravel-side shoulder, Claire guessed, that the dogs had first alerted on the scent of the toddler who, his mother claimed, had disappeared from a nearby swap meet—the Southland Snatcher's fourth alleged victim.

But Jennifer Kirkendall had failed her lie detector test. That much Claire had been able to draw from Dan before he parked the car, slammed on the hand brake and got out, warning her to stay put.

He was at the bottom of the ridge now, being brought up to speed by a couple of uniformed cops and plainclothes officials whom Claire had immediately marked as FBI. Next to Dan stood a tall, slim woman in a pantsuit, who could only be Laurel Madden. Her shining blond hair fluttered in the sunlight. From time to time, Dan glanced her way as she tucked it behind her ears, only to have it slip free in the next gust.

Watching them together, Claire felt every bit as voyeuristic as she had gazing at the wedding picture Mrs. Kazarian had brought to show her. Dan and Laurel, too, made a handsome couple, if you let yourself think about it that way. She shuddered, trying to convince herself that her rising anxiety was ridiculous—that the very idea of anything ever developing between those two was laughable. That they were supervisor and subordinate, period; and that her being stuck up here on the ridge had nothing to do with the fact that she'd cast Laurel in a critical light. Except—

Except Dan was nothing if not loyal, to friends and co-workers alike. Laurel was beautiful, to boot. As for Dan's own qualities—well, he was the kind of faintly scarred guy who might have had a few skin problems when he was a teenager, and hadn't a clue how attractive he was now. Claire had noticed the surreptitious looks he often got from women, but Dan was a little obtuse in that department—a guaranteed turn-on and challenge to a certain kind of female. Like Laurel Madden, maybe?

Get a grip, girl!

He'd warned her from the outset, Claire reminded herself, that she would have to hang back once they arrived. Letting her ride along had been a huge favor, one she knew he'd granted only out of friendship for her father. No doubt he was regretting the decision now, she mused bleakly—her own regret degenerating rapidly into angry self-recrimination. How could she have so clumsily dredged up the Madden/Doucet/Kazarian mess?

The thought of having disappointed Dan made her heartsick. She'd known him most of her life. Even after Dan left to join the Bureau and her father died, the Sprague and Gillespie families had kept in close touch. Claire had seen Dan laugh, work, play and grieve. But before today, she had rarely seen him angry—and certainly never at her.

She was trying to decide how to apologize, or explain herself, or *somehow* make Dan understand that she'd never intended to blindside him with trick questions about Laurel Madden, when suddenly, down below, there were flashes of movement and the unmistakable signs of something happening.

Heads snapped up, and the crowd on the bank moved to the water's edge. The flat-bottomed boats had slowed their pace to a dead crawl. They circled slowly, then came to a stop about ten yards from the shoreline and from one another. In the bow of one, a black-and-tan bloodhound crouched even lower, stretching out a forepaw and smacking the water's murky surface. The ruddy hound in the other boat alerted in his own unique way, sticking his face into the water right up to his eyes, his wagging tail balancing the other end of his loose-skinned body.

The handlers signaled to each other, then gestured to a third boat standing by in a cove. It moved out as its two passengers, police divers in black neoprene wet suits, snapped on weight belts and wrestled their feet into flippers. Positioning the dive boat near the others, the cop at the tiller cut the outboard. The divers proceeded to shrug into tank harnesses, pulled on masks and clamped their teeth around regulator mouthpieces. Then, one after the other, they pitched themselves backward, over the gunwales and into the water.

Caught up in the tense excitement, Claire completely forgot about Dan's orders, climbing out of the car and positioning herself on the front bumper for a better view. She cupped her hands over her eyes to shade them from the sun. Two lines of air bubbles and a trail of churning brown water rose to the surface in a zigzag pattern between the boats as the divers groped their way along the murky bottom.

Suddenly, the bubbles' advance halted. The water simmered in one place for a minute or so, then a buoy popped through to the surface. It was followed a moment later by a single black hood. While his partner remained below to mark their find, the diver oriented himself toward shore, lifted his mask, removed his regulator and wearily raised one clenched fist into the air.

The sign for a hit.

The coroner's van had arrived and the stretcher had been loaded when Dan finally headed back toward the car, supporting Laurel's arm as they stumbled their way up the brush-covered ridge. Pausing at the top, he glanced over at Claire, but if he was annoyed that she'd gotten out of the car, he gave no indication of it.

Not surprising, she thought. It was a shaken, subdued crowd that had watched the police divers emerge and gently lift the tiny, waterlogged body into the boat. A misdemeanor like hers was a minor infraction next to such a tragedy.

Dan released Laurel's arm, and they moved toward the line of cars. Claire studied the other woman. Her expression was grim, her skin pale as death. When they reached the car, Dan hesitated a moment, then introduced them.

"Agent Madden, Claire Gillespie. Claire's a reporter for *Newsworld,*" he explained. "Also, an old friend. She came along for the ride to get an off-the-record briefing on TOTNAP."

Laurel nodded distractedly but said nothing, as if she didn't trust her voice after what they'd witnessed below. If she'd ever heard Claire's name before, it wasn't apparent. Claire felt Dan's eyes on her, though, almost daring her to say anything.

No way. Not here, not now.

Claire nodded instead at the stretcher bearers making their way slowly up the bank. "The Kirkendall baby?" she asked quietly.

Dan nodded. "Looks like."

Laurel pulled a set of car keys from her pocket. "I'd better be going. I'll stay down for the autopsy and let you know what turns up."

Dan shook his head. "Oz will send someone else. They won't likely do it till tomorrow morning, anyway."

"I don't mind coming—"

"No. I want you back working on TOTNAP. But not now," he added, his voice gentler. "That's enough for today. Go home and get some rest. Will you be all right to drive?"

"I'm fine, but—"

"Home. That's an order."

Laurel hesitated, glanced at Claire once more, then nodded and walked away. Dan watched until she'd gotten into her car and pulled out. Only then did he turn back to Claire, his own face drawn. "Ready?"

"If you are."

He exhaled wearily. ''More than ready.''

''Dan?''

''What?''

''I'm sorry about before—on the drive down. I really didn't mean to put you on the spot.''

''Forget it. We'd better get going. Bridget and the others will be waiting with that dinner.''

He opened her door, his expression unreadable. Claire slipped past him and into the front seat, feeling like a stranger, weighed down by an inexpressible sense of loss—loss of the child. Loss of innocence. And maybe, too, the loss of an old trust that might never be rebuilt.

Dan closed the door and walked around to his side of the car. Claire buckled her seat belt, then sat quietly, waiting for him to get in. Westward, the spreading gleam of estuary waters spilled into the wide Pacific, reflecting an orange sun and a sky shot with blue and purple shards of offshore clouds. It was an obscenely pretty sunset forming above the horizon. What business did nature have, Claire wondered, celebrating the end of a day so somber?

She turned away from it, watching instead as the last of the men from below trudged up the embankment. Suddenly, coming from the far side of the estuary, a flash of light caught her eye.

Peering across, scanning the silhouetted ridge, she could just make out an indistinct figure—a man, she thought, though it was hard to be certain. Wearing a baseball cap? The glare of the setting sun bounced off twin circles of what appeared to be binoculars—trained in their direction, Claire realized.

Dan was reaching to turn the key in the ignition when Claire put a hand on his arm. "I think someone's watching us," she told him.

"Where?"

She pointed through the windshield. "Way over there, on the far ridge. See? Looks like a man with a pair of binoculars."

Dan draped his arms across the steering wheel and also peered at the figure. "Probably just a looky-loo," he said, frowning. He watched for a moment longer. The figure never moved. "Maybe press. But just to be on the safe side…" He slipped a radio microphone off its hook. "A-2, this is A-1. Come in, over."

The radio crackled. *"A-2, over."*

"Yeah, Oz, we've got company on the north ridge. You see him? Over."

The air was silent for a moment, and then the radio crackled again. "Yeah, got it. You want us to take a look? Over."

"Just get the locals to check it out, will you? Over."

"Ten-four."

"Thanks. A-1, over and out."

A moment later, another of the radios on his console crackled with the relayed message. A sheriff's cruiser a couple of cars down from them roared to life and careened back out of the turnoff, heading down Backbay Drive. As it disappeared around a bend in the road, Claire watched the figure across the way lower his binoculars, turn and disappear from view.

14

Poor Bridget, Dan thought. She'd prepared a spectacular dinner to welcome her big sister—fresh-baked bread and homegrown tomatoes, minted peas and wild rice with almonds, a crisp green salad, and a chicken dish with dried fruits, olives and a sauce so amazing that the recipe had to have come from God's own kitchen. But when Claire, Chris, Dan and his daughters all finally wandered in, hungry, tired and late from their respective afternoon efforts, they squeezed around the table in Bridget's tiny breakfast nook and devoured everything in sight with the single-minded enthusiasm of locusts—appreciative, but sorely lacking in leisurely civility, as dinner companions went.

Afterward, it was a subdued, satiated and shrunken group that retired to the apartment's postage stamp–size living room. Erin and Julie made teenage time-to-go excuses, pleading homework that should have been done before Sunday evening, Dan thought grumpily, but somehow never was—not that it would get in the way of long telephone conversations. How they ever made the grades they did was a mystery to him.

Claire and Bridget launched into a friendly argument about whether or not Bridget should accompany her husband to a medical conference in Santa Barbara the next weekend. As part of his internship, Chris McCabe was doing an emergency-room rotation at the medical center. That afternoon, the department head had offered him the weekend perk when the resident had had to back out because of another commitment.

"It's perfect timing, Britty. How often do you guys have a chance to get away on your own? And on an all-expenses-paid boondoggle, besides."

"But you've got work to do, Claire."

"No problem. I file on Wednesday. The weekend's free, and I can't think of anything I'd rather do than hang out with Lexie. We'll be fine, won't we?" Claire added, tugging the toddler's sleeve.

"Annie-Care baby-sit?"

"Yeah, what do you think?"

Lexie turned to her mother. "Annie-Care baby-sit me," she said firmly.

Bridget shot Chris a hopeful glance, then turned a worried look to her sister once more. ''Are you sure? It would only be for two nights—''

''And you'd be, what? An hour away? Go, go!'' Claire said, laughing and making sweeping-off motions with her hands.

Bridget leaned over and planted a kiss on Chris, who'd settled into a recliner in the corner of the room. ''Well, maybe,'' she said.

Chris grinned and nodded sleepily. He'd changed out of his hospital greens, cold-showered and drunk coffee all evening in a valiant effort to be a good host. But he was obviously wiped after another long shift, and it wasn't long before the battle to stay awake turned into a rout. As the others talked, his cropped blond head, propped in one hand, nestled deeper and deeper into the cushions. The ever-amiable smile stayed in place, Dan noted, like some trusted old retainer standing guard over an empty house, but the pale gray eyes, after much-determined, slow-motion blinking, finally abandoned the watch. Score one for the sandman.

That left Dan and Claire to hold up their ends of a conversation that expressly avoided, after the briefest of updates, any mention of TOTNAP or the depressing developments at Newport Bay. By unspoken mutual agreement, they'd decided that Bridget didn't need to have the wits scared out of her, especially when her own child was about the same age as little Ryan Kirkendall and not much older than the TOTNAP victims.

Dan watched Lexie empty her toy box, item by item, bringing things to show Claire. She was sitting on the carpet with her back against a wall, Bubba draped across her stretched-out legs like some hairy, hundred-pound throw rug. Much to Lexie's delight, Claire proceeded to deck him out in a necklace of brightly colored plastic pop beads, with a doll-blanket kerchief for his blocky head.

"I cover him up," Lexie decided, running off to retrieve another flannel blanket from her doll cradle. She dragged it across the room, flopping down to arrange it over the tiny portion of the dog's body that the thing actually covered. He lifted his nose to sniff at it dubiously, but Lexie's small hands cupped his kerchiefed head and pressed it down again onto Claire's lap. "Go to sleep, baby."

The dog lay back, enduring the indignity of it all with a martyred look and long-suffering sigh.

"Poor Bubba," Bridget crooned.

Claire laughed and stroked him, then leaned

over to kiss Lexie's cheek. But when she sat back and caught Dan watching her, a flicker of discomfort passed through her eyes. She looked away quickly and busied herself with helping Lexie groom the dog with a doll brush.

Nice going, Sprague.

Despite declaring the incident over and forgotten, he thought guiltily, his blowup that afternoon obviously still rankled. He found himself trying to fathom why on earth Claire would take an interest in loose Bureau gossip about Laurel Madden. And what was all that about Kazarian? What was his claim on Claire? The agent's murder was more than just another news item to her; Dan had seen it in those pained blue eyes when she'd mentioned his name. But why? Just because she'd met him before he died? Maybe. The faces of the dead did have a tendency to haunt the living.

Or was it because the Kazarian case was still open, his murder every bit as unsolved as Sean Gillespie's? Feelings of doubled treachery, first by a killer, then by the system that fails to find him, often made for angry embers, smoldering on in those whose lives were scarred by unpunished crime.

Claire had been eighteen when her father was gunned down late one night, sitting alone in his squad car, quietly doing his paperwork under the lights of a minimall parking lot. Months and months of dogged investigation had produced no more than speculation that the murder was the work of a frustrated stick-up thief or some drugged-out drifter. No one ever had solved the apparently random crime. Given the special bond between Sean and his eldest, Dan felt certain that Claire, even more than her sisters, carried deep inside her an intense fury and frustration over his senseless death.

Then Dan had another disastrous thought. Was it possible she'd fallen for Mike Kazarian? That she'd gone from the frying pan of Alan and Nicky's betrayal into the fire of an emotional entanglement with a married—and doomed—undercover agent? Kazarian had had a reputation as something of a ladies' man. God forbid that he'd ever laid a hand on her, especially at a time when she would have been so vulnerable. Claire was worth more than an Alan, a Nicky and a Kazarian combined, even though she had no idea of her own appeal. Never had, Dan reflected, mystified as ever by people's apparent inability to read themselves or anyone else.

As he watched her playing with Lexie and talking to Bridget, the sense of unease he'd been carrying around since the argument proceeded to make a tangled knot of his gut. Part of it was guilt over lashing out at someone for whom he'd long felt an indefinable protective attachment. But there was more to it than that, he knew. The mysterious Laurel was beginning to haunt him, too.

He thought about her stubbornly defending a young mother against unthinkable suspicions, then swallowing her shaken faith to conduct a deft interrogation that yielded the information on the location of her son's body. And the look on Laurel's face when she watched that tiny form being lifted, wet and dripping, from the water…

What about his duty toward her? Dan asked himself. She was his colleague and his subordinate. She had every right to expect the same support he gave every other one of his people, didn't she? Why hadn't he defended her more strenuously against the innuendos Claire had raised? Or had he? Maybe too strenuously? He couldn't even recall the exact words he and Claire had exchanged.

The devious mental gremlins that wreak havoc under conditions of stress and fatigue were playing nasty games with his mind, he realized. He glanced at his watch: a little after eight. If he took off soon and got to bed early for a change—

Just then, the dormant pager on his belt came to life, beeping hysterically, demanding his attention. Dan was tempted to throw the thing against the opposite wall.

''Wazzat?' Lexie asked, pulling herself to her feet and toddling over to him.

''It's my beeper,'' Dan told her.

Chris stirred in his chair, while Claire and Bridget watched Dan unclip the pager. Lexie held out one hand as the other rubbed her eyes sleepily. ''Lemme see.''

Bridget came over and scooped her up. ''No, honey, that's not a toy. Uncle Dan's work is calling. And you need to get into your jammies.''

Lexie looked down at him from the safe aerie of her mother's arms. ''You gotta go ho'pital?''

''I sure hope not, sweetie.'' Dan hit the Message Retrieval button. The number on the readout was a familiar one: Oz Paterson's. He sighed. ''Can I use your phone, Bridget?''

In the quiet of Sunday evening, Dan made the trip from his house in Santa Monica to Brentwood in five minutes. It took another ten of cruising up and down unfamiliar streets, missing signs in the dark and making illegal U-turns before he finally arrived at the address Paterson had given him over the phone. When he pulled up to the condominium complex, the evidence technicians were already packing up their cameras, gloves and Baggies, and the violent-crimes squad leader was standing at the front gate, keeping a watch out for him.

Oz Paterson's rimless glasses, thinly covered pate and the twin puffs of snow-white hair over his ears gleamed brightly under the glow of tiny white Christmas lights massed on trees at the entryway to the sprawling, Mediterranean-style complex. Paterson's first name was actually Calvin, but, short and stocky, he'd been called Oz for as long as anyone in the Bureau could remember, thanks to his resemblance to the wizard of Dorothy and Toto fame. As a Kansas boy himself, Dan had always appreciated the aptness of the nickname.

"She didn't want me to call you," Paterson said as Dan strode toward him, "but I figured you'd better see this for yourself."

"Where is it?"

Paterson whistled through the gap in his front teeth and gestured to John Quinn, one of the technicians, who approached with some labeled evidence bags and a pair of tweezers. The squad leader pulled a flashlight out of his pocket.

''The envelope was stuck to the mailbox with duct tape,'' he said, opening one of the bags and showing Dan a carefully folded-over piece of the gray adhesive. ''Looks similar to the tape they found with the Morales baby, but who knows? We'll get the lab to run a comparison.''

Dan nodded. When the bagged body was found in the aqueduct, it had been bound with duct tape. Made by only a few manufacturers, the all-purpose tape was so widely distributed that identifying any particular purchaser was like looking for a needle in a haystack. But if the brand or rip marks on the tape matched up between different crime scenes, or between crime scene evidence and a roll found in the possession of a suspect, then it became a potential forensic nail to help close a case.

''And the note?''

''Here's the envelope,'' the technician said, reaching into another evidence bag to withdraw a standard white number ten envelope. Three words were scrawled on the outside in felt marker: *To LOREL MADEN.*

''Guy can't spell for beans,'' Paterson observed dryly. ''Wait'll you see the note.''

''The envelope was taped to the *outside* of the mailbox?'' Dan asked. ''Not in it?''

"Nope. The boxes for all the units in the complex are right here," Paterson said, stepping back inside the gate. Dan followed him through and saw four rows of four boxes set into a freestanding brick wall with a master access door on the back.

"Laurel said she stopped to check her box after coming back from running an errand around six-thirty," Paterson said. "That's when she saw the thing taped to the top. We found the adhesive marks left behind where she ripped it off."

"Okay, so presumably the guy knows she lives here, but doesn't know in which unit. That's a relief, anyway." Dan frowned. "What was she doing looking for mail on a Sunday evening? There's no delivery today."

Paterson shrugged. "She said she forgot to check yesterday. We went door-to-door to see if any other residents noticed anything—the note or anybody hanging around the mailboxes—but of the ones we found at home, nobody'd seen a thing. I'll send someone out tomorrow to follow up with the rest. We did find one guy who picked up his own mail this afternoon around two, and he said the note wasn't there then, far as he noticed."

"So that means it was probably put there sometime between two and six-thirty. See if you can narrow that range when you do the follow-up to-morrow, Oz. Let me see the note, please,'' Dan added, turning back to Quinn.

Using the tweezers once more so as not to smudge possible fingerprint evidence, Quinn withdrew a single piece of eight-and-a-half-by-eleven unlined paper creased by multiple fold lines.

''Don't think the guy knows how to stuff an envelope too efficiently,'' he said. ''Looks like he made several tries before he figured out how to get the thing to fit.''

Dan pulled a flashlight from his own pocket. ''Hold it steady, please.'' He shone the light on the paper along with Paterson's, squinting at the words scrawled with what looked to be the same felt marker.

DEAR LOREL,

I SAW YOU ON TV WITH THAT OTHER FBI GUY. I'M FLATTERED THEY'VE GOT SOMEBODY LIKE YOU ON THE CASE. THEY SAID YOUR REAL SMART & THAT YOU CAUGHT SOME CRAZY KILLER BACK IN DC. BUT THAT WAS THEN, THIS IS NOW, LO-

REL. SORRY—YOU WONT CATCH ME—THO MAYBE I MIGHT DECIDE TO CATCH *YOU!!!* I'M A LITTLE DESAPPOINTED IN YOU PEOPLE, THO. YOU HAVEN'T FOUND THAT FIRST KID, AND I LEFT HIM RIGHT OUT IN AN OPEN FIELD. KNOW WHAT ELSE? THAT KID AT THE SWAP MEET? IT WASN'T ME WHO TOOK HIM. HA, HA. SORRY YOU HAD TO WASTE YOUR TIME ON SOME DUMB COPYCAT. BUT I WANT TO HELP YOU OUT, LOREL, SO TELL YOU WHAT—I LEFT THE LAST ONE THERE TODAY, TO SAVE YOU SOME TIME LOOKING. DONT SAY I NEVER DID NOTHING FOR YOU. SEE YOU SOON!!!

YOUR GREATEST FAN,
S.S.

There was a big smiley face scrawled next to the initials.

"S.S.?" Dan said.

Paterson shrugged. "Southland Snatcher?"

"I guess. 'Left the last one there?' That supposed to mean he left the Goodsell baby at the swap meet?"

''Could be.''

Dan shook his head. ''This could all be an ugly hoax. To be on the safe side, though, you'd better call the sheriff's department and have them get the bloodhounds back out there tonight.''

''This is turning into a full-time job for them.''

''No kidding. We'll have to think about that other comment about the first victim being in an open field.''

''You know how many open fields there are in the whole of L.A. County? About a gajillion.'' Paterson ran a hand over the stubble on his jaw. ''You really think there's a chance this is a hoax?''

''It's possible. Except for the duct tape, which could easily be a coincidence, there's nothing here any twisted sister with a television set couldn't have concocted for kicks.''

''Yeah, but that twisted sister tracked Laurel home.''

Dan nodded soberly. ''I know. I don't like that at all. I'm going to call the duty officer and put a watch on her place until we get to the bottom of this. Is this the only entrance?''

''No, there's another one out back by the parking area. You'll need at least two cars to cover the place. You want me to wait till they get here?''

''No. I'm going to go talk to her, and I'll wait for them. Just turn in the evidence and make that call to the sheriff, then call it a day, Oz. You've had a long one.''

''I guess we'll ship this stuff to Quantico if anything turns up at the swap meet?''

''No, I want it shipped, regardless of what happens down there. As a matter of fact, get the duty officer to overnight it, and mark it top priority. No son of a bitch is going to stalk one of my people and get away with it. I want a photocopy of the note and the envelope made before it goes out, please.''

''You got it, boss. Come on, folks,'' Paterson called to the others. ''Let's turn it in.''

''See you guys.'' Dan started up the sidewalk, then paused and turned back. ''Hey, Oz? What number is she in?''

''Eight. Last unit down on your left.''

''Got it. G'night.''

'''Night, Dan.''

Dan watched them load the cars and pull out. Then he turned, moving slowly up the walk with a doomed feeling weighing heavily on his chest.

15

The sight of his leash was apparently a signal for Bubba to begin performing gravity-defying leaps of joy. His exuberant vertical liftoffs under the Spragues' back porch lights put Claire in mind of a four-legged Baryshnikov performing virtuoso onstage jetés.

"Bubba, sit!" Erin commanded.

He immediately plopped his bottom down, but his liquid brown eyes danced with anticipation as she handed the leash to Claire. "He'll be all right once you get it on him. He loves his walks. Thanks for taking him."

Claire clipped the lead to his collar. "I need the exercise. The kitchen's cleaned and Bridget's putting Lexie to bed, so I thought I'd work off dinner. See you in a while," she added, heading down the drive behind the waving banner of Bubba's tail.

"Have fun!" Erin called.

Content to let the dog lead, Claire followed his loping pace up the street, knowing from past visits and past walks that he'd head for the park a few blocks away. At that late hour, she could let him off-leash there to run a few happy laps and sniff for the wild rabbits he never quite knew what to do with once he found them—his retriever instincts exceeding the grasp of his urban life-style, guaranteeing a bunny-bowser standoff.

The night was comfortably warm, like August in Manhattan, but with a dry, dusty breeze whipping up loose paper and errant seed pods. The air smelled of the distant Mojave Desert. This was not the salty Pacific wind she'd come to know. That could only be a Santa Ana blowing in, Claire thought.

She gazed at lighted windows as she passed house after house, wondering at the lives of the people who lived in them. Just blocks from the Santa Monica Pier and the ocean, Dan's house was a renovated prewar bungalow, nestled cozily among three or four square miles of similarly modest but pristine properties, interspersed here and there with fancier rebuilds. Regardless of how much it aged, Santa Monica would never be anything less than a cushy corner of prime coastal real estate—not equal to the pricey, status-conscious levels of nearby Brentwood or Malibu, maybe, but none too shabby. Handy for Dan, too, not to have to make a long L.A. freeway commute into the office every day.

As her thoughts turned again to him, Claire recalled the strain on Dan's face as he'd hung up Bridget's phone and told them he had to go out again. As if sensing Claire's questions, he'd shot an oddly self-conscious look in her direction, but said nothing. The call had something to do with TOTNAP, she was certain, but if she thought he'd let her in on the latest development, she was sorely mistaken—not that she entertained any such illusion. It was only too obvious that the pall of the afternoon still hung over them. From here on in, if she wanted the FBI position on the Southland Snatcher, she was going to have to take whatever pap Alice Wentzl was authorized to dish out. So much for old friends and inside tracks. Some boundaries you didn't cross, but somehow, unwittingly, she'd done just that with Dan the moment she'd brought Laurel Madden's name into the conversation.

When Claire and the dog came to an intersection, Bubba, well-trained fellow that he was, stopped and looked up at her expectantly, waiting for the go-ahead. Claire let a couple of cars pass on the cross street, then nodded to him. "Okay, big guy, we can do it now."

They traversed the street at an angle, turning down toward the park. Bubba's pace quickened as it came into sight.

A car drifted slowly by them—a Mercedes, Claire noted by the familiar, pie-cut chrome circle on the trunk. She'd picked up another bicoastal cultural habit of late, she realized. In Manhattan, where almost no one she knew kept a car, the only vehicles she bothered to pick out of the street melee were buses and yellow cabs. But here in auto-loving L.A., where your wheels were your calling card, it was vanity plates and luxury models she'd taken to ticking off in her mind like some mental motor scavenger hunt.

When they reached the edge of the grassy park, she bent to unclip the lead from Bubba's collar. But instead of bounding away, he bristled and plastered himself against her leg, a low growl building deep in his throat as he stared straight ahead into the night. Claire followed the direction of his gaze. The Mercedes had pulled up to the curb about twenty yards ahead, and the driver was getting out to call at one of the houses on the opposite side of the street from the park.

"It's okay, Bubba. Come on, let's have a run."

She flipped the leash over her shoulder and started moving forward. The dog kept pace with her, but he never took his eyes off the man or let up on his worried grumbling. Claire peered at the figure again. He wasn't crossing the street, after all. Instead, he came around the car to the passenger side at the curb and leaned back on the hood, watching them. Waiting.

They gave him a wide berth as they approached, the dog crouching lower and pressing even closer to her leg with every step. Claire couldn't decide if Bubba's stance was meant as a threatening, protective display, or if he was looking for her to defend *him.* She suspected the latter. So much for night strolls with a big dog—although when she finally made out the face of the stranger, she acquired new respect for Bubba's canine instinct for danger.

"Doucet!"

He nodded laconically. "Hey there, Claire. Taking the night air?"

"What are you doing here?"

"Pretty much the same as you, I imagine. Nice evening for a stroll." He leaned forward, patting his leg. "Hey there, pooch!"

Bubba growled.

"You want to watch your step," she said. "He doesn't like strangers."

"Oh, go on. Not this guy." Doucet's knees bent, and he slid down the side of the car. Leaning against it, he slapped his thighs. "Come here, buddy! Attaboy!"

Claire watched, dismayed, as Bubba inched forward, head and tail cowed submissively. His nose stretched forward and he sniffed Doucet's hands a couple of times. Then Bubba rose and snuggled next to the rogue agent, his tail picking up altitude and speed as if he'd discovered a long-lost friend of his youth. Since that was impossible, all Claire could conclude was that the dog had no damn sense.

"Thanks a lot, traitor," she grumbled.

Doucet ruffled the animal's ears. "Never met a retriever I didn't like. You want to fetch a stick, fella? Come on, let's go find one."

He stood again and wandered off across the park, searching the ground as he went. Bubba padded along beside him, completely clueless but more than delighted to join in whatever game his new friend was playing. Claire rolled her eyes and traipsed behind. There was a lot to be said for rottweilers, she decided.

Doucet reached down and grabbed a piece of

broken tree branch, then waved it in front of the dog's nose. "Ready?"

Bubba woofed.

Doucet drew back the best pitcher's arm Claire had ever seen outside the pros and whipped the branch farther across the park than she would have thought possible. Bubba bounded off after it.

Doucet watched him for a moment, then turned, grinning. "That'll keep him busy for a while. Nice dogs, golden retrievers, but they've got moss for brains."

Despite his smile, the dark eyes glinted in the light from the distant street lamps, as alert and calculating as Claire recalled from their meeting in Brooklyn. She took a nervous step backward. What an idiot she was, following him blithely to the center of the park, far from neighboring houses and potential help. Now that they stood face-to-face, she could see that he towered an easy foot over her, with every bit of that extra height devoted to legs.

Good luck trying to make a run for it on your stubby gams, dimwit!

She studied him warily. He'd lost that grubby ski jacket he'd been wearing in Brooklyn, and she could see that it was a buffed-to-standard special agent's body he had under that denim shirt. Make that *ex*-special agent. Should she let on she knew he'd been axed? she wondered.

Not yet. See what he's up to.

She planted her hands on her hips, feigning a bravado she didn't feel. "You look a little cleaned up compared to the last time we met." She cocked her thumb over her shoulder at the car. "And you've got better wheels."

He shrugged. "Well, that was then, this is now. My daddy always used to say, 'If you're gonna go tracking game, son, make sure you blend into your surroundings.'"

"And exactly what game is it you're tracking?"

"The very question I was going to put to you. You left New York awfully suddenly, Claire. What brings you out here?"

"I don't see that it's any of your business."

Far behind him, Claire dimly made out a flash of light-colored fur. Bubba had already lost interest in them and the stick, and had wandered off to sniff the bushes. She whistled. Intent on his hunt, he ignored her. Claire turned, anyway, moving back toward the light of the street.

Doucet proceeded to amble alongside. "You're staying at your sister's, I see."

''Is that so?''

''Yes, ma'am. Mary Bridget Gillespie McCabe, thirty-one, television reporter, but on extended maternity leave at the moment. Husband Christopher John McCabe, thirty-two, intern, UCLA Medical Center. Daughter Alexis Claire McCabe, two years old—named after you, I see. You and your sister must be close. She even followed you into journalism.''

Claire stopped dead in her tracks, her heart pounding. ''What are you trying to prove, Doucet? Why are you spying on my family?''

''Not spying. Just doing my homework.''

''Doing your homework—is that what breaking into my apartment back in New York and stealing my files was about?''

He didn't admit it, but didn't deny it, either. ''Like I said, I'm curious what makes you tick.''

''Why?''

''You're an interesting case. You know what else I found out about you? You tried to enroll in police academy a year after your father was murdered. Never got past the physical, though. Why was that? Too short?''

She grimaced. ''As a matter of fact, no, that wasn't it. They were hiring midgets that year, believe it or not. Go figure.''

"So?"

"If you know so much about it, you should know that, too."

"Missed that detail in my research. Just found out you were rejected after the physical."

They'd reached the edge of the park again, closer to streetlights and the comfortable proximity of neighboring houses. Doucet stopped next to a picnic table and hiked himself on top, planting a pair of serious-looking black leather boots on the bench. He leaned forward, elbows on his knees. "So come on, Claire, fess up. Why'd you wash out of the police academy? Flat feet?"

"If you must know, a busted tailbone."

He hooted. "*What?* How'd that happen?"

She sighed. "I broke it when I was nine, playing paratrooper. I jumped off a roof and landed on my tush. When it healed, apparently, it fused to my bottom vertebra. The academy doctors figured after a couple of years in a cruiser, I'd just end up another long-term back-disability claim, so they turned me down."

"Ouch! Why did you want to be a cop?"

She turned away, not answering. As the wind tumbled dry leaves across the grass, Claire spotted another broken branch on the ground. She bent over and picked it up, slapping it against her thigh. That was another rule from *Gillespie's Guide to Getting Out in One Piece:* "Find something to use for a weapon." Just in case.

"You wanted to join up so you could hunt for your dad's killer, didn't you?" Doucet said.

She nodded reluctantly. "Yes."

"But that didn't work out, so eventually you got over it and on with your life."

"You never get over something like that."

"I suppose not. But you did move on and became a crime reporter, instead. What's that all about? Trying to fight the bad guys by other means?"

She fixed him with a hard look. "I fight crooked law enforcement officials, too, Doucet. I've nailed a couple so far."

"I know. And now you've come out here to check up on Laurel Madden, is that it?"

"Who says?"

"I do. You met her today."

She thought of the figure with the binoculars on the Newport ridge. Had that been him? "If you know that, then you know I was assigned by my magazine to cover the Southland Snatcher case."

He nodded. "That's your official reason for being out here. But it's really still about Mike Kazarian, isn't it?"

She studied him for a moment. ‘‘You know what, Doucet? You’re not the only one who does your homework. I’ve learned a thing or two about you, too, since the last time we met. Like, for example, you have no right to be carrying that FBI badge you showed me the other day. You were canned. ‘Conduct unbecoming a federal agent’—I think that’s the category your firing fell under, wasn’t it? For having an affair with another agent’s wife—your best friend’s wife, to boot. And that’s just for starters, because I hear the other shoe may yet drop. I suspect Ivan Ivankov was telling the truth, and it wasn’t his goons who did Michael in at all. I think maybe it was you.’’

‘‘You do, do you? So you couldn’t do anything about your father’s killer, but you’re going to solve the mystery of Mike Kazarian, is that it?’’

‘‘Sounds like a plan to me.’’

‘‘Fine. But as long as you’re doing your homework, little lady, maybe you should take a closer look at that fella you’re so intent on turning into a martyr.’’

‘‘Don’t patronize me, Doucet. What do you mean?’’

‘‘Well, for starters, you might want to check out the possibility that Mike Kazarian cheated on his wife.’’ He shook his dark head. ‘‘But, on second thought, you researched that one firsthand, didn't you?''

''I told you before, I had no idea he was married until the day of his funeral.''

''You know, I really wonder about you, Claire. For such a smart lady, you are one god-awful judge of men. That ex-hubby of yours is a real piece of cake, too.''

''You mind your own business.''

He held up his hands apologetically. ''Okay, okay—*pardonnez-moi.* I can understand why that would be a touchy subject. Fair enough. Let's stick to Mike. Since you're already acquainted with the adulterous side of his nature, how about the fact that he was an abusive husband?''

''Did Laurel tell you that?''

''She didn't have to. I saw the bruises.''

''Was that before or after you started sleeping with her?''

His black eyes narrowed, but he let her comment pass. ''Here's another charming thing about the guy—had an ego from here to Mexico. She was a trophy for his shelf, not much more. And you know what's interesting about trophy wives? Their real value as an ego booster only exists if other men covet them. What would you say if I told you Mike tried to market Laurel to his friends?''

''Oh, I see! He *forced* you to have an affair with his wife, is that it? How very convenient for you.'' Claire laughed out loud. ''You're a riot!'' She spotted Bubba loping across the field and whistled. ''Bubba! Come on, boy, let's go.'' He ran up happily this time, and she hooked the leash onto his collar. ''This has been highly entertaining,'' she said, turning back to Doucet, ''but I have to be going now.''

''Hold on a minute, would you?''

''Why?''

''Because I came to offer you a deal.''

''What kind of deal?''

''How about if I give you back your files?''

''You'd do that?''

''You want to go ahead and do your exposé on Ivan Ivankov and the Russian mob in Brooklyn, don't you?''

''And what do you want in exchange for returning my own property that you have no business having in the first place?''

''I want you to leave Laurel Madden alone.''

''That's it?''

''Yes.''

''And what about you? I'm not doing the Ivankov story without looking into who car-bombed Michael Kazarian. And right now, Doucet, you're at the top of my list of suspects.''

He sat back and patted his chest. ''Give me your best shot, *ma chère.* I can take it.''

''Just leave Laurel out of it, is that the deal?''

''That's about it.''

She shook her head. ''Nope. Come on, Bubba, let's go.'' The dog gave Doucet a regretful look, as if inviting him to join them, then loped happily off at Claire's side.

''Claire?'' Doucet called after her. ''Leave her alone!''

She turned. ''Or what?''

''Just stay away from her, I'm warning you.''

Claire and Bridget sat outside on the stoop at the top of the stairs, drinking hot herbal tea and talking quietly while Chris and Lexie slept in the apartment.

''I'll tell Dan about it when he gets home,'' Claire said. ''I'm certain Doucet's just trying to intimidate. God knows, I've run into that before. I don't think there's any real risk, but I'm thinking maybe I should move to a hotel tomorrow, Britty.''

''Don't. You'll just give this character the

sense of power he craves. The only thing to do with a bully is stand firm.''

''He did break in to my apartment in New York.''

''Well, if he's been checking up on things as closely as you say, then for sure he knows whose property this is, and he's got to know you're going to pass his name on to Dan. You think he's going to run the risk of trying anything now? This is the best possible place you could be.''

''Maybe,'' Claire said grimly. ''But if he was looking for my Achilles' heel, he sure found it when he mentioned you guys.''

Bridget put an arm around her shoulders. ''Don't give him the satisfaction of worrying. I'm not.''

Claire sat gloomily, raising her cup to her lips and watching her breath move steam over the rim. ''Britty?''

''What?''

''Do you think I'm a lousy judge of character?''

Her sister gave her a puzzled look. ''Not at all. You wouldn't be as good a crime reporter as you are if you weren't terrific at ferreting out lies and dissembling.''

''I don't know,'' Claire said ruefully. ''I always

flattered myself that I was good at it, but sometimes I think it works like the finicky electronics on a sports car. It's got a real nasty habit of cutting out on me at inopportune moments—like whenever I fall for a guy."

Bridget rubbed her back. "I think you do have a tendency to see only the good in those you love," she agreed. "Tell you the truth? I could never understand what you saw in Alan."

"I wonder about that myself, these days. But he really is an amazing writer, you know. Whatever else I may have misjudged, I know I wasn't wrong about that."

"Could be. But talent alone doesn't cut it if you're not prepared to invest the sweat equity. That's ninety-nine percent of what success is all about. Look how hard you work, Claire. Chris, too. That's what it takes to get anywhere, no matter how much talent anyone has."

Claire exhaled wearily. "I kept thinking that if I gave Alan enough space and support, he could do it. In the end, he just got lazy. But you know what the funny thing is?"

"What?"

"I think Nicky might be good for him. No way are there going to be two prima donnas in that family. She might actually whip him into some kind of shape.''

''Oh, I think she's already trying. From what Mom tells me, I'd say old Alan's on a very short leash with a very demanding taskmaster. One way or another, his coasting days are over.''

Claire looked over at her sister. ''The sweetest revenge,'' she said, eyebrows dancing.

Bridget burst out laughing.

16

Dan knew he was sunk the moment Laurel opened the door to her cream-stuccoed town house and he spotted the tear-stained cheeks.

She was as prickly as ever, though, and made an exasperated sound when she saw who it was. ''I *told* him not to bother you. There was no reason to bring you out again tonight.''

''Oz did the right thing, calling me. I would have been annoyed if he hadn't.''

She wiped her face and peered around the doorjamb, painted brick red to match the door. ''Are they still out there?'' she asked, glancing down the leaf-strewn walkway.

''No, they packed up and went back to the office. We're going to ship the evidence off to the lab. Meantime, until we get to the bottom of this, I'll have cars stationed at the front and rear entrances.''

She held her wind-whipped hair out of her face,

and nodded. Her miserable, emerald eyes were almost at the level of his own. Dan felt his stomach plummet.

"Can I come in for a minute?"

She hesitated, then pulled away from the opening to let him pass into the black-and-white-tiled foyer. A filigreed wrought-iron banister ran up white-carpeted stairs to the right, while to the left, mahogany-trimmed French doors led into what appeared to be a living room. Through a broad archway at the end of the hall ahead of him, Dan saw tall wooden stools tucked under the shelf of a large kitchen island. Filled plastic grocery bags and flowers in a cellophane wrapper looked to have been abandoned, unopened, on its marble top.

The door latched softly behind him, and Dan turned to find Laurel watching him, one hand still on the handle. She glanced away quickly, self-consciously tucking a loose strand of hair behind an ear. She'd changed her clothes since Newport Bay. Now she had on an ivory-colored sweater—long, in some kind of nubbly wool—hanging loose over a flowing, multicolored skirt that went almost to her ankles. Her feet looked bare in soft, slip-on loafers.

Sunk, sunk, sunk.

He cleared his throat. ''Oz said you found the note about six-thirty?''

She nodded. ''I'd just gotten back from the grocery store and ran down to get the mail. I forgot about it yesterday.''

''The envelope wasn't on the box when you left?'' he asked hoarsely, the words deteriorating into a rasp.

''I didn't go out the front way. Do you need a glass of water?''

Eyes watering in the effort to hold back a cough, he nodded and wheezed, ''Please.''

''Follow me.'' She led him to the kitchen, taking a glass from a shelf and filling it from a bottle of Evian off the fridge door. ''Here.'' As he drank it to the bottom, she watched him as if he'd just dropped in from some distant and very gauche planet. ''Better? Do you need another one?''

He waved a hand, feeling as stupid as he ever had. ''No, it's fine, thanks. Sorry. I don't know where that came from.''

She shrugged as he returned the glass to her. ''The wind's picking up. I hear these are the famous Santa Anas. They say people go a little crazy when they blow in off the desert. That true?''

"If the last couple of days are any indication, I'd say so."

"No kidding. Have a seat," she said. "As long as we're here, I think I should put away the groceries before the frozen stuff completely melts."

He pulled out a stool and settled onto it, trying not to stare as she moved from counter to fridge to cupboard. "What did you make of that note?"

"Are you asking me in my capacity here as resident profiler or sitting duck?" she asked dryly.

He smiled. Clearly, she was shaken but not defeated. "Both, I guess. Do you think it's from the Snatcher?"

"I'm not sure. It's a bid for attention, obviously. If it is our UNSUB, then he's upping the ante on this game of hide-and-seek he's been playing with us. Like we're not moving fast enough, or playing cleverly enough for him."

"That note doesn't look like it came from any rocket scientist. It was full of spelling mistakes."

"Doesn't necessarily mean anything. Some clever people are lousy spellers. It's also possible that the spelling mistakes are deliberate. We had a case like that in Michigan last year, where a serial killer was taking out young college women and leaving crude, misspelled notes on their bodies. Turned out he was an English professor trying to throw us off his track.'' She reached into one of the plastic bags and lifted out a round of cheese. ''The TOTNAP suspect's been playing it very safe up to now by choosing victims at random—knowing, I'm sure, that by targeting complete strangers, he decreases dramatically his chances of getting caught. That's a very thought-driven perp.''

''And the note?''

She paused, holding the cheese in her hand. ''There's a vague sexual undertone there that seems aimed at me. It's strange, given that his targets up to now have all been small children, as far as we know. But the power trip he seems to be on is consistent. Even if his method is in the process of shifting, it's a consistent criminal signature.'' Dan must have given her a strange look, because she grimaced. ''I don't make this stuff up, you know,'' she said. ''I've learned it from other people smarter than me. It's just the way a criminal mind works. This guy's signature is the power thing—that, and the shock value he seems to be going for.''

''So you do think it's the same guy?''

''Very possibly. If it is, he's becoming rapidly more unstable, and I have a feeling I know why.''

''Why?''

"I've been thinking about the Morales case, and the way the child was suffocated inside an opaque plastic garbage bag. Typically, when a killer hides his victims' faces—like when a terrorist, say, puts sacks over his captives' heads—it means he wants to depersonalize them. He doesn't want to think of them as human beings with a life and feelings same as him, someone maybe he can relate to. They're simply objects to be dispatched on the way to achieving whatever twisted goal he has in mind."

"But in this case, it was the whole body that went into the bag."

"Exactly," Laurel said, frowning. "It's not like any pedophile I've ever heard of. It's more like somebody putting kittens in a sack and tossing them off a bridge. Like he can't stand to look at what he's doing. I've been thinking maybe he's going for shock value, knowing there's nothing more certain to get attention than targeting babies, but he still has enough…I don't know…conventional values, I guess, to feel badly about what he's doing." She fell silent and stared at the counter, lips pressed tightly together.

Through her lowered lashes, Dan saw the glimmer of fresh tears. He reached across the counter and placed a hand lightly on hers. "This is tough, I know. We don't have to do this right now."

She looked up again, tearful, defiant and very angry. "Feels bad about what he's doing—but it doesn't stop the bastard, does it?" She withdrew her hand and carried the cheese over to the refrigerator. "And that bragging tone in the note—it's disgusting."

"It may not be the Snatcher at all," Dan said, reaching for any hopeful note, "just another, garden-variety pervert who's piggybacking on TOTNAP."

She closed the door and turned to him. "Well, thanks. That makes me feel a whole lot better."

He felt his face flush. "I didn't mean—"

She waved a hand. "Never mind. I know what you meant." Back at the island, she lifted the cellophane-wrapped flowers and hefted them in her hand, grimacing. "I bought these in a dim effort to cheer myself up after what we found in the bay this afternoon. Pretty pathetic, don't you—" Her voice broke and she slapped them back down on the counter, dropped her head and braced herself with both fists. "Oh, hell! Bloody, bloody, hell…"

She made no sound, but when the first tear splashed on the marble countertop, Dan got up and pulled her into his arms. She stiffened instantly.

"It's okay," he said quietly. "Go ahead and cry. You've earned the right."

She resisted a moment longer, then gave it up. Folding her arms in front of herself, she dropped her head to his shoulder and let him rock her gently. Dan patted her back, feeling strangely bifurcated—his heart wrenched by the ugly situation, and by the realization of how disastrous it must feel for her to be pulled into another twisted felon's game, after what she'd already gone through with the Beltway Ripper. But at the same time, a small corner of his mind was distracted by the oddity of holding a woman almost as tall as he was. Fiona had tucked neatly under his arm when they'd walked beside one another, and when he'd held her like this, he could rest his chin on her head. Laurel, on the other hand, almost had to bend at the waist to lay her cheek on his shoulder. For all her height, though, she was surprisingly fine-boned and delicate. If he squeezed her, Dan had the sense she'd shatter in his arms.

She shuddered, then straightened and pulled away from him, wiping her eyes, looking slightly mortified.

"You know what?" Dan said.

"What?"

"I think a strong belt of something might be in order right about now. Have you got anything to drink in the house?"

She smiled vaguely and gave his chest a couple of indulgent pats, shaking her head. "I don't think that's a good idea."

"Why not?"

"Because..." Taking a deep breath, she took another step backward, resting her hands behind her on the countertop. "I think you should go home. Don't get me wrong. I appreciate your support and concern, I really do. In fact, I think you're the nicest man I've met in a long, long time—"

"I hear a 'but' coming on."

Laurel nodded. "But if you and I have a drink together right now, I'm afraid it might..." She paused. "Let's just say I'd rather not destroy the very nice image of you I have in my mind."

"What image is that?"

"The last decent married man on earth."

Dan felt the blood drain from his face.

"I'm not suggesting you had anything improper in mind," she said quickly. "It's just...well, things have happened to me before. And in your case—" She smiled a little. "I didn't mean to eavesdrop when I came by your office yesterday. But when I heard you on the phone to your wife, it was really nice, you know? And you've got all those family pictures in your office—''

''I was talking to my daughter.''

''Pardon?''

''Erin. She's nineteen. I have another daughter, Julie. She's sixteen.''

''Oh. I thought—''

''You don't know about my wife?'' He shifted uncomfortably. ''Of course you don't. How would you? I guess I just thought someone in the office might have said something to you, or…I don't know.''

''I'm not much for office gossip, maybe because I've been the brunt of it too often. I haven't really talked to anybody there about anything except ongoing cases. What about your wife?''

''She died two years ago this past October. It was cancer.''

Laurel's hand went to her mouth. ''Oh, God—I'm sorry. I had no idea. You wear a ring and everything, and I just assumed—''

He looked down at his wedding band. ''My daughters have told me I should think about taking it off.'' He gave it a tug, but it jammed, skin pillowing against knuckle. ''I've worn it for twenty-three years, and it doesn't come off any-more. I guess my knuckles have gotten bigger or something. I mean, I *could* get it off, I suppose. I could have it cut off, but...''

''But that would feel disloyal. Like you were cutting her out of your life, right?''

He looked up at her gratefully. ''I guess that's it, yes.''

''I can understand that.''

''Thanks. Anyway, you're right, I should get going and leave you alone.'' He turned and started for the door, then glanced around. ''I haven't called about that surveillance. If I could use your phone for a minute—or, no—'' He patted his pockets, and found his cell phone. ''Never mind. I'll go outside and make the call, and just wait out there till—''

''Dan?''

''What?''

''You're right, you know. I really could use a stiff drink. How about you?''

''It started with a note the last time, as well,'' Laurel said, handing him a double scotch, then settling onto the bar stool next to his. Despite the comment about needing a stiff drink, she'd poured hardly a finger's worth in her own glass, he noticed. ''Randy Harkness had seen me on television, too.''

''Harkness being the Beltway Ripper?''

She took a sip and nodded.

''I didn't really follow the case too closely,'' he said apologetically. ''It happened right around the time my wife got sick, and—''

''And you had more important things on your mind. Understandable.''

Dan took a slow drink from his own glass, then set it down. ''Did this Harkness character write to you at home?''

''No. He sent it to me in care of headquarters. He didn't realize at first that I was out at Quantico and not in the Hoover Building.''

''But this was after he'd already killed some people?''

''Yes, four, in fact. I'd been asked to stand by at a press conference called to review the steps the Bureau was taking to find the guy. We'd put together a profile based on what we knew about his victims and methods, and at one point I was called on to summarize that profile. We were hoping someone might recognize something familiar in it, maybe think of a neighbor or co-worker who fit the bill.''

"It started out as an IRS beef, didn't it?"

"That's right. Harkness was a small businessman, but his trophy-making operation had been seized for back taxes. After that, he started drinking. His marriage broke up, a few other things went wrong in his life, and at that point things went south fast. Next thing you know, he decides to go after an IRS employee—any IRS employee would do—to pay the organization back. He picked out a midlevel manager he'd dealt with during his audit. Followed the guy home, stabbed him in front of his own house and drove off. Nobody saw or heard a thing. Harkness figured he'd gotten away with it, so he decided to take out another. This time, it was a clerk who worked the front desk in the service's downtown D.C. office. Just picked him at random, we think. It wasn't clear Harkness had ever dealt with him. Got the guy while he was out jogging in a park early one morning. Once again, no witnesses. Next, Harkness remembered that the Social Security Administration had gotten after him for nonsubmission of employee benefits. He picked his victim there pretty much at random, too. Pretty soon, he decided all of Washington was his enemy, including the FBI."

"But, in this case, it wasn't a random choice? He targeted you specifically?"

She nodded. "When I was asked about the UNSUB's motivation during that news conference, Harkness was watching, apparently, and somewhere deep in that twisted mind of his, he decided I understood him. That, somehow, I sympathized with what he was doing. So he started sending me these notes that, over time, grew increasingly bizarre—and obscene."

Dan watched her shaking hand lift the glass to her lips. "We don't have to talk about this," he said.

She drained the glass, then set it down. "There isn't much more to it, anyway. He finally read somewhere that the Behavioral Science Unit was at Quantico, not downtown, so he started hanging out over on the Virginia side. One day, he spotted me driving by. After that, it was just a matter of time."

She got up and carried her glass to the counter, as if she was going to refill it from the bottle she'd left there. Instead, she turned away at the last moment and started pacing restlessly.

"He slipped into my car at a convenience store where I'd stopped on the way home one night. To this day, I don't know whether I left the door unlocked or whether he jimmied it. All I know is that he popped up in the back seat after I pulled out, put a knife to my throat and made me drive to a secluded field.''

Laurel returned to the counter and picked up the bottle of scotch, crossing back to Dan. ''And the rest, as they say, is history. I walked away from that field. He didn't.''

It was an admirable bit of bravado, Dan thought—except when she went to unscrew the cap, the bottle slipped from her trembling hands and dropped to the island's marble countertop. Miraculously, it didn't break, but spun around on its side, spewing liquor all over the island, Dan and Laurel herself.

''Oh no!'' she cried, leaping out of the way. ''I'm sorry!''

Dan grabbed the bottle, righting it, while Laurel ripped paper towels off a roll on the island, trying to dam the flow.

''I'm sorry! Did you get wet?''

He found the cap and screwed it back. ''No damage done.''

She didn't seem to hear. ''What a stupid, clumsy thing to do,'' she cried, dabbing frantically at the rivulets long after they were mopped up.

"It's okay," he assured her. When she didn't stop, Dan reached out and grabbed her wrists. "Laurel! It's all right. Take it easy."

She froze. He let go of one wrist, removed the towels from her hand and dropped them on the counter. Under his fingers, Dan felt her pulse pounding. Her hands trembled, her breathing rapid and thready. "It's just a spill," he said quietly. "Nothing to worry about. Honestly. Take a deep breath and relax."

Her gaze darted, avoiding his.

He dropped his chin to see her face. "Laurel? You okay?"

She nodded and inhaled slowly. Then her eyes closed and her arms went limp. Dan watched her for a moment. Still holding her hand, he moved closer, leaning forward until their foreheads touched.

"I got you all wet," she whispered. "I'm sorry."

"It doesn't matter."

Slowly, she drew up one of his hands, hesitated a moment, then touched it to her lips. She turned it over, and as she kissed his wrist, Dan felt every tense, long-suppressed, erotic nerve in his body come to life. Her mouth passed over his palm. Slowly, one by one, she took his fingers into her mouth, tasting them, caressing them with her tongue, softly murmuring his name.

Dan watched, agonized, until finally, he had no choice but to lift her chin and claim that mouth for his own. The liquor was sweet on her lips and tongue as they kissed, lightly at first, tasting. Then harder, over and over. He backed her up against a wall, pressing her there with his hips as a hand moved under her sweater, wanting more of her. Laurel's arms slid around his neck, pulling him tighter, clearly as desperate as he was to close the last distance between them now. To merge. To forget everything else, if only for a while, and swim in the warmth of another human's touch.

It was after midnight when Dan awoke to the waxy smell and dim flickering light of candles. As he glanced at the bedside clock, he remembered he hadn't called home. The girls would be asleep by now, the house locked up. They'd think nothing of it. It wasn't the first time he'd stayed out till all hours—only the first time he'd spent those hours in a bed other than his own, rather than in his car or office.

He also hadn't called to set up the surveillance. He looked down at Laurel, lying next to him, her head on his shoulder, one arm draped across his chest. Even asleep, she was beautiful. Her breathing was deep and regular, her face smooth, unlined. Untroubled, at last.

Glancing around the room, debating what to do, he dimly made out several framed photos on the bureau and the walls, all of the same subject—an infant, alone or in her arms. Her son, he realized sadly. As far as he could see, though, there were no pictures anywhere of the child's father. Her murdered husband.

A phone sat on the table next to the bed. With a small sigh, Dan slipped his arm out from under her and sat up, dropping his feet to the floor. When he lifted the receiver, the keypad lit up, obscenely bright. He punched in the field office main number, and the duty officer picked up on the third ring. As Dan identified himself and issued the order for two unmarked units to stand guard over the Brentwood condominium, he felt the bed move.

"Until the source of the threat is identified," he added, "I want a bodyguard on Agent Madden anytime she's outside the Federal Building." Laurel's arms slipped around his waist, her lips exploring his neck.

"Did you want those in place immediately, sir?" the duty officer asked.

Her tongue found Dan's earlobe, sending shivers through his entire body. When he felt her hand slip down to his thigh, he covered it with his own and held it still, clearing his throat sternly.

''Sir? Shall I send that surveillance team in immediately?''

''No,'' he said. ''This watch is covered. Have them in place for 6:00 a.m., would you?''

''Yes, sir.''

He hung up the phone and turned back to the brightest green eyes he'd ever seen, shining in the dim light like a mischievous cat's. He grinned back at her. ''What's so funny?''

'''This watch is *covered?*''' She rose to her knees and pushed him gently back down on the bed. His hands held her hips as she settled astride him, whipping a blanket around her pale shoulders like a velvet cloak, her hair sweeping his cheeks and shoulders as she bent low to brush his mouth with her own.

''Oh, yes,'' she said, laughing softly. ''It most definitely is.''

17

"It's all a matter of perception," Alice Wentzl said, spearing a fat pink prawn in her salad.

When Claire had phoned her that morning, the FBI press rep had willingly agreed to meet for a long overdue lunch date and catch-up session. As they gave their orders to the waiter, Alice insisted on salad—determined, she said, to wrest back control of her diet after a weekend of holiday partying. That hadn't stopped her from ordering the giant seafood number, then drowning the lot in croutons, bacon bits and heavy cream dressing, Claire noted, bemused. One thing you could say for Alice: she'd always had a good appetite.

Alice's recent transfer to the FBI's Los Angeles office had put her in charge of one of the Bureau's largest and most sensitive media relations units. Far from just another PR flack, however, she was an agent in her own right, with sixteen years of experience working every detail from violent crime to racketeering. She'd found her true calling almost by accident, when the Bureau had stuck her temporarily in the backwater of media relations while she recovered from gallbladder surgery. Alice, it turned out, had an easy manner with reporters and a gift for spin control—talents her controversy-prone organization was more than grateful to take advantage of. She'd been handling the troublesome press ever since. She was like everyone's favorite old spinster aunt, Claire thought, alternately indulgent and crotchety, but always coming to the rescue with a helpful quote when ugly deadlines threatened.

They were halfway through lunch, and had long since run through the official Bureau line on the Southland Snatcher. More friend by now than business acquaintance, Alice understood about Claire's relationship with Dan Sprague and wasn't surprised when Claire said he'd taken her to Newport Bay the previous day and given her some background. Claire didn't think it necessary or appropriate to mention their argument—nor Dan's odd behavior that morning.

Her body clock still on New York time, Claire had woken early and was already dressed when she heard his car pull into the drive a little after six. She'd slipped down to tell him about her worrisome encounter in the park with Gar Doucet, but Dan's ashen reaction had taken her completely by surprise. She was still trying to fathom what to make of it, and of the distinctly boozy odor she'd noticed rising off his clothes. He'd never been much of a drinker, but something strange was going on there, Claire decided—intuitively sensing that whatever it was, Laurel Madden was somehow mixed up in it.

Now she was anxious to get Alice's take on the office's resident profiler and her curiously dual reputation—strictly off the record, Claire promised. It was a measure of Alice's trust that she would even consider discussing another agent, but it was trust Claire had earned by her long-standing refusal to practice ambush journalism or betray a confidence.

Alice held a prawn aloft between them, its fantail bobbing at the end of her fork.

"How do you mean, 'a matter of perception'?" Claire asked.

"Well, take this thing, for example. Is it a gourmet delicacy? Or a disgusting, buglike bottom feeder?" She ripped off the tail, popped the prawn into her mouth and shrugged as she chewed. "Myself, I'm willing to overlook a few bad habits. Not everyone is, though."

Claire smiled and went back to pushing rice around her own plate of Mexican fajitas. ''And Laurel Madden?''

''She's beautiful, intelligent and talented. No disagreement about that. Also ambitious, scheming and cold, according to some. Or, alternatively, professional, focused and very shy. Take your pick. Problem is, when a woman looks the way she does, it tends to invite extreme reactions. Everything she does falls open to conflicting interpretations. Like I said, a matter of perception.'' Alice poked the air with her fork. ''You may have noticed, however, that this problem doesn't arise anywhere near as often with good-looking men.''

''That's true. So what's *your* take on Madden?''

''I think she's had a very tough personal life, and I feel sorry for that. On the other hand, sometimes I just want to give her a good shake and tell her to lighten up already. She can be her own worst enemy.''

''Vintage Aunt Alice,'' Claire said, grinning.

''Well, *really.*'' Alice rolled her eyes in mock exasperation. Then she leaned across the table and peered sternly at Claire. ''And what about you? You've officially rid yourself of that no-good bum of a husband, I hope.''

Claire couldn't help laughing. ''You've never even met him!''

She waved her fork dismissively. ''Hey, if he walked out on a nice kid like you, he's obviously an idiot.''

''You're so good for my ego. But yes, legally, we're history.'' Claire pulled a face. ''Of course, that doesn't mean I won't have to see the schmuck at every ruddy family reunion from here to eternity. To be honest, though, now that it's all over and done with...? It's kind of a relief not to have to wonder what kind of crummy stunt he's going to pull next. Not my problem anymore.''

''And so—?''

''What?''

''Anyone else?''

''Not these days.''

Alice prodded her salad. ''And this curiosity about Laurel,'' she said. ''That wouldn't have anything to do with Michael Kazarian, would it?''

''Why do you ask?''

''Because you told me you'd run into him again in New York before he died. And because I knew him, Claire. He was a charmer, that one. Even an old bird like me felt a flutter when he turned those baby blues in my direction.''

Claire felt her face go warm, and she took a

sudden interest in the pedestrians passing on the Brentwood side street beyond their window table. "Off the record?"

"It's only fair. You keep my secrets, I keep yours." Alice leaned forward once more and lowered her voice. "But you should know, it was common knowledge that marriage was all over but the shouting."

"Well, maybe, but it was news to me—and I mean all of it. I suppose I should have asked him point-blank if he was married, but frankly, we didn't spend that much time together, and somehow, it never came up. Hard to believe, I know, but true."

"You were going through a rough time yourself."

"That's no excuse. I think I was just being willfully stupid."

"It takes two to tango, my dear. And Michael could sometimes get carried away by his own power and sense of entitlement."

"How so?"

"Oh," the older woman said vaguely, "I wouldn't speak ill of the dead. But I knew Michael from the time he joined the Bureau, and if anyone was on a fast track to the top, I would have sworn it was him. Everyone felt that way—

including Michael, though he always pretended to be too modest to admit it. He was the golden boy. But somehow, he never quite lived up to the promise. By the time you met him at Quantico that first time, his career seemed to have stalled out. Like he'd peaked too soon.''

''He wasn't a good agent?''

''He was good. He just wasn't as great as everyone expected him to be. I think he found it hard to accept his own limitations—especially when some younger agents started passing him by in the promotion stream.''

Claire frowned, drumming her fingers on the table. ''Alice?''

She'd taken a mouthful of sprouts. ''Mmm?''

''Did you ever suspect Michael of being an abusive husband?''

Alice's eyebrows shot up to somewhere in the vicinity of her hairline, and she swallowed hard. ''Michael? No. Who told you that?''

''Gar Doucet.''

''You know him, too? My, my, girl, you do get around.'' Alice put down her fork and arranged her utensils, frowning. ''Why on earth would Gar say such a thing?''

''Maybe he has a vested interest in making Michael out to be a villain.''

"They were good friends."

"You knew Doucet was fired?"

The other woman was obviously troubled. "Yes, but you could have knocked me over with a feather when I heard. Gar, of all people!"

"You like him, then?"

"One of the sweetest guys I know. Don't you?"

Claire frowned and debated whether to explain the circumstances under which she and Doucet had met. But Alice was in a voluble mood, and it seemed like one of those occasions where discretion was the better part of valor, and receiving might be more educational that giving. It also occurred to her that Alice was the human equivalent of Bubba—she simply liked *everyone.*

"I would say we did not hit it off. I find him sly and annoying, with that dumb Cajun routine he pulls."

"Dumb? Gar?" Alice shook her head emphatically. "Not remotely. Not as flashy as Michael, admittedly. Cajun, definitely," she added, smiling as she drawled, "born and bred on the bayou. But Gar attended Yale Law School on a full scholarship and graduated top of his class."

It was Claire's turn to be flabbergasted. "Doucet? You're kidding."

"Nope."

"What kind of work did he do in the Bureau?"

"Various things. For the last two years, he'd been in OPR, the Office of Professional Responsibility. They're—"

"I know who they are. They're the FBI equivalent of an internal affairs division, the guys who police the police." Claire shook her head. Curiouser and curiouser, she thought. "That's like asking the cat to watch over the canaries."

Alice shook her gray head firmly. "Gar was an excellent agent."

"Well, maybe, but he obviously slipped up, big time. If he got fired, it could only be because OPR itself decided he was one of the rotten apples in the Bureau barrel." Claire frowned. "You know what I don't understand? He was fired for allegedly having an affair with Laurel Madden, right?"

"So I heard," Alice demurred. "But I couldn't—"

"So why wasn't Laurel fired, too?"

Alice hefted her shoulders. "Got me. OPR can seem like a star chamber sometimes. It's a little terrifying to be the target of one of their investigations. I have no idea how they came to their decision on this one. That's revealed strictly on a need-to-know basis. I can only assume that whatever transgression Gar committed was ruled to have far exceeded Laurel's."

"But what sort of transgression? Surely this is about more than just a roll in the hay."

"I honestly don't know."

Claire pursed her lips, thinking. "Was he married?"

Alice shook her head. "No, although he was involved with someone for years. I met her a couple of times at various functions. She's a lawyer at the Justice Department—a nice woman. They split up a while back, though. Last time I talked to Gar—it was over the summer, I think—he mentioned that she'd gotten married. I think she just got tired of waiting for him. He was working cases all over the country. By the time he got transferred back to headquarters, she'd found someone else. Too bad."

"Maybe he was involved with Laurel even then?"

"I don't know. I know they were all friends—Gar, Michael and Laurel—and that Gar felt really bad when their baby died. He was very supportive, I think, during that business, and then, when Michael went off to work undercover. But Gar was good to a *lot* of people," Alice added firmly when she caught Claire's knowing nod. She sighed. ''I feel terrible about what happened to him. I can't help thinking he got caught up in something bigger than he was, and somehow, it just spun out of control.''

Claire sat back and drummed her fingers on the table, perplexed. This was a whole different take on someone she'd come to think of as the villain of the piece. Talk about conflicting perceptions. ''When Doucet worked in OPR, what was his job, do you know?''

''Only in a general way. He was responsible for investigating certain categories of operations in the field offices.''

''Which field office was he investigating last, before he was fired?''

Uncomfortable silence.

''Alice? Please?''

''I don't know if I should say any more, Claire. Really, I've already told you way too much.''

''Just tell me this, yes or no, and I won't ask another thing, I promise. Was it New York?''

The older woman exhaled heavily, and gave a very reluctant nod.

18

On Monday afternoon, the kidnap response team squeezed around the small conference table in Dan's office to update the TOTNAP file. Oz Paterson came with half his investigative team, plus Ron Younger, the polygraph examiner.

Alice Wentzl was there to review the media situation. She mentioned to Dan on her way in that she'd just had lunch with Claire Gillespie. He nodded, keeping his expression noncommittal, but he was less than thrilled about the notion of those two exchanging notes, especially after the conversation he'd had with Claire in his driveway that morning. His mind was still wrestling with what to do about that situation.

Laurel was last to arrive. Hair pulled back severely and wearing an expression as sober as her tailored black suit, she avoided eye contact as she walked in, settling into a seat at the table that put Oz Paterson between herself and Dan, with the squad leader blocking any direct line of vision between them.

Dan was thankful for small mercies. Tied up with bank squad meetings all morning, he hadn't seen her since slipping away shortly before dawn to await the surveillance units. On the team's arrival at the condominium complex, Dan had briefed them on the note, the stalker and the possible connection to TOTNAP, doing a passable job, he thought, of avoiding any overt lies, but still leaving the impression that he and others had spent the night following up evidence and securing the premises.

Now, in the harsh light of day, he found himself gripped by serious second thoughts and grave self-doubts. He'd never approved of workplace romances. They complicated the chain of command and held the potential for all kinds of messy office conflicts. And what about Erin and Julie? The last thing he needed was one more distraction from his responsibilities and the little time he had with them. Where could this thing with Laurel possibly go, anyway? And what about this Doucet character, who'd apparently turned up again like a bad penny—still harboring, according to Claire, the same obsession for Laurel that had gotten him sacked in the first place?

As long as he didn't look at Laurel or think about last night, Dan was convinced he'd made a serious mistake by letting things get so out of hand.

"The Kirkendall case is definitely off the scope," Oz Paterson was telling the group. "The autopsy showed the child was drowned, but not in Newport Bay. It wasn't estuary water in his lungs. It was soapy water."

Alice Wentzl leaned forward. "Soapy?"

"Yeah. Like bathwater."

"The mother failed the polygraph," Younger explained to her and the others, "but she stuck firmly to her story about her son being kidnapped at the swap meet. Laurel had established a good rapport with her, though, so she did the post-test interview, and she managed to get the girl to speculate on where a 'kidnapper' might leave a body. That's what directed the search to Newport Bay. It was a nice piece of work," he added appreciatively, glancing over at her.

Laurel sat quietly as the others nodded.

"After the autopsy," Paterson continued, "Ron here and a couple of sheriff's deputies went to Jenny Kirkendall's apartment this morning. She finally admitted that little Ryan drowned in his bath on Friday evening."

''An accident?'' Alice asked.

''The exact circumstances are hazy, but I doubt it,'' Younger said. ''She was apparently distraught over being dumped by a boyfriend. She said she was giving Ryan a bath when he threw a typical two-year-old temper tantrum and somehow slipped under the water.''

''More likely was dunked in a fit of rage,'' Paterson said.

Younger nodded. ''Could be. At the very least, she admits she lost it and froze up temporarily. By the time she finally pulled him out, Ryan was dead. She sat for a couple of hours, trying to work up the courage to turn herself in. But the TV was on, and she saw the reports about the kidnapping at South Coast Plaza and the discovery of the Morales baby in the aqueduct. That's when she hatched the scheme to toss Ryan's body in the bay, then go to the swap meet Saturday morning and claim he'd been snatched.''

On the other side of Oz Paterson, Dan saw Laurel's knuckles turn white on her tightly gripped pen. ''I gather the girl's been arrested?'' Dan asked.

''Second-degree murder,'' Younger said. ''Her lawyer will probably try to cop a manslaughter plea.''

''And the press line?'' Alice asked Dan.

''I think we should make it clear that we're no longer looking at this one in connection with TOTNAP and refer all additional inquiries to the Orange County authorities.''

She nodded.

''Okay, moving on,'' Dan said, ''what about the note?''

''What note?'' Alice asked.

Dan explained about the taunting note found taped to Laurel's mailbox the previous evening. ''We overnighted it to Quantico.'' He turned back to Paterson. ''Any word, Oz?''

''I just got off the phone to the lab. The document examiners have given it a quick once-over, but there's not much to report so far on it or the envelope. The duct tape, however, is another matter.''

''What about it?''

Instead of answering, Paterson pushed back his chair, rose and crossed the room. As he vacated the space between them, Dan and Laurel made brief eye contact. They turned away quickly, focusing their attention on the squad leader as he removed Dan's tape from the dispenser on his desk and selected a metal ruler from an organizer on the credenza. Paterson hefted the ruler in his hand once or twice, then walked back to the conference table, sat down and balanced the roll of tape on its side, steadying it lightly with one finger to keep it from rolling away. His right hand, meanwhile, lifted the ruler a foot or two above the table and smashed it down like a blade on the edge of the roll.

Dan raised an eyebrow. ''Are you upset with my tape for some reason, Oz?''

Paterson held it up between two fingers to show them how the ruler had indented the roll on one side, right down to the cardboard center. ''When we sent them the wrappings the Morales baby's body was found in, the material analysis folks noticed something odd about the duct tape that had been used to seal the garbage bag. They used a solvent to detach it, and when they laid it flat, they discovered it had a defect—something like this.''

He unrolled a foot or two of tape, holding it aloft. All along the strip, at regular intervals, they saw a whitish stripe and a small kink.

''Same thing, more or less, on that duct tape—a crease that reoccurred at regular intervals, every 38.4 centimeters along the sample.''

''As if the roll had been damaged,'' Laurel said.

''That's right. Like it had been banged against

a sharp table corner, maybe, or was kept in a trunk, and somebody dropped a tire iron on it or something, putting a bend in the roll. When we sent them the duct tape sample from Laurel's place, they opened it up, and guess what they found?''

''The same crease?''

''You betcha. In two places, just a hair under 38.4 centimeters apart.''

''Under?'' Alice said.

''Yes, because as the roll runs down,'' Laurel told her, ''its circumference decreases, so the interval between the defect on the tape also decreases marginally.''

''Precisely,'' Paterson said.

''So the note-writer probably is our UNSUB,'' Dan said. He sat back in his chair and exhaled heavily. ''Goddammit.''

''Sorry, Laurel,'' Paterson said, patting her arm ruefully. ''Looks like you found yourself another wacko fan.''

''What about that business of leaving the Goodsell baby at the swap meet?'' Dan asked quietly, almost afraid to hear the answer.

''The sheriff's department and the bloodhounds searched the fairgrounds. They didn't find anything.''

There was a collective and audible exhalation of relief around the table.

Paterson held up a hand. ‘‘But—the dogs did alert on the little girl's scent. The trail led out of the grounds and onto the freeway.’’

‘‘He took her there and left again?’’ Alice asked, looking visibly shaken.

‘‘Either that, or her body was carried off undetected when the swap meet shut down yesterday. Maybe with the trash.’’ Paterson added grimly. ‘‘The sheriff's people are following up on that possibility this afternoon.’’

No one in the room had any doubt, Dan knew, what the sheriff's people would find.

It was a quiet group that filed out of his office sometime later.

‘‘Hold back a minute, would you, Laurel?’’ Dan said. ‘‘I'd like a word.’’

She stood aside to let the others pass.

In the outer office, Dan saw Gwen, his secretary, glance up briefly, then turn back to her word processor. He turned to Laurel. ‘‘Close the door, please.’’

She hesitated, then stepped around the door and swung it shut. Moving to the center of it, away from the window that ran alongside, she leaned back. Only then, satisfied, apparently, that she couldn't be seen from the outer office, did she allow herself to reveal a small chink in that formidable armor. Like black storm clouds breaking just enough to let a single ray of sunlight shine gently through, her grave expression dissolved into a shy smile. ''Hi,'' she said quietly.

Dan sank, figuratively and literally, settling himself on the edge of the table. ''Hi,'' he said. ''How are you doing?''

''Fine. How about you?''

''All right. A little bewildered,'' he confessed.

She nodded. ''Me, too.'' Her skin was wan, her eyes shadowed with fatigue. But her smile deepened, and two lines appeared at the corners of her mouth. Dan remembered touching them in the dark.

How was he ever going to give her up?

''I'm sorry the note turned out to be from the UNSUB, after all,'' he said, for lack of knowing what else to say.

''Well, like you said, it was either him or some garden-variety pervert. One way or the other…'' She shrugged resignedly.

''The surveillance stays on your place round the clock until we catch the guy. And you'll have protection every time you leave this building. It's not going to unfold like last time, Laurel. He won't have a chance to get close to you, I promise.''

She nodded. ''I appreciate it. Although maybe...''

''What?''

''Maybe it's better if he does come after me.''

''What do you mean?''

''I was just thinking maybe we could draw him out. Goad him on somehow, and get him to make a move.''

''With you as bait? I don't think so.''

''If we could control the circumstances—the place and the time—it wouldn't have to be too dangerous. Maybe I could use a press conference to connect with him—''

''Forget it.''

''—counter his challenge, get him really mad—''

''No way.''

''Listen, Dan, this makes sense. If we can goad him into targeting me, just to prove how tough he is, then he won't be going after babies, will he?''

''No, dammit!'' Dan's glance shot to the window and the outer office. Gwen's head had popped up in surprise, and she was watching him. He rose from the table and walked toward his desk. When he turned back to Laurel, his voice was low but firm. ''I'm not putting you in this guy's path.''

''We have to do something. I didn't hear any other brilliant ideas coming out of this meeting, did you?'' She stepped forward and leaned on the table. ''He's not a pedophile, Dan. I'm sure of it now. He's picking on babies because they're an easy target and yet, perversely, the most sensational target he can choose at the same time. Maybe there's some other significance to his choice of victim, too, I'm not sure. But it's not sexual. Those notes are like the preening of a cock before a hen. He wants my attention. He wants all of our attention, and he wants to make us look like fools.''

''I'm sure you're right. And if we build on the physical and psychological evidence, sooner or later, we'll find the key that'll lead us to him.''

''When? Next week? Next month? Next year? How many more mothers will have to bury their babies before we nail this son of a bitch? At least this is worth a try.''

He shook his head slowly. ''I don't know. Let me think about it.''

''We can't wait too—''

''I *said,* I'll think about it, Laurel. In the meantime,'' he added heavily, ''there's another problem I need to talk to you about.''

''What problem?''

He must have looked as uncomfortable as he felt. As she waited for a response, Laurel's expression—her whole physical carriage—shifted. The newfound ease Dan had come to see in her vanished. Something flashed across her features—fear? Pain? Then, like a curtain closing, the old veil of wariness dropped over her once more.

She turned away from him, feigning an indifferent shrug. ''Look,'' she said, ''if it's about last night, don't worry. I'm certainly not going to say anything. In the first place, who would I tell? And in the second, if last night was only about last night and nothing more—fine. I'm not looking for involvement. Believe me, from your perspective, I'm the safest person this could have happened with. I have even less interest than you in becoming fodder for in-house gossip.''

Dan shook his head. ''It's not about last night. It's about Gar Doucet. He's in town.''

Laurel spun around, her skin even paler than it had been, if that was possible. ''How do you know?''

''Claire Gillespie told me.''

''That woman you brought to Newport yesterday? The reporter?''

''Yes. She's staying at my place, and she ran into Doucet last night. It wasn't the first time. He seems to be stalking her.''

''Stalking her? I don't understand. Why would he do that?''

Dan exhaled heavily and perched himself on the edge of his desk. ''Claire lives in New York. She's a reporter, as I said yesterday, and she's been looking into your husband's murder. She thinks Doucet may be mixed up in it somehow.''

''How did she know Michael?''

''I'm not exactly sure. She says she'd met him at Quantico a couple of years back, then ran into him again shortly before he was murdered. Since then, apparently, she's been following the investigation into his death.''

Laurel backed against the wall. ''Is that why she's out here? To check up on me and the rumors I had something to do with it?''

''I don't know. She said she was here to cover TOTNAP for *Newsworld.* I only found out about the other business later.''

''And you led her straight to me? You didn't even warn me, Dan! How could you do that?'' Her green eyes narrowed suspiciously. ''What's really going on? Does headquarters know about this? Are they just throwing me to the wolves, is that it?''

''No, Laurel, no one's throwing you to the wolves. I told you, Claire's a friend. I wasn't aware she knew your husband. When I found out, I told her that whole subject was off-limits.''

''But she's staying with you?''

''Not with me, with her sister. Bridget lives in the apartment over my garage.''

''How very cozy.''

''Her *married* sister, and her husband and their daughter. Claire and Bridget's father was my partner, years ago, when I was a cop in Kansas City. He was killed on the job, and I've always—well, I've got a responsibility toward his family. Anyway, that's all beside the point.''

''Exactly what is the point?''

''Doucet's making threatening noises in Claire's direction, and I don't like it.''

''What do you expect me to do about it?''

He raised his hands, exasperated. ''Tell me where he's coming from! What's he up to? Why is he so protective of you?''

''Of me?''

''Yes. Claire says that's what seems to be worrying Doucet—the idea that she's trying to unearth negative information on you.''

''Is she?''

''Is there anything to find?''

Laurel reared back, stricken, but when she spoke, her voice was measured and cold. ''If you have to ask me that, I shouldn't even be here.''

He pushed a chair toward her with his foot. ''Look, just sit *down,* would you?''

''No, thank you. If this is an inquisition, I'd rather stand.''

''It's not an inquisition.''

''It feels like one.''

Dan sighed. ''All I want to know is what Doucet is up to.''

''And I already told you—I don't know.''

He watched her stubborn expression, feeling his jaw muscles begin to ache as his back teeth ground together. Rising to his feet again, he walked to the window. Outside, the wind had shifted. The towering Italian cypress trees posted like sentries all around the Federal Building swayed and bent, as a bank of thick, dark clouds massed in the western sky. A winter storm was moving in.

''You were transferred to this office with a letter of censure on your file, Laurel. I knew about that, and something about the circumstances that led to it, but I accepted your transfer, anyway. People make mistakes. You're not the first agent it's happened to, and it's not an insurmountable barrier—especially not for someone with a track record as solid as yours.'' He turned to face her again. ''But I also know you were lucky to get off with only a letter of censure. I was told you displayed a distinct lack of candor, refusing to answer questions or cooperate in any way with an official investigation.''

''I refused to credit a lie with the dignity of a response.''

Dan watched the glimmering, angry eyes that he knew would not cry—not now, not over this. He leaned wearily on the table. ''Tell me about you and Gar Doucet, Laurel. Please.''

''Who wants to know?'' she asked bitterly, her hands clasping and unclasping. ''My boss? Or my lover?''

He thought about that for a moment. ''Probably both,'' he admitted quietly.

She shrugged. ''It really doesn't matter. Either way, official business or prurient interest, I can't help you. Gar was my friend. My constant, *loyal* friend,'' she added pointedly, ''who stood by me, through good times and bad. As far as anything else he may or may not have done, or be up to now, I don't know. I don't speak to him anymore, and he's no longer part of my life.''

''Then why—''

''But neither will I speak against him. Don't ask me, Dan, because I won't. Not for the OPR. Not for your reporter friend. Not even for you.''

With that, she turned on her heel and yanked the door open, nearly colliding with Doug Zellerbach as she stormed out of Dan's office. ''Whoa!'' the bank squad leader said laughingly, putting a hand out to steady her. ''Slow down there, pretty lady!''

''Get out of my way, idiot!'' she snapped, smacking his hand away.

Zellerbach watched her retreating form, then came in, head shaking. ''Man! What's got into her?'' He glanced around the office as if he expected to find blood on the walls, then dropped himself into a chair and tossed a file on the table. ''I dug out those robbery stats you were asking about. I thought we could—'' He stopped and studied Dan for a moment, then leaned forward, looking amused. ''Well, hey, Dan-o, you sly old devil! Been sparring with the Ice Maiden, have you? Didn't I tell you that was one—''

''Z?''

''What?''

''Shut the hell up, would you?''

19

"It never rains in Southern California," or so said the old pop hit. But the author of that brilliant lyric, Claire decided, obviously hadn't stuck around long enough to discover the error of his premise.

She emerged from the L.A. Hall of Records at closing time on Tuesday, stiff-necked and itchy-eyed, only to find a torrential downpour turning streets into rushing rivers. Keeping sheltered beneath the building's canopied entrance, postponing the inevitable ruination of her favorite black pumps, she watched the umbrellas of departing city staffers as they scurried across the slick plaza and disappeared into the night like rats deserting a sinking ship. Obviously, other people paid closer attention to weather reports than she did—but who knew pop music could be so factually flawed?

The rainstorm had crept up on her while she

was deep inside the bowels of the dusty, windowless municipal office, standing in one line after another, waiting to speak to bored, clock-watching clerks, who eventually directed her toward the real-estate records division and the files she was after.

Before that, she'd spent most of the previous twenty-four hours coordinating input on the Southland Snatcher story with the local *Newsworld* stringers and photographers assigned to cover various angles of the case, as well as conducting her own interviews with the LAPD, the San Bernardino and Orange County sheriffs' departments, and a criminal psychologist—though not the one she'd wanted, since Dan wouldn't let her anywhere near Laurel Madden. Then, confident that she was in good shape for her filing deadline the next day, Claire had decided to take a little time off to research the other, more personal business that had brought her out here in the first place.

She'd gone to the Hall of Records to look for evidence of any recent property acquisitions by a certain federal employee who might have come into a large insurance settlement of late—or be in possession of a Russian mobster's misplaced half-million dollars. The idea of Laurel Madden blowing blood money on real estate wasn't as far-fetched as it seemed. After all, Claire reasoned, it was an expensive house purchased with payoffs from his Russian handlers that had helped expose a midlevel mole in the CIA a few years back. What was the point of ill-gotten gain if you couldn't use it to aspire to a more comfortable life-style? Or so went the reasoning of your average conspiratorial traitor.

Ruined shoes or no, she had found what she'd come for, although what she'd discovered raised as many questions as answers. Now, with the information safely stowed in her tote bag, Claire searched in vain for a solution to her lack of foresight in the precipitation department. Back in New York, at the first drop of rain, hawkers sprouted on every street corner like entrepreneurial urban mushrooms, selling cheap but serviceable umbrellas that generally lasted her a storm or two before being forgotten in some cab. No such luck here, though. Of course not—street vendors presumed pedestrians. In L.A., nobody walked, unless you counted the armies of the homeless, who did not make for a great customer base.

Claire was plotting a wet dash to the parking lot when she suddenly remembered a more serious problem than her about-to-be-drenched shoes and clothes. "Oh my gosh! The car!"

She'd left the top down on the rented Mustang convertible. The Civic Center lots had been filled to capacity when she'd arrived late that afternoon, so she'd parked the car a couple of blocks away, in an outdoor lot across the street from Parker Center, confident no one was going to mess with a vehicle in the shadow of LAPD headquarters. She hadn't reckoned on vandalism by deluge.

Contemplating the waterlogged convertible she was about to face, Claire sought solace in the knowledge that it wasn't hers, but rented on an expense account that would surely cover drying-out charges—or not, given Serge Scolari's penny-pinching and the like-minded gnomes in *Newsworld*'s accounting department. Well, she thought, sighing resignedly, even if she couldn't make the case for reimbursement, she still had a new experience in locomotion to look forward to: driving and swimming at the same time.

As she readied herself to make a run for it, Claire studied the water flowing down the street, then her doomed shoes, then the water again. The shoes came off. She slipped them into her tote bag, flipped up her jacket collar, took a deep breath and sprinted across the plaza and down the broad steps to the street. She ignored the cold, wet shock to her stocking feet, wincing at the occasional stone, but otherwise running a decently fast slalom around slow-moving umbrellas. She made it through two well-timed traffic lights, but got caught at a third intersection. Jogging in place while she waited for the signal to change, enduring curious stares from passing drivers, she watched the red light's reflection on the fast-running water, turning it to something resembling a sparkling river of blood.

Finally, the light changed to green. She made a dash for the lot, fishing in her pocket for the car key as she ran so that she could get the door open, jump in, turn on the power and raise the roof as quickly as possible. But when she located the aisle where the Mustang was parked, her plan dissolved into confusion. The car was intact and secure—the roof firmly in place and closed, the driving rain bouncing harmlessly off the waterproof black canvas.

Alice Wentzl was fond of saying that middle age meant having days when the blood just didn't seem to wash over the brain. If a mental lapse like this was typical, Claire thought, she was already having her first midlife crisis at the positively tender age of thirty-five. She *knew* she'd driven the car into the lot with the roof down. She could have sworn that was the way she'd left it, too.

It was only when she reached for the door handle that she noticed that the windows were steamy. That was not a figment of her imagination, and could only result from the breathing of someone sitting inside the car—waiting. Primed to bolt, Claire pulled the latch and swung the door wide, backing away even as she ducked to see who it was.

"Hey there!" Gar Doucet called cheerfully. "Come on in, girl! Get out of the rain!"

"Doucet!" she yelled over the din of the downpour. "What are you doing in my car?"

"Waiting it out. I got your roof up just in time, but as soon as I got the thing latched, the rain started coming down like the dickens. Figured I'd just sit tight. This is a real toad-choker, isn't it? You enjoy a soaking, do you?" he asked, grinning at her drenched clothing and soaked feet. "Maybe I should have left things well enough alone."

Claire followed his gaze down her front. Her jacket was flung wide and her white silk blouse was plastered to her like a second skin, leaving nothing to the imagination by way of her lingerie choices. She pulled the jacket across her chest with one hand, while the other pushed hair and water out of her eyes. "You can get out now!"

"After the favor I did you? Thank you very much. Get in here!"

She glanced around the dim, virtually deserted lot, then back at him. Exhaling resignedly, she tossed her bag in the back, dropped into the seat and slammed the door. Her hands pushed her wet mop of hair off her face, then crossed over her chest and tucked themselves under her armpits, as much for warmth as modesty. As she swiveled in her seat to face him, her teeth began to chatter. "If you're planning to bonk me over the head or something, just get it over with quick and put me out of my misery, would you?"

"I have no such plans, *ma chère.* Why don't you get the heater going before you catch your death?"

She nodded and withdrew her shivering right hand, holding the key. But before she could get it in the ignition—

"Wait just one minute," she said suspiciously. "This is an electronically controlled roof. How did you raise it with no key to turn on the power?" She poked at the ignition with her fore-finger. The housing seemed a little loose. She gave him an incredulous look. "You *hot-wired* my car? Right in front of LAPD headquarters?"

"How else was I going to get the roof up?"

"I can't believe it! First you break into my apartment, steal my files and crash my computer, now you hijack my car!"

"I didn't hijack it, it's right here. And I put it back together after I was done, didn't I? You're a most unreasonable woman, you know that? Are you going to turn on that heater or not? It's downright clammy in here."

Claire turned the ignition and cranked up the heating controls, then wedged herself back against the door. "For a former federal agent, you have an extraordinary range of illegal skills."

He shrugged. "My uncle Rosaire had a junkyard back of his place down there near Grand Chenier. That's in *Louisiane*."

"I think you mentioned that was home. So, Uncle Rosaire taught you how to hot-wire, did he? What was that, some sort of inventory-acquisition procedure?"

"No, wise guy. But every wreck I ever drove when I was a kid came from that lot. Ol' Rosaire used to say, 'You get her to run, boy, she's yours.' Except the wrecks didn't always arrive on the yard with keys, so—"

When he shrugged again, Claire got a whiff of the cobbler-shop smell of his brown leather jacket. It was a little heady in such close quarters—although her sense of disorientation could simply be delayed shock over finding him there. She found herself keeping a cautious watch on those big hands, and on that angular face, with its black, watchful eyes that gave away nothing—and missed nothing, she suspected, like some stealthy old gator, lurking quietly beneath the surface of a swamp, biding his time, waiting for his moment to pounce. Not someone you wanted to turn your back on.

"So," he said, "did you find what you were looking for in the records division?"

"You tell me. Is there *any* move I've made in the last few days, or weeks—months, for all I know—that you aren't aware of? Any particular moment that you haven't been spying on me?"

He seemed offended. "It's not like I don't have other things I could be doing, you know."

"Well, don't let me stop you. What are you waiting for? Go!"

"I told you back in New York, Claire—I'm waiting for you to give up this crusade of yours and move on. You didn't find the dirt on Laurel you were looking for in there, did you?"

''What makes you so sure?''

''Because I know that all you could find out was that she bought a two-hundred-and-eighty-six-thousand-dollar, two-bedroom, three-bath condo in Brentwood on which she made a hundred-and-ninety-four-thousand-dollar down payment. The balance she's carrying on a mortgage she can quite easily afford on her salary. That doesn't exactly qualify as evidence of an outrageous life-style.''

''It's a decent down payment.''

''Financed on the sale of the house she and Mike owned in Virginia.''

''I thought as much,'' Claire conceded. ''But that doesn't mean she hasn't stashed the money somewhere else.''

''What money?''

''Ivankov's missing half-million—or the large insurance payoff she would have gotten after Michael's death. Take your pick. Of course, I still haven't ruled out the possibility that you're the one with Ivankov's cash.''

''The cash I lifted after I murdered Mike?''

''If you say so.''

He watched her for a second, his expression ominous. Suddenly, his hand shot out, easily enveloping her neck in the soft area just under her chin, and he moved closer, his dark eyes boring into her from a distance of a scant inch or two. ‘‘Aren’t you afraid to be alone with a murderer, Claire? No one nearby to hear you scream?’’

She’d done prison interviews with psychopaths, whose moods shifted in the blink of an eye, and she knew about those who fed on fear. Her heart was pounding, but Claire had no intention of giving this guy the satisfaction of cowering. ‘‘I’ve told people about you, Doucet. Anything happens to me, your mug and prints will be wired from here to Timbuktu. Won’t do *me* much good,’’ she admitted, ‘‘but you’d never get away with it.’’

He watched her for a moment, then his grip loosened, and his fingers moved up her cheek, his gaze settling on her lips. Claire found herself watching his mouth, too, wondering if he intended, incredibly, to kiss her. Wondering, too, about the traitorous instincts that could make her curious, in spite of everything, to know what that would feel like—and almost to wish that he would.

Instead, he withdrew his hand with a sad shake of his head.

She hadn’t realized she was holding her breath, but it escaped now in a slow sigh of relief. As her wits returned, Claire found herself tempted to hit him. "You know, for the life of me, Doucet, I cannot understand why Alice Wentzl likes you. She usually shows better judgment."

He broke into a broad smile—and quite an amazing transformation it was, too. "How is old Alice?"

"She's fine." Claire frowned. "Shaken about you getting fired, though."

"She's a great old girl. Bit of a gossip, mind you, but a good one 'for true,' as they say back in my neck of the woods. I'll bet the two of you really bent each other's ears at lunch yesterday."

Well, Claire thought, so much for wondering whether he'd been tailing her the previous day. "She tells me you went to Yale Law School."

"That's a fact."

"And that you graduated top of your class."

"Near the top. Number two, actually. There was this girl from Boston—real quiet, glasses like this—" he held his thumb and forefinger about four inches apart, obviously partial to gross exaggeration "—at least, until she got her contact lenses. Good thing, too. At first glance, with those Coke-bottle glasses, you'd think she was dumb as a duck. But I could *not* best that girl, no way, no how."

"Ah, we have a competitive streak in us, do we? So where is she now?"

"Justice Department, married to a real nice guy, and about to become a mom for the first time."

"You kept in touch. That's nice. Is she the old girlfriend?"

He looked at her askance. "Alice really does talk too much."

Claire smiled a little, rubbing her arms for warmth.

Doucet bent low and peered out the window. "It looks like it's letting up a little. I should probably make a dash for it, and let you get going home to your sister's so you can dry off."

He shifted to go, but Claire put a restraining hand on his arm. "Wait! You have to tell me—what happened between you and Laurel and Michael? You were friends, all three of you. What went wrong?"

If she expected a direct reply, she should have known better by now. Sure enough, instead of answering the question, he asked one of his own. "You ever hear of the *fifolet?*"

"The fee-for-who?"

"The fee-fo-lay. They're eerie, glowing lights

that some people claim to see out on old Atchafalaya swamp, down there in Cajun country. See, the story goes,'' Doucet said, his voice downshifting into a veteran storyteller's soft lilt, ''that there was this old man named Medeo—a wizard, don't you know, who lived on the banks of the Atchafalaya. And every night, ol' Medeo, well, he'd shed his skin and go out casting evil spells on village folk. For true, he did. Turn himself into a beautiful *fifolet,* a will-o'-the-wisp, all soft and glowing. And he'd dance and tempt good folk, till they'd follow him right down into that ol' Atchafalaya swamp and sink straight to their destruction—nobody ever imagining that beneath an appearance so lovely could be a force so evil. At dawn, Medeo would slip back into his skin and carry on like nothing had happened, everybody wondering but nobody able to figure out the mystery of that ol' *fifolet.* And so it went on, for a long, long time—him bewitching good folk, them following him to their doom. But ol' Medeo was outsmarted, at last.''

''What happened?''

''Well, now, it was a young woman named Zula who finally figured out that ol' wizard. She followed him secretly one night, trying to see what he was all about. And when Medeo shed his skin like always and turned himself into the *fifolet,* sailing out over the swamp, why, that clever Zula, she just grabbed up that skin he'd left behind, filled it with hot-hot cayenne pepper, then left it there on the ground, like nothing had happened. When Medeo returned at dawn, he slipped back into that skin, thinkin' nothing of it—and wasn't he just burned right up by that hot-hot pepper? Burned up to nothing.''

Mesmerized up to then by his voice and by the strange, unsettling nearness of him, Claire suddenly felt her blood run cold as she realized the words Doucet had chosen. ''Burned up? Like Michael, Gar? Was he like the evil Medeo? Because you think he hurt Laurel?''

''Man had no right to treat her that way,'' he said quietly.

He stared out the window, saying nothing, while Claire studied him closely: a complex man, who feigned simplicity and transparency, yet was full of contradiction and mystery.

As if returning from a long journey in his mind, he turned back to her, but when he spoke, his question took her by surprise. ''Did you love him, Claire?'' By the way he watched and waited for her answer, it seemed a weighty matter to him, something he felt compelled to know.

She thought for a long moment before replying. ''No,'' she said finally. ''I don't think I did. I was touched by something in him. A sense of his isolation, perhaps—though that could just have been my own loneliness that I was projecting onto him. Or maybe it was Michael's sense of mission, and his belief in the rightness of what he was doing. It was refreshing to find someone so focused after being married to a man who believed in nothing—not in me, not in our marriage, maybe not even in himself.''

Doucet touched her cheek gently. ''You've got the kind of heart that wants to take care of people, *ma chère.* But some people aren't worthy. You have to be on your guard against that ol' *fifolet,* you know. There's some say Medeo takes on other forms—that he's still out there, playing his old, cruel game.'' He pointed to her wet stockings. ''Your feet will be slippery on the pedals. Put your shoes on, and drive home carefully, now.''

He was out of the car before she could say a word. ''Gar!'' Claire called after him.

He dropped his head back down. ''What?''

"Was Michael not worthy? Even of living?"

The black eyes went hard once more. "Grieve for your father, Claire, not for Mike Kazarian. He doesn't deserve your tears." With that, Doucet closed the door softly and disappeared into the night.

20

Wednesday dawned sunny and bright after the previous day's storm, but the mood in the conference room was gray and gloomy, after the discovery of the body of little Erica Goodsell in an Orange County landfill site. The kidnap response team was having its morning update meeting before team members dispersed to follow up on the latest evidence.

Oz Paterson looked apologetic as he handed Dan the composite sketch of the man who'd been seen leaving Macy's with the child the night she disappeared from South Coast Plaza. It showed a man, probably dark-haired, wearing a baseball cap and glasses whose lenses obscured his eye color.

''This is about as helpful as that old Unabomber sketch,'' Dan said, examining the blank, generic face in the charcoal composite.

''The witness is elderly,'' Paterson said, ''and tiny—four-ten or thereabouts. She said the man towered over her, which wouldn't be hard. The bright lights in the store were glinting off his glasses, and she didn't see—or couldn't remember—his eye color. Said she spent more time looking at the baby than him, anyway."

"What about the clothing? Is this accurate?" The figure in the sketch had on a dark-colored shirt and jacket.

Paterson shook his head. "Not entirely. She wasn't sure about the shirt, and once we located the security video, it turned out he actually had on a sweater. We're getting a revised sketch out today. But the jacket was definitely leather—black or maybe dark brown. She wasn't sure, and the video was in black and white, so it's hard to be sure. Once we knew it was our UNSUB, a couple of our people went down and spent a few hours with her yesterday, trying to draw out additional details. But other than noting how friendly and polite he seemed, she just drew a blank. The old girl's real shaken up, not surprisingly, since it turns out she was probably the last person to see that child alive."

"No accent, nothing unusual about his choice of words?"

Paterson shrugged. "Not that she could recall."

"Where are we at on analyzing the store's security videos?'' Laurel asked. She was sitting at the far end of the table. Dan hadn't spoken privately to her since she'd stormed out of his office on Monday.

After the discovery of the Goodsell child's body yesterday, accompanied by a second, taunting note from the Snatcher addressed to Laurel, Dan had gone by the violent-crimes squad room to see how she was bearing up. He'd found her with Paterson in his office, on a speakerphone call to the Behavioral Sciences Unit in Quantico, discussing the note's contents. When Dan had walked in, she'd avoided all eye contact. He'd sat down and listened quietly, amazed at her detached, analytic tone—as if that weren't her name on both notes, and this psycho had made someone else the object of his boasting challenges.

''Quantico's got the video now and they're doing a frame-by-frame analysis to see if they can pull anything useful off it,'' Paterson told her now. ''The store security system caught him entering with the little girl, then walking past jewelry and makeup, then again at the exit, where he stopped and spoke to the old lady. But the guy seems to have deliberately kept his head down and his face partially hidden under that ball cap in every single shot. The lab's working on it now with their computers, trying to see if they can block out the hat and maybe, between the video and this police sketch, piece together enough information on his features to make a better guess at his appearance than what we've got so far. They'll also do some triangulation to determine his exact height.''

''Meantime,'' Alice Wentzl said, ''we distributed copies of the store video and the sketch to all the media outlets last night. By now, those images have appeared in every newscast and paper in the country in the hope that someone will recognize something on there.''

''The tip line's going crazy,'' Paterson said. ''We got sightings of this guy from here to Canada. The Rapid Start team's burning the midnight oil, trying to separate the wheat from the chaff. It only takes one accurate report for us to zero in. The trick is to figure out which one it might be.''

Dan frowned. ''It's like he knew about the location of the security cameras and planned in advance how to get past them without leaving his face as a calling card.''

''I've got somebody over at Macy's today, checking out that possibility,'' Paterson said. ''They're looking at all their surveillance tapes on those areas from the last couple of weeks to see if they can spot this guy earlier, maybe doing a little advance recon as he planned his next snatch.''

''Sounds to me like Laurel could be right about him being a police buff,'' Wentzl said. ''Maybe military?''

''It's possible,'' Laurel said. ''We're thinking some of the things he's said in the notes may—''

Dan cut her off. ''We'll discuss the notes later. First,'' he said, looking at the others around the table, ''let's review the autopsy results and any additional physical evidence since the discovery of the latest victim. I don't want to hold you guys up from your work.''

There was a brief, awkward silence, the kind that always occurred when it became obvious that certain pieces of information related to a difficult investigation would be shared on a need-to-know basis only, creating a kind of caste structure, dividing those in the loop from those who were not. It couldn't be helped, Dan decided. Idle speculation and loose revelations had sunk more than one case in the past. Until they had a firm strategy for responding to the Snatcher's taunts, he had no intention of giving the impression that this braggadocio had thrown the investigation into a tizzy.

Of course, if anyone was going to call him on the decision to play some cards close to his chest, Dan knew it would be straight-shooting Alice Wentzl. Sure enough, he saw her iron-gray head shake. "You may not be able to keep a lid on the note angle much longer, Dan. I'm getting nonstop calls from reporters looking to confirm the rumor that the Snatcher's been in touch with us. I know you've ordered a total gag, but with the Orange County authorities aware of the latest note, it's only a matter of time till somebody lets something leak."

"I've got a thought about how to deal with that, Alice, but I'll talk to you about it later."

Wentzl nodded. Laurel, Dan observed from the corner of his eye, had been watching him closely throughout the exchange. He fought the sinking feeling in his gut. A decision had been made and now there could be no postponing the inevitable. It might have been a little easier if he hadn't let things get out of control the other night, but probably not. Deliberately placing one of his people in harm's way ran counter to every instinct he possessed, but at this point, risking the one to protect the many seemed the best—and only—card he had to play.

* * *

''Oz and Laurel, you two hold back, please,'' Dan said as the rest of the team filed out of the conference room twenty minutes later. Alice Wentzl also paused and gave Dan an expectant look. ''I'll be over to see you in a while,'' he told her.

She nodded and left, closing the door behind her. The others settled back down, and Dan leaned toward them.

''Okay, about the latest note. I've been talking to the front office, and we had a conference call late last night with the director and some of his people. The upshot is, we've come around, with much reluctance, to Laurel's notion that we should try to get our UNSUB to narrow his focus to her, and maybe draw him out.''

''You want to make her a target?'' Oz said.

''Under carefully controlled circumstances, yes, if we can. But only if Laurel's absolutely certain,'' Dan added, turning to her.

She nodded without hesitation—less a deer caught in headlights than a deer volunteering to stand in front of a Mack truck, he thought. If he could have taken her place, he would have, gladly.

''Show me the latest note again,'' he said, ''and tell me what your take is on it.''

Laurel opened a manila folder and handed him a photocopy of the two-page note found taped to the garbage bag in which the Goodsell child's body had been found.

It had taken the better part of Monday to re-search the Orange County fairgrounds, then track down the trash disposal company and determine which trucks had serviced the site and to which landfill they would have taken their load. After a manual search had failed to turn up anything, the bloodhounds had been called out yet again on Tuesday, finally alerting on a scent around midday. A storm-caused power outage affecting the Orange County morgue had delayed the autopsy until late that night, but in the end, there had been no surprises. The cause of death had been ruled suffocation, probably by the same plastic bag in which the body was found, and probably very soon after the child had been taken.

Dan smoothed the two sheets Laurel handed him and laid them side by side on the table before them.

DEAR LOREL,

THIS DIDN'T HAVE TO HAPPEN. THE PAPERS CALL ME A MONSTER, BUT I'M NOT. THEY HAVEN'T UNDER-

STOOD YET. HAVE YOU? HERE'S A HINT: ITS NOT JUST ABOUT BABIES. *ANYONE* CAN BECOME THE NEXT VICTIM, IF I DECIDE. BUT THERES NOTHING LIKE A MURDERED BABY TO MAKE PEOPLE SIT UP AND TAKE NOTICE, IS THERE?

DO I HAVE YOUR ATTENTION NOW?

YOU ARE POWERLESS AGAINST ME, ALL OF YOU. I KNOW ALL YOUR LITTLE TRICKS. I AM THE ONE TO MAKE YOU ALL SEE THE ERROR OF YOUR WAYS.

I'M SURE THERE ARE MANY, MANY QUESTIONS YOU WOULD LOVE TO ASK ME, LOREL. I KNOW I MUST BE FASCINATING TO YOU, IN YOUR LINE OF WORK—ALTHO AT THE RATE YOUR GOING, YOU COULD BE OUT OF A JOB SOON. THIS HAS NOT BEEN YOUR FINEST HOUR, HAS IT?

DON'T FEEL TO BAD ABOUT IT. I'M JUST BETTER AT THIS THAN ANY OF YOU. I WILL TEACH YOU WHAT YOU NEED TO KNOW.

YOURS TO THE END,

S.S.

"I don't think there's much doubt anymore that he's doing this for shock value," Laurel said, "and not out of any kind of deviant sexual predilection for young children. Nor, I think, is there any doubt that he's trying to humiliate the law enforcement community in general—maybe the Bureau in particular. Hard to say."

"But why?"

"How about because he's a psycho?" Paterson said.

"There's a perfect internal logic to what he's doing, you can be sure," Laurel said. "There always is with obsessives. But it's a logic written in cipher, and the key to the code is locked up deep in his mind."

"And his fixation on you?" Dan asked, forcing a detachment he didn't feel. "Is it sexual, do you think? And how does it relate to this anti–law enforcement bias?"

She shrugged. "People fall in love with faces on the screen all the time. Sometimes, they decide the face looking at the camera is looking right at them. If they're in a state of psychological flux, they might bond to it. The more interesting thing is this guy's arrogant tone. I'd say there's a good chance we're looking for someone who's worked—or wanted to work—in law enforcement. Who puts a high value on his own worth, but feels alienated because the community didn't recognize it. There's anger here, and it's the anger of rejection."

"Like our guy was overlooked for advancement? Maybe even fired for incompetence?"

"It's very possible, yes."

Dan turned to Paterson. "This is an angle we should be pursuing, Oz. Let's get somebody looking into recent law enforcement personnel records, starting with local area forces and moving out from there."

Paterson nodded.

"I still say we should be talking back to him," Laurel said.

"I agree," Dan said. "Obviously, the media's the way to do it, and I've had an idea about how to deliver the message. The question is, what message? You can't exactly invite the guy to tea, can you?"

"No. What's more, since we know he's security-conscious, he's going to be on the lookout for a trap."

"So how do we flush him out of the woodwork?" Paterson asked.

"By doing just the opposite of what he wants,"

Laurel said. ''He wants to be seen as important—we denigrate his significance. He wants to be feared—we write him off as a coward. He wants to be seen as brilliant—we call him an idiot.''

''He wants you,'' Dan said quietly.

Laurel shrugged. ''So I reject him. And you drop—or significantly reduce—the overt surveillance on my place, like we've analyzed the threat and written it off as not worthy of serious concern, like our forces are best deployed elsewhere.''

''That should get him thoroughly ticked off,'' Paterson agreed, ''but what if he just goes after another kid?''

''We have to keep him focused,'' Laurel said. ''Stoke the fires of his obsession. Work him up into a rage, if we can. I think he prides himself on keeping cool and analytical, and always one step ahead of us. If he loses his cool, he might just make the fatal error that allows us to put our hands on him.''

''You really think we can get him to come after you?''

''If we play our cards right, yes,'' Laurel said, ''because there's one thing you can always count on with obsessives—what they can't have or control, they'll try to destroy.''

21

"Have laptop, will travel," had been Claire's motto for more than a decade. She carried vivid memories of writing to tight deadlines on police barricades, in careening taxicabs, on cold park benches next to sleeping winos, and even, on one occasion, outside the viewing room of the New York city morgue.

Compared to those work environments, her sister's compact, cheery kitchen in Santa Monica was a veritable creative paradise, its only drawback being the smell of the cookies Bridget had left cooling on the counter when she and Lexie took off for their Wednesday morning play group. Claire could easily conquer distractions like police bullhorns or snoring winos. Oatmeal chocolate-chip cookies, however, were proving to be her Waterloo—especially given the need for some sort of diversion, regardless of caloric risk, from the heartrending work at hand.

Her third comfort cookie was securely between her teeth when she typed "-30-" to mark the end of her story on the Southland Snatcher. It was one of the most depressing pieces she'd ever done—three kidnapped babies, two found murdered, the third still missing, but no doubt also dead; the death of another child in a bizarre copycat case, and the authorities seemingly stumped by a psychopath who, if unconfirmed rumors were true, was sending them taunting letters.

At times like these, Claire could only recall what her father had once said about a cop's duty to remain emotionally detached: "It's not that it doesn't hurt like hell to see victims or their grieving families, but it's not our tears they need. They need us to solve the crime and see that justice is done for them."

A reporter, too, she thought, had to muster up some detachment, so that victims weren't forgotten, the public was warned and informed, and pressure was kept on law enforcement to get the bad guys off the streets. The trick was not to fall into the trap of promoting mass hysteria or, worse, glorifying the deeds of some sick perp who might revel in his own dubious fame or inspire another twisted, vulnerable mind. Her first editor at the *Kansas City Star* had taught her that responsible journalism meant always walking a slippery tightrope, never more than a tiny misstep from falling into the hack's pit. Every word, every quote, every inference had to be weighed for accuracy and its potential to do damage rather than good. The problem was, you just never knew for sure.

Moving her laptop to the kitchen's recessed nook and setting it on the counter, she unplugged the telephone wall jack, substituting the line from her computer modem. It had taken a couriered software package from Serge Scolari a couple of days earlier, then three hours of frustrating tinkering with Chris's help to get her computer up and running again after the damage done during the break-in at her apartment. But when she'd finally dialed into her Internet server and the *Newsworld* editorial office, the magazine's logo had popped up on her screen and she'd breathed a sigh of relief. She was wired and back in business.

Now she clicked the "send" icon, and her story was on its way, a digital rocket spanning the three thousand miles between L.A. and New York in milliseconds.

"Ain't technology grand?" she murmured, taking another bite of cookie.

The piece would be on Scolari's own desktop system momentarily. Then, all she had to do was stand by the phone in case he called with follow-up questions. Claire watched the screen. After the automated confirmation of receipt from *News-world*'s internal computer system flashed across it, she unplugged the modem and reconnected Bridget's telephone. She was just heading to the refrigerator for some milk when the phone rang.

"That was fast," she said, walking back.

But it was Alice Wentzl, not Scolari on the other end of the line. "Claire? I know you're filing your TOTNAP story today, but if you have time, I have some additional information for you."

"I just submitted my piece. Can you tell me over the phone? If it's important, I can still call it in."

"You'll need to come down to the field office."

"Too late. It's already midafternoon in New York. The magazine is printed and shipped overnight, and hits the stands tomorrow. They're finalizing content and layout as we speak."

"I promise, this will be worth your while."

Claire shook her head. "I hate to tell you this, kid, but 'Stop the presses, we've got a new lead' only happens in the movies. I can't—"

"Do you want to see the Snatcher's notes?"

She froze. "It's true? He really *has* been in touch with you?"

"Yes."

"And you've decided to publish the notes?"

"Not entirely. Not yet, anyway. For now, no one else gets access to them but you."

"An exclusive?" Her mind reeled. "Can I quote from the notes and get the Bureau's take on them?"

"You can even interview our resident profiler—on the record. Dan will be there, as well."

"Dan agreed to let me be in the same room with Laurel Madden?"

"Strictly to discuss TOTNAP," Alice warned. "That's the only ground rule, Claire. You can even bring a photographer, if you want."

"Wow. Okay, fair enough." Claire hesitated, knowing she was a fool to look a gift horse in the mouth, unable, nonetheless, to believe such good fortune. "You know, Alice, last time I checked, Santa Claus was dead. Pardon my suspicious nature, but why are you doing this?"

"To be honest, we have a message we want to get out. Your stuff gets wide enough dissemination that our UNSUB's bound to pick up on it. At least, we hope so. We could go the televised route, but the danger there is that our message might get edited down to nothing more than a four-second sound bite on the eleven o'clock news. That may not be sufficient to accomplish what we want."

"What's the message?"

"The Snatcher has put something like an offer to deal on the table. We want to send him a reply."

Serge Scolari was beside himself when Claire called to alert him. "An exclusive? The same babe who took down the Beltway Ripper? And *pictures?* Oh, Lord, I've died and gone to heaven!"

"So I gather you're interested?"

"Oh, yes indeed. I *knew* sending you out to cover this story was the way to go. If this pans out, girl, I'd say you've knocked the pope off the front cover. But we'll have to move fast. I'll talk to head office and Production. We've got maybe a three-hour window of opportunity at best, so you've got to get back to me fast."

"I'll take my laptop. I'm guessing there'll be no problem getting a corner to work in over there and a phone line once I've done the interview with Madden. You'll need to contact a photographer, Serge, and have him meet me at the Federal Building. There's a full-time press contingent camped outside, so you'd better tell him to play it really low-key so they're not tipped off. Tell him, if he's asked, to say he's working on an immigration story. Once he gets inside the building, he should report to the Bureau's seventeenth-floor reception area and say he has an appointment with Special Agent in Charge Dan Sprague."

"Got it. Now, go!"

"'Obsession shrink-wraps the soul.' That's the best description I've ever heard for the phenomenon," Laurel Madden said.

She was sitting across from Claire, hands clasped tightly, the Snatcher's photocopied notes lying on the table beside her, misspellings, taunts and all. After Claire had been allowed to read them through, Laurel had taken the notes back and set them aside without a glance, as if their mere proximity was loathsome—or dangerous—and the sight of them would turn her, like Lot's wife, into a pillar of salt. Claire had no doubt, however, that every word in them was burned into Laurel like a tattoo of hate.

Alice Wentzl sat next to her, Dan at the end of the table, in a conference room next to the Emergency Response Center. Outside the door, long rows of tables and workstations, some with computer monitors, were arrayed in front of a podium and a long blackboard, a couple of the computer monitors labeled Rapid Start. On the way into the meeting, Claire had noticed agents manning phones and feeding data into them. Apparently, this was where the TOTNAP tip line leads were reviewed and analyzed, in the hopes that someone, somewhere, might have seen the man whose sketched image was being plastered across the nation, and would call in before he struck again.

"There's no doubt the notes are genuine?" Claire asked.

"No doubt at all," Laurel said. "They led us straight to the bodies of the two missing children. The clue on the first victim still hasn't panned out, but the reference to a field and a canyon still leaves a lot of terrain to search. With five weeks having passed since the Jefferson child disappeared, it's even possible that the body could have been carried off by animals. But this is definitely our guy, and he wants us to know it."

"How does a person descend into this kind of depravity?"

"He probably functioned for quite some time like a reasonably normal human being," Dan said, "by outward appearances, at least. But somewhere along the way, something snapped. An anger took hold in him, and now it's smothered out everything else."

Claire was typing notes on her laptop as fast as she could. "So you think he's deteriorated to the point where he's no longer even functional, holding down a job, interacting with friends or family, that sort of thing?"

"He's basically a loser," Laurel said. "My view is he's never had what anyone would call a normal relationship in his life. He goes after kids as a substitute for the adults he's incompetent to deal with."

"I don't think he wants to hurt children," Dan said. "It seems clear from the notes he feels bad about that, but he thinks it's the only way he can get anyone's attention."

Claire's fingers paused on the keyboard, and she glanced up at him, checking for facial signs of the sarcasm that she wasn't hearing in his voice. The Dan Sprague she knew had never wasted much sympathy on anyone who chose to follow a criminal path. The idea that he would have the slightest empathy for a baby killer was unthinkable.

There was also the distracting matter of the raw tension he and Laurel were generating in the room. They seemed, on the surface, to be focused on the matter at hand, yet Claire had the distinct sense of two people with eyes only for one another, trying desperately to convince themselves and everyone else that such was not the case. Her encounter the other morning with a distracted, boozy-smelling Dan came to mind, and Claire suddenly knew, with the absolute certainty of a professional observer of human foibles, that if they hadn't already slept together, they were on the brink and fighting a losing battle against the inevitable. The notion was not a happy one. Laurel Madden had already gotten her hooks into Michael Kazarian and Gar Doucet, and look what had happened there. How could Dan have let himself fall under her spell?

"He goes after defenseless babies because it makes him feel powerful and in control," Laurel said contemptuously. "A blowhard like this is particularly inept with women. I think his own sexuality is very much unclear. He sounds like he's trying to impress me about his potency, but I think the person he's really trying to convince is himself."

"And his line of work?" Claire asked, forcing herself to keep her mind on her deadline. "You think he might have been in the police or security fields?''

''Or aspired to be,'' Dan said. ''Maybe applied and was turned down. Whatever the case, he feels slighted. He may have been fired from a job. At the very least, he might have felt his contributions were being put down, his opinions overlooked.''

''He would have been blown off because he's fundamentally an idiot,'' Laurel said. ''But oh, what a hero in his own mind!''

Claire's hands had already abandoned the keyboard, her head pivoting from one to the other as they argued back and forth. Finally, with an exasperated sigh, she pushed the laptop away. ''Hold it right there, folks. This is not going to fly.''

''What do you mean?'' Alice asked.

Claire looked at her. ''This game these two are playing—good cop/bad cop, simpatico/heavy, whatever it's supposed to be.''

''We're not—''

''The bleeding-heart role doesn't suit you, Dan. Sorry, but I've known you too long. And as for you, Agent Madden—well, I don't know you at all personally, but I do know a little about your professional reputation, so I certainly don't buy this unsubtle ball-buster routine you're performing here.'' She glanced at her watch. ''We're about ninety minutes away from missing my publication deadline completely, so if there's a message you want to get across, people, my advice would be to tell it straight and quit jerking me around.''

The three agents exchanged glances, Dan's eyebrows arching in an I-told-you-so look.

Alice sighed. ''Sorry, Claire, it's my fault.''

''What's going on?''

''I was afraid of insulting your professional integrity. I thought you might feel you were being used for a mouthpiece if we said outright how we wanted this to come across.''

''Tell you what,'' Claire said. ''Why don't you do just that, and let me worry about my own professional integrity?''

She was sitting alone in the conference room a while later, her laptop plugged into one of several phone jacks on the wall, when Laurel leaned around the open door. ''Alice said you had more questions for me?''

Now *there* was an understatement, Claire thought. But she'd made a promise not to deviate from TOTNAP, so that was what she intended to do, despite the temptation to grill this woman—

and to warn her off Dan Sprague. Despite her teenage crush on him, Dan had evolved since then into the closest thing to a big brother Claire would ever have, and she desperately hoped he would find a new love one day to fill the void in his life left by Fiona's death—as long as it wasn't Laurel Madden.

"Are you all done with the photographer?" Claire asked her.

"I just walked him out. I let him hook up to one of the modems in our squad room to send his pictures before he left."

"That digital camera boggles my mind. The photo department in New York will be examining those pictures right now, choosing, cropping and fitting them into the layout."

Laurel nodded. "Pretty incredible."

"I spoke with my editor," Claire said. "They'll use your picture to accompany a sidebar he's pulled together from our files, relating the last time you got caught up in a situation like this." She turned the laptop and slid it across the table. "I wanted to show you what he's written on the Beltway Ripper incident so you could check it for factual accuracy."

Laurel approached the machine as if it were a ticking bomb, wrapping her arms around herself as she read the text, reaching out nervously a couple of times to scroll down the screen. There were deep blue shadows of fatigue under her eyes, Claire noted, as well as noticeable lines around her mouth that marked her, if you looked closely enough, as well past the ingenue stage. Despite that, the photographer's shots had no doubt turned out beautifully. Good bone structure went a long way toward overcoming the ravages of stress and the passing of years.

"Looks about right," Laurel said, straightening.

Claire pulled the machine back. "It can't be easy to let yourself be set up like this, after what you went through last time."

"If it works, it's worth it."

Claire typed a confirmation note and E-mailed it back to Scolari. "Do you think the Snatcher will take the bait?" she asked Laurel.

"What you've put in your piece should certainly bruise his ego. What about you? You don't mind reporting quotes like that from me, knowing they're deliberately calculated to get a rise out of him?"

"Like you said, if it works, it's worth a little fudging." Claire closed the files on her screen and sat back in the chair. "I have to wait a few more minutes until they call back to confirm the thing's been put to bed, if that's all right.''

''Alice had another call coming in when I spoke to her. I'll walk you out if your call comes before she gets back.'' Laurel perched on the edge of a chair, and they sat in awkward silence. ''Did you tell your editor what we were doing?'' Laurel asked finally.

''No, it seemed more prudent not to. He's a little amazed that the normally staid FBI is playing gunslinger here, and did ask me to confirm those quotes you made about the Snatcher's lack of *cojones,*'' Claire said, smiling a little. ''But if I'm willing to stand by them, it makes for great copy. Of course, if this all blows up in our faces, I'll make a handy scapegoat.''

''Let's hope it doesn't. You've put your career on the line here.''

Claire shrugged. ''You're putting your life on the line. I presume you'll be a little more prepared this time if he does come after you?''

''I've been under surveillance since the first note showed up, but it's being stepped down now to reflect our apparent underestimation of the threat. We have no choice. He won't come close otherwise.''

''Has Dan set up electronic surveillance?''

At the mention of his name, a flicker of something uneasy passed across Laurel's features. "Let's just say, if the need arises, help should arrive reasonably quickly. I'll just have to hold the guy off until it does."

"You fought off Randy Harkness and won."

"Barely. And only because..." Laurel hesitated, her hands clasping and unclasping in her lap. "I had just found out I was pregnant a few days before the attack," she said quietly. "I was sure I was going to die out in that field. He had me on the ground, and he'd already stabbed me once. But when he started to rip at my clothes, I realized he planned to rape me before he finished me off. That's when I got it—the adrenaline surge they say allows people to lift cars. I thought about my baby, and I became enraged. I managed to get my hands around a rock and hit him over the head. He was only dazed, but it was enough. I ran. I made it back to the car and found the sidearm he'd taken off me when he first ambushed me." She shook her head. "Still, he came after me. I warned him to stop, but he just kept coming."

"So you shot him."

"Yes."

"Good," Claire said firmly.

Laurel looked up and gave her a rueful, almost grateful nod. At that moment, the image Claire had been holding in her mind of the evil black widow began to fade. In its place appeared another of a woman about her own age, with a stubborn temperament not unlike her own—someone she might, conceivably, under other circumstances, have been able to call a friend. It was the same phenomenon she'd experienced sitting in the car with Gar Doucet in the middle of the downpour, listening to him weave his tale of the *fifolet.* Maybe they weren't monsters, after all, but simply people who, as Alice had suggested, got caught up in something bigger than they were. And why should that be so surprising? Some crimes were committed by psychopaths, sociopaths and habitual criminals, but not the majority of murders. The truth was, given sufficient motivation, anyone could kill—even people with as much to offer as a Laurel Madden or a Gar Doucet.

"I understand you knew my husband," Laurel said.

Lost in her own complicated thoughts, Claire was taken by surprise, and she had the distinct sense of the tables being turned. She studied Laurel, trying to decide whether the comment—a statement, not a question—was meant in the biblical sense. She would have preferred not to have to think about that. She'd never before found herself in this situation with another man's wife, and other considerations notwithstanding, it wasn't something she enjoyed or ever hoped to experience again. On the other hand, since Laurel herself had raised the subject, it was an opening she'd be a fool to pass up.

"I met him briefly a couple of years ago when I was doing a story on the FBI academy. I ran into him again in New York last spring while I was investigating the mob he'd infiltrated."

"You recognized him?"

Claire nodded.

"Then I have to ask you a question," Laurel said. "Do you think your recognizing him might have been what gave him away to the mob?"

Claire shook her head incredulously. "That's a pretty astounding question, under the circumstances."

"Why is that?" Laurel asked. And then she gave a short, bitter laugh. "Oh, I see. Because you've been operating under the popular assumption that I had something to do with Michael's murder, is that it?"

"Did you?"

"No," Laurel said without hesitation. If she

was a liar, she was pathological. "So I repeat—did you give Michael's identity away?"

Good question, Claire thought. How to answer? That she'd believed she had, and then that she hadn't, and now she wasn't sure?

"To be honest," she said at last, "it's something I agonized over for a long time after he was killed. But I'm reasonably certain now his murder had nothing to do with me. Last week, I interviewed Ivankov, the Russian mobster I thought was responsible. I walked away from that meeting with two firm convictions. One, he'd never heard of me before I asked for that interview, so obviously he wasn't aware that I'd also interviewed the man he knew as Misha Kurelek."

"And two?"

"Ivankov didn't murder Michael, either."

"You're certain of that?"

"Yes," Claire said. "I am."

Laurel stared at her for a moment. Then this woman—normally so cool, so assured—slumped back in her chair and covered her face with her hands.

"Laurel?"

Her green eyes were damp when she slid her hands away from them, looking up with as miserable an expression as Claire had ever seen.

Claire leaned across the table. ''It was Gar Doucet who killed Michael, wasn't it?''

Laurel's voice was an agonized whisper. ''I don't know.''

''But that's what you believe?''

''Dan said you've seen Gar?''

''Yes. He's been watching me for some time. He broke into my apartment in New York and stole all the files and records related to the story I was working on when I met Michael that last time.''

''Oh, God! This has gone too far.''

''What's gone too far? Laurel, you have to come clean. This is never going to end until you do. Doucet has made it perfectly clear he's obsessed, and that he'll eliminate anything and anyone he thinks poses a danger to you.'' Claire had a sudden, chilling thought. ''What about Dan?''

''Dan? What do you mean?''

''Look, forgive me, but I know him pretty well, and I can tell something's going on between the two of you. I happen to care a great deal for that guy. What happens if Doucet decides Dan's a threat? Will he go after him, too?''

''Dan a threat? To me?''

''No, to Doucet! A threat to take his place with you.''

''Gar has no place with me.''

''Does he know that? Does he accept that you're not interested in him?''

Laurel shook her head. ''You don't understand. It's not about *me* with Gar. It's never been about me.''

''Then what—''

The phone in the center of the conference table rang. Both women shot it an irritated glance. ''It's probably my editor,'' Claire said.

''Go ahead, answer it.''

Sure enough, the duty officer reported that a Mr. Scolari was calling. While Claire reviewed alternative lead lines and quote attributions with him, Laurel got up and paced.

When Claire hung up the phone a few minutes later, Laurel turned to her expectantly. ''Done?''

''Yes. Congratulations. You just made the cover of *Newsworld.*''

22

Dan had assumed Claire was finished with writing and sending her article and long gone from the building, but when he wandered back across the seventeenth floor to talk to the Rapid Start team, he was surprised to see through the conference room window that she was still there, deep in conversation with someone hidden by the door—Alice Wentzl, he guessed. He opened the door, startled to find Laurel, instead. The conversation stopped and the two women looked up at him with equally apprehensive expressions. Not a good sign.

"What's going on?" he asked, knowing by the look that passed between them that Claire had overstepped some boundaries here.

"You need to tell Dan," she said to Laurel.

Laurel nodded.

"Tell me what?"

Their nervous faces turned again in unison toward him. It reminded Dan of when Erin and Julie were younger and had done something they were afraid to tell him about—except in this case, he sensed the problem was far more serious than a broken window or a dog let loose in the neighbor's geraniums.

''If you can spare the time,'' Claire said to him, ''I think you'd better sit down and hear this, Dan.''

He couldn't, really, but neither did he dare leave the two of them alone any longer. He closed the door and pulled out a chair. ''What's going on?''

''Laurel and I have been talking about Michael Kazarian and Gar Doucet.''

''Claire, I thought I made it clear—''

''She didn't raise the subject,'' Laurel said. ''I did. I've been thinking about what you told me about Gar stalking Claire, Dan, and I realized it's gone too far. I did something terrible. I didn't mean for things to get so out of control, or for anyone to be hurt, but they have. I should have said something before now, I know. But we'd been punished and I tried to convince myself it was enough. It's not.''

''Punished? Who are we talking about?'' Dan asked.

''Gar and me. He lost his job. I lost the few friends I had and most of my professional credibility. But it isn't over. It won't be until Gar's pulled in and we both pay for what we did.''

''Maybe you'd better start at the beginning, Laurel,'' Claire said quietly.

Dan nodded. ''Please.''

Laurel rose from her chair and moved to the window, laying her forehead against the glass. ''It was Michael. I was crazy about him when I first met him. He was confident, attractive and charming. Everyone loved him. I was awkward and gawky—''

Dan started to protest, but she held up a hand.

''I know what you're going to say. I have mirrors. Objectively, I know what I look like, but that's someone else in the mirror. The real me, inside here,'' she said, pressing a clenched fist against her chest, ''feels like the homely beanpole even my own mother belittled. So when Michael wanted to marry me, I was amazed and grateful—and maybe too starstruck to pay attention to the warning signs.''

''What warning signs?'' Dan asked.

''That he was jealous and possessive, and had a temper. I saw it even before we were married, although it was a side of himself he kept carefully hidden. He shoved me up against a wall once, shortly after we got engaged. I'd been away on a case, and he got the idea something had gone on with another agent in the Chicago field office. I tried to tell him he was being ridiculous, but he didn't believe me. The argument spun out of control and he lost it. Afterward, he was so contrite that I forgave him. Stupidly. I should have known better. After we were married, things were fine for a while, except he did things."

"Things?" Dan asked. "Like what?"

"Strange things. If I had a new dress, for example, insisting in front of other men that I stand up and turn around, like I was on display—like a new car or some prize-winning fish. Discussing details of our personal relationship—" She glanced uncomfortably at him. "—and worse. It made me horribly uncomfortable. I asked him to stop. He always apologized, but brushed off my concerns. He said he was proud of me and liked to show me off. He'd let up for a while, but pretty soon he'd be at it again."

Laurel turned to the window once more. "At the same time, he became more and more jealous. Every time I had to go out of town on a case, he'd phone me at all hours, day and night, wanting to know if I'd had dinner with anyone, imagining he heard another voice in my hotel room. Once, he even showed up unexpectedly when I was working a case in Atlanta. He said it was to surprise me, but he acted more like he'd expected to catch me doing something I shouldn't. It got to be ridiculous. Finally, I told him I wanted a separation."

"Did you separate?" Dan asked.

Laurel shook her head. "Not for long. I moved out, but after a couple of days he came to me, crying, promising to go for counseling. He did go a couple of times, and things got a little better. And then, I got pregnant, and Randy Harkness showed up."

"It must have been terrifying," Claire said.

Laurel gave her a grim look. "The media circus afterward was almost worse than the attack itself."

Claire winced apologetically.

"Was Michael upset by all the attention you were getting?" Dan asked.

"Him?" Laurel gave a rueful laugh. "He loved it. Played it to the hilt—the poor, desperate husband whose pregnant wife was kidnapped and nearly murdered." Her expression darkened. "He was the one who spoke to the movie people. It made me cringe, personally and professionally, to have the incident raked over in the media, again and again. And then, that stupid movie business. Michael loved it, though. He started talking about a career as some Hollywood technical consultant. Envisioned his name in the publicity when the movie was made—'Harrison Ford as Michael Kazarian,' that sort of thing. It was such a joke. Just your typical fifteen minutes of fame, of course, and then it was over. Thank God, thought I."

"But not Michael," Dan said.

Laurel moved back to the table and sat down. "You have to understand, there were such high expectations for him—from his family, friends, everyone. He learned to crave the limelight. When he was in college, NFL coaches were even courting him."

"But he turned them down," Claire said, nodding. "His mother mentioned that."

"Oh, you've met Alma, have you? A nice lady, but she spoiled Michael rotten. He always made out that he turned down an NFL career, but I discovered that it was they who turned him down. He might have had a shot, but he injured his right knee in one of the last games of his junior year. Nothing permanent. The knee was more or less fine after surgery and a few months of recuperation, but the injury was enough to scare off the pros. The insurance companies thought it was just too great a risk.''

''He never quite made the grade in the Bureau, either,'' Dan said. ''He joined a couple of years after me. I remember people predicting he'd be the first in his class to make SAC, and that he'd be an assistant director by the time he was forty. He seemed golden.''

Laurel nodded. ''The problem was, when you looked closely enough, Michael was really just brass.''

''What about Doucet?'' Claire asked.

''Gar and Michael joined up at the same time. They stayed friends, although their assignments took them to different field offices. Maybe that's why the friendship lasted for so long. If Gar had been around more, he might have gotten disillusioned earlier with Michael. As it was, it was only a couple of years ago, when he was assigned to work back at headquarters, that things really began to unravel.''

''Was that after the baby?'' Dan asked quietly.

''About that time,'' Laurel said. ''It was a difficult birth, for me and the baby. The doctors thought it might have something to do with the injuries I'd sustained during the attack by Harkness, but you never really know about these things. Anyway, the baby and I were in the hospital for nearly a week. When we were finally released, I went home to discover that Michael had sold my car."

"What?" Claire exclaimed.

"I can prove it, too. The car was in my name, but he forged my signature on the pink slip."

"Why would he do that?"

"He said it was because he wanted to buy me a new one—but, of course, he never did. It was just his way of exerting control."

"What did you do?"

"I was furious. But I was also weak after the baby's birth, and worried about Theo, too. He was jaundiced, and there were some breathing problems. I was too preoccupied to fight Michael over my car right then. I let it pass, but I felt like a prisoner. Michael took his car to work every day. If I needed to go somewhere, he took time off to drive me—the dutiful, long-suffering husband," Laurel added bitterly. "All the women in his office thought he was henpecked, and that I was the world's most demanding wife. It went on like that for months, and we were fighting again. When I told Michael I'd decided to go back to work, he never said a word, just hauled off and hit me across the face. He knocked out a molar and blackened my eye.''

''Did you call the police?'' Claire asked.

''And tell them what? That FBI Special Agent Madden, who defeated the Beltway Ripper, was being held captive and abused by her husband?''

''You're not the first woman it's happened to,'' Claire said.

''Don't you think I know that? Me, who'd made a career out of going after control freaks? I was humiliated.''

''So what *did* you do?''

''I called Gar for help. I knew he'd understand.''

''But he was Michael's best friend.''

''Yes, but he also has four sisters. Gar's close to all his family, but his youngest sister was always his pet. When he was away at college, she started seeing a guy who pushed her around. Gar went home for Christmas that year and threatened the guy to within an inch of his life if he ever came near her again. But after Gar left, this fellow started hanging around again. Finally, the sister moved in with him. A few weeks later, this creep beat her up so badly that he fractured her skull. She ended up paralyzed and permanently brain-damaged.''

''Oh, Christ,'' Dan breathed. It was his worst nightmare. There was a good reason he grilled and ran police checks on every guy Erin or Julie went out the door with.

''When Gar saw my black eye, he was ready to kill Michael. He wanted me and the baby to move out right then, but Michael had left. He'd just volunteered for the undercover assignment, and had gone to start setting up the operation.''

''It seems funny, him leaving right then,'' Claire said, ''given how nervous he was about you slipping away.''

''Not really. He left feeling quite certain he'd made his views clear about my going back to work. Knowing, too, that I'd be too embarrassed to go out of the house for a while, looking the way I did. It seems ridiculous, I know, but you have to understand, I was sleep-deprived, because of the baby, and completely isolated. Michael was confident he could maintain control of the situation, even from a distance. And then, too, that undercover assignment was something he really wanted. It was a chance for him to be a hero. To go play Serpico, and bring down a big mob operation. He couldn't resist.''

''And Gar?''

''He took me out that very day to buy another

car. He also tried to persuade me to report Michael to the OPR, if not to the police.''

''But you didn't,'' Dan said.

''No. To this day, I wish I had, but as I say, I was humiliated. And, in spite of everything, I still cared about Michael. My parents had divorced when I was a kid, and I'd always blamed my mother for driving my dad away. I thought if I was just a better wife, and understood what he was going through—his fear of getting old, his worry about his career—and didn't do anything to make him jealous...well, you know the story. So do I, really. It's such an old one.''

''But you still did return to work,'' Dan said.

''Yes. I called my unit and asked to go back part-time, once I'd found a sitter for Theo. I waited to tell Michael until he came home for the weekend. Gar made sure he was there when I did, and it was a good thing, too. Michael went ballistic. That was when I finally realized that it was never going to get any better. Gar tried to reason with him. Michael told him to butt out, and he probably would have hit him, except Gar was working as an OPR inspector by that point, and Michael was afraid he'd report him. Gar warned him, though, that if he touched me again, he himself would file an internal report, with or without my cooperation. The Bureau's an old boys' club,'' Laurel said to Claire, ''but it's better than it used to be, and that kind of behavior isn't much tolerated these days.''

Claire nodded.

Laurel took a deep breath. ''Michael backed down and returned to New York. I didn't hear anything for a while. I started having doubts again about breaking up the marriage, though. I was a child of divorced parents, as I say, and I didn't want that for my son. I thought, when Michael's assignment was over, we could go for counseling and get back on track.'' Her expression darkened. ''But then I found out Michael was telling people Gar and I were having an affair.''

''Were you?'' Claire asked. ''Not that it makes a difference as far as Michael's behavior is concerned, you understand. I'm just trying to figure out where Doucet's coming from now.''

Dan watched Laurel fix her with a steady gaze. ''It's impossible to prove a negative in the court of public opinion, Claire. If people are determined to believe that what Gar did for me means I must have been sleeping with him, then nothing I say or do will convince them otherwise. All I can tell you is the truth. It never happened.''

''Then what do you have to feel guilty about?''

Dan asked. ''As far as I can see, you're blameless here. As for Doucet, if he's hanging around now because he's fixated on you—''

Laurel held up a hand. ''There's more. There's my son's death. It happened a couple of months later.'' She closed her eyes. ''I don't know why I just didn't kill *myself* that morning, too. It would have been so much easier than continuing on.''

Claire felt a chill. ''Kill *yourself,* Laurel?'' she asked quietly. ''Did you kill the baby?''

Laurel's head snapped up. ''What? No! My baby? My God, no! How could I kill my own baby? When I found him—'' Her voice cracked and she began to cry.

Dan moved next to her and put one hand over hers, the other stroking her hair as she struggled for control.

''I'm so sorry,'' Claire said. ''I misunderstood.''

Laurel looked up again and nodded miserably. ''Michael came home as soon as he heard. We both knew it was all over between us. At least, I thought so. But then, when the pathologist did the autopsy and said he suspected Theo had been smothered, things got crazy. Michael stood by me, and basically bullied the man into backing down. I was cleared, and the cause of death was listed as SIDS. But once an accusation like that gets around, people never really look at you the same way again.''

''It drew you and Michael back together?'' Claire asked.

Laurel gave her the oddest smile. ''Oh, yes. Permanently, Michael thought. That's what he said, 'Now you'll *have* to stay with me.'''

''What the heck is that supposed to mean?'' Dan asked.

''Ah, well—it meant he had me over a barrel, you see. Two days before the baby died, I had phoned Michael in New York to tell him I wanted a divorce. Afterward, when he'd stood beside me like that, he just assumed the divorce was off. When he realized I hadn't changed my mind, Michael said if I tried to leave him, he'd go back to the police and say that I *had* killed the baby. That he'd once caught me putting a pillow over Theo's face to stop his crying—which was a complete and total fabrication. He'd say I was depressed after the baby's birth, and isolated myself, refusing to see our old friends, except Gar, whom I proceeded to have an affair with. Michael would tell the police, pained and reluctantly, of course, that I wasn't in control of my own actions anymore. That I was suffering from postpartum depression, and being manipulated by Gar. That Gar had convinced me I'd be happier if only I were single and free and with him, unburdened with another man's baby. Michael would admit that I'd made some crazy call to him about wanting a divorce. But, the story would go, he hadn't been able to bring himself to believe that I'd actually go so far as to hurt the baby. Even after our son died, he hadn't wanted to believe it, but now, he'd say, after much soul-searching, he'd decided he had to turn me in so I could get help.''

''Son of a bitch,'' Dan muttered.

''So you turned to Gar once more for help?''

''A few days later,'' Laurel said, nodding. ''I didn't want to pull him into it again, after what Michael had already put him through with his lies about us, but I was desperate. Only, I went too far.''

''How do you mean?''

Laurel got up and moved back to the window. ''The more I thought about what Michael had said, and how he had everything so figured out, the more I began to wonder whether maybe the baby really did die of unnatural causes, only not at my hand, but at his.''

''But he was in New York when it happened,'' Claire said.

''Working undercover and out of pocket for long periods of time. Gar actually looked into it, but Michael had an alibi for that night,'' Laurel said, grimacing.

''Another woman?'' Claire asked, knowing even as she did what the answer would be. This would have been long before she and Michael had become involved, so obviously she hadn't been his only extramarital fling.

''Yes,'' Laurel said. ''But if she was lying for him—and that's not so hard to believe, knowing Michael as we do—''

Claire felt her face go warm.

''—he could easily have slipped away overnight to Virginia and returned without anybody being the wiser. He'd warned me the night I called him about the divorce that he'd never let me take his son away. When I pointed out there was little question who'd get custody, he just said it again, 'I won't let you have him.'''

''Did it never occur to you when your son died that Michael might be involved?'' Dan asked.

''No, not for a second. Even if I could imagine anyone killing a helpless baby, Michael's son was as much a trophy to him as I was. Only later did it start to make sense that he could and would do such an awful thing.''

"So what happened when you spoke to Gar Doucet?" Claire asked.

"He told me to leave it with him. I didn't hear anything for a couple of weeks, not from him or Michael. I started to worry."

"Why?"

"Because I told Gar that I wished Michael were dead. I meant it, too, but I wasn't thinking straight. Michael seemed to be lying so low that I thought Gar may have threatened him. When I finally asked him point-blank, Gar put his hand on my shoulder and said the strangest thing."

"What?" Dan asked.

"He said, 'You won't have to worry about Mike anymore, Laurel. He's going down.' A couple of days later, Michael was car-bombed. They said at first that it was the mob's work—that they must have found out Michael was an undercover agent. That's why I asked whether you might have given him away," Laurel added to Claire.

"But you suspected all along it was Gar, didn't you?"

"Yes."

"Laurel, why didn't you ever say anything about this before?" Dan asked. "You knew Doucet was under investigation. Yet you flatly refused to speak against him."

She raised herself to her full height and turned to them both, her expression defiant. ''Because I was grateful to him. I believe Michael killed our son, and that he did it out of sheer spite. So when I heard he was dead, I was glad. No matter who was responsible, I still am.''

23

The *Newsworld* article on the Snatcher hit the stands Thursday afternoon, in an issue that featured an eye-catching photo of Special Agent Laurel Madden on the cover. *The Southland Snatcher: A Top FBI Profiler Goes Head-to-Head with a Killer,* the cutline screamed. The full-page color shot had Laurel standing against a backdrop of Most Wanted posters, a tall, blond Amazon with arms folded defiantly, her sober green eyes fixed on the camera as if issuing a direct challenge to the Snatcher: ''Come and get me—if you dare.''

Say what you will, Claire thought as she sat on the staircase below Bridget's apartment the next day, sunning herself and flipping through the issue one more time—the woman made for great copy.

The steps vibrated as her brother-in-law pounded down, lugging suitcases. Claire squeezed herself against the rail to let him pass. ''Can I take that with me to read by the pool?'' he asked, nodding at the magazine.

''Sure, but I thought this was supposed to be a medical conference.''

''Oh, I'll take in a seminar or two, long as they don't get in the way of Jacuzzi time with my wife,'' he said, grinning up the stairs.

Bridget had just stepped out on the landing with Lexie in her arms and a brightly colored tote bag slung over her shoulder. ''Sounds good to me,'' she said, returning the smile. He went to load the Toyota as she started down. ''I've left the number for the hotel in Santa Barbara by the phone. Also, the car phone, the pediatrician and Chris's pager. There's spaghetti sauce and stew in the fridge, and plenty of fruit in the bin. I think Lexie's got more than enough clean clothes to last, but if you think—''

''We'll be *fine,* Britty.'' Claire laughed, reaching out to her niece. ''C'mere, you. We've got a busy weekend planned ourselves, don't we?''

''Take Bubba to the park?''

''Right away, soon as we say bye to Mommy and Daddy.''

''I go get him!'' The toddler wriggled her way to the ground and ran over to the Spragues', a blur of blue overalls, her long-sleeved white shirt covered with bright blue geese in beribboned Mother Goose bonnets.

"Ring the bell, sweetie!" her mother called as the little girl clambered up onto the back porch. They watched until the door opened and Erin took Lexie into the house to find the dog's leash. Then Bridget's smile faded, and she turned worried eyes on Claire. "Are you sure you'll be all right?"

"We're going to have a ball. And you'd better do the same, you hear me?"

"Yes, ma'am."

Claire handed her the issue of *Newsworld.* "Take this. Chris wanted to read it."

Bridget examined the cover. "It's ironic, under the circumstances, isn't it? Her ending up on the front like this?" She rolled the magazine and put it into her bag. "Do you really think her career's over?"

Claire nodded. Late the other night, after filing her piece and returning from the field office, she'd quietly confided to her sister the whole saga of Laurel, Michael and Gar Doucet, and how she herself came to be bogged down in that quagmire of complex relationships. It was a story she'd never write for publication, regardless of how things ended for Laurel and Gar. There was nothing to be gained by opening up that much private pain to public scrutiny, especially since she knew Dan, too, was going through his own quiet, personal agony over Laurel and what was going to happen to her.

''Since it's already in play, they're going to let this gambit with the Snatcher run for a few days to see if he takes the bait,'' Claire said. ''After that, Laurel's been ordered back to FBI headquarters to face the music. Dan intends to stand by her and speak on her behalf, but it probably won't be enough to save her career now. They've also issued a warrant for Doucet's arrest.''

''But do they actually have proof he killed her husband?''

''I don't know. He's been under suspicion all along, it seems. Depending on what the investigation's found so far, Laurel's testimony might be enough to bring down an indictment, at last.''

Bridget studied her closely. ''You don't seem too happy about that. I thought you wanted Michael's killer found and charged.''

''I did. Knowing now what I do, though, and that Michael worked his charisma and lies on me the same way he did so many other people, it's small comfort. And if Laurel's right about their baby—'' Claire shuddered. ''If he did what she suspects he did, then he should burn in hell.''

''But what if she's still lying? Maybe she and Doucet were in cahoots all along to get rid of her husband, and the business about the baby is just smoke.''

''If that were so, why confess that she may have pushed Doucet into it?''

''Maybe just to get you off their backs. After all, if Doucet hasn't been arrested up to now, maybe there never will be enough evidence for a conviction, and they both know it. All they have to do is ride this out, take their pink slips from the Bureau, retire to Fiji and live out the rest of their days on that stolen money and the insurance payoff.''

Claire shook her head, unconvinced. ''Laurel claims she didn't know about the insurance until after Michael's personal effects were returned to her and she found the policy. She says she didn't want anything from him, so she burned it without ever filing a claim.''

''You believe her?''

''I'm inclined to, although that isn't saying much. I believed in Michael, too.''

''Sounds like they were a pair.'' Bridget ran a hand through her fair hair. ''Maybe she couldn't collect on the insurance as long as there was some doubt about the circumstances surrounding his death. And she might have deliberately set up this poor sucker Doucet, planning to stand back and let him take the fall alone. Did you ever think about that?''

Claire laughed as Chris returned, jangling car keys. ''You know, fella, this wife of yours has a very Machiavellian mind. You want to make sure you treat her right, because if not, she's got some real nasty 'how-to-murder-a-husband' scenarios mapped out in that sweet head of hers.''

He flung an arm around Bridget's shoulders. ''That's my girl,'' he said proudly. ''Now, where's that little peanut, so we can say goodbye and cruise on up the Coast Highway?''

A person should really be in possession of three sets of eyes, Claire decided as she stood next to the sandlot play structures, watching her little niece. At the moment, she needed one pair to supervise Lexie on the slide, one to keep tabs on Bubba, who was off-leash again and sniffing bushes in the deserted park, and a third, vigilant pair, preferably in the back of her head, to keep a wary watch out for Gar Doucet.

Her bristling instincts told her he was due to

put in another of his surprise appearances, and strangely enough, she knew she'd feel cheated if the police or Dan's own people picked him up first. She told herself she merely wanted to ask him some more questions, and see firsthand his reaction to Laurel's claim that he may have murdered Michael. But the truth was more unsettling. Doucet's face had been drifting uncomfortably through her mind ever since their rainstorm encounter. He had a gift for melodrama, that one, Claire thought ruefully—showing up in driving rain and deathly ice storms, or on the kind of dark, starless night when a hot wind blew through the trees and you could swear you heard ghosts sighing. As much as she tried to rationalize and minimize his effect on her, Claire was finding, as she lay restlessly awake at night listening to Lexie's snuffles and flops in the next bed, that her thoughts dwelled on his smoky eyes that seemed to see so much yet gave away so little. On the remembrance of his big hand on her skin and a touch that could shift from threat to caress in an instant. On that lilting voice, spinning the tale of the *fifolet,* those shimmering wizard lights that lured good people to their doom. Who was the real *fifolet* here? she wondered.

Laurel's revelations about Gar's sister put his

stubborn defense of her in an entirely different light. But was Laurel telling the truth, about that or anything else? Whether or not Gar had a battered sister was easily enough checked, Claire reasoned, so presumably, that much could be fact. As for an affair between him and Laurel, true or not, it was relevant only if it had led to a long-term game plan to get rid of Michael and snag a small fortune for themselves in the bargain. But did Laurel and Gar necessarily have the *same* game plan? Or had she cleverly seduced him, as Bridget suggested, and planted the idea to kill Michael, thinking to make off with the money herself and leave Gar to take the rap?

Another thought occurred to Claire: might that also mean that Michael *wasn't* the abuser they'd made him out to be? After all, history is written by victors. With no other witness to the alleged abuse besides Laurel and Gar, who was to say it ever really happened?

She sighed wearily, shading her eyes as she watched Lexie at the top of the slide, starting another run down. There were almost too many possibilities and permutations to hold in her mind. What if she never discovered the truth about what had gone on there? Was this destined to be another senseless crime that would haunt her until the day she died?

An engine revved on the quiet street behind her, and Claire spun around, but it was only a landscape gardener's truck lurching to a stop in front of one of the houses across the way. Three Mexican day workers spilled out of it, carrying rakes and clippers, their gazes watchful under broad straw hats—nervous, no doubt, of the roving immigration checks that Californians loudly demanded, even while they took full advantage of the cheap labor the illegals provided, guaranteeing a steady flow of migrants across the border from Baja California seeking work and the American dream. The gardeners went to work, clipping, mowing, watching—the only sign of life on the street.

Claire turned her attention back to Lexie, and to the puzzle spinning through her mind. One thing was certain: Laurel and Michael's infant son had died. And no matter what other doubts she might have, Claire believed that Laurel had been and still was devastated by her baby's death. That rightly or wrongly, she held Michael responsible. And that she hated him passionately for it.

Enough to kill? This was like the nesting *matushka* dolls Michael had given her that past summer, Claire thought, layer after layer of illusion hiding a core of truth. But what was illusion here, and what was truth?

Head spinning in confusion, she groaned, "What *happened?*"

"Nuffin'," Lexie said. Claire looked down, startled to see the toddler by her side, rubbing her eyes. "Don't wanna slide no more. Wanna swing. Annie-Care push me?"

Smiling, Claire picked her up and snuggled her warmly. "You bet I will, sweet ducks." She carried her over to the baby swing and settled her into its soft leather pouch, standing back to push her gently. Thinking it was a game of catch-the-baby, Bubba came running up, bobbing and weaving and trying to snag the swing in his teeth.

"Bubba," Claire said sternly, "go lie down."

Disappointed, the dog padded a little way off, then turned and plopped onto the grass, head still swiveling from side to side as Lexie swung, back and forth, back and forth. Finally exhausted by the repetition, he dropped his head onto his paws, only his big brown eyes keeping up the to-and-fro movement.

As she pushed the swing, Claire scanned the street again for the low-slung Mercedes Doucet had been driving the other night. It had been hard to make out in that dim light, but the color had been dark. Black? Deep blue, maybe? Gray? She wasn't certain, and in a city overrun with Mercs, one more was just the proverbial needle in a haystack. In any event, except for the inevitable gardeners, the neighborhood was quiet, streets and yards nearly as abandoned as the park.

Lexie's head began to loll forward on her arm, so after a few more drifting passes, Claire let the swing coast to a stop and lifted out the drowsy toddler. She carried her to the stroller, reclining the seat as she laid her into it. Lexie stirred without opening her eyes, shifted sideways, slipped her thumb into her mouth, and then was gone, a picture of peace and contentment.

"Come on, Bubba," Claire called softly. "Time to go."

The dog padded over and stood quietly, his chin resting on the arm of the stroller as Claire snapped the leash onto his collar. Hooking its looped end over her wrist, she headed toward the street with dog and stroller, plotting a circuitous route home that would ensure Lexie was sound asleep when it was time to lift her out and carry her up to bed. Bubba maintained a sober, steady pace at her side, his playful energy forgotten for the time being, as if he were some hairy military escort who bore heavily his responsibility to guard the sleeping child.

When they finally turned into Dan's driveway, however, the fur along his back bristled visibly, and a low growl sounded from somewhere deep in his throat.

"What's the matter, fella?" Claire murmured.

She scanned the yard and street. Nothing much to see. Her rented red Mustang was in the drive, but Dan's Jeep was gone. Erin was studying for college midterms, Claire knew, but must have decided to take a break and go out for a while.

The dog's growling picked up intensity, and he crouched into a full-alert stance, head and tail extended, ears back, nose sniffing the air. He inched forward, ahead of the stroller, taking point position for this cautious charge into whatever danger it was he sensed coming from the Spragues' backyard. This was exactly the way he'd behaved the night they'd approached Doucet at the park, Claire realized.

She debated retreat, but where? And on what grounds? Because a notoriously goofy retriever smelled something? It could be a cat, a stray possum, or even a skunk. Was she going to call in federal troops for that?

"Bubba, shush," she whispered impatiently.

"You'll wake Lexie. Come on, we'll go see what it is."

She unhooked the leash from his collar, and Bubba made tight circles around her and the stroller as they moved up the drive. At the corner of the house, Claire peered around it and over an azalea bush, toward the Spragues' back door, then across the lawn to the garage. Still nothing. She looked down at Lexie, fast asleep. Tiny beads of sweat had collected on her brow, and her blond curls stuck damply to them. Should have put a hat on her, Claire thought, squinting up at the glaring sun. Skunk or no, she really needed to get this little one upstairs and into her bed.

She parked the stroller in the shade of the garage, next to the bottom of the stairs, then ran back to the Spragues' door, hoping Julie had gotten home from school and could take Bubba in. Claire knocked, then tried the knob. Locked. She rang the bell, once, then twice. Clearly, no one was home.

Bubba, meanwhile, was pacing back and forth between the house and the garage, becoming more agitated by the second. She should put him inside, anyway, Claire thought, just in case it *was* a skunk. But since the spare key to the Spragues' house was hanging on a hook in Bridget's pantry, securing the dog would have to be the second order of business. If it was a skunk, then the dog was in for a tomato-juice bath, like it or not.

''Bubba, stay,'' Claire whispered. ''Let me put Lexie to bed, and then I'll come and we'll look around.''

Instead, the dog ran for the stroller, teeth clamping onto the footrest. As he hunched down and tugged at it, the carriage teetered precariously to one side.

''Bubba, no! Drop it!'' she cried, racing to catch it before it tipped over. Lexie started as Claire righted it. ''It's okay, sweetie,'' Claire reassured her softly. Sleepy, half-opened eyes looked around, unfocused and confused. Claire grabbed the dog's collar. ''What is *wrong* with you? Come here!''

Struggling mightily against a hundred pounds of reluctant canine, she dragged him away from the stroller, looking for somewhere to tie him out of reach while she took care of Lexie. Finally, she spotted the handle of the garage door and led him there. Holding his collar with one hand, Claire looped the leash through the metal handle and then back on itself, then hooked it to the collar ring.

''There!'' she said, breathing heavily from the

exertion of wrestling with him. ''Now, just sit for a minute, would you? I'll be right back.''

She moved toward the side of the garage and the staircase, praying that Lexie was still sleepy enough to finish the nap Bridget had insisted she needed. For that matter, Claire thought ruefully, she could use one herself. This domesticity schtick was more tiring than she'd imagined. ''Okay, sweetie, up we go,'' she whispered, turning the stroller toward her to lift the baby out.

It was empty.

Panicked, Claire wheeled around. How could those tiny legs have clambered out so quickly? Suddenly, the dog howled. Overhead, a hinge creaked, and Claire looked up at Bridget's door just in time to see it close behind a man's large, black boot.

Then, from the apartment upstairs, she heard her little niece cry.

When Claire burst through the door of the apartment, she found Doucet slouched on a kitchen chair, watching her through lazy, half-lidded eyes. ''Gar, damn you! I knew you were skulking nearby. Where is she?''

''I tried to warn you,'' he said quietly.

Lexie shrieked again.

''Where *is* she, dammit!''

In answer, his gaze drifted to the nook at the far end of the kitchen, the part of the room's inverted el that was hidden from Claire's line of view, just as another man emerged from the recess. But she had eyes only for the panic-stricken toddler locked effortlessly in the crook of one of his big arms—and for the gun clenched in his free hand.

''You can have whatever you want,'' she said as evenly as she could, ''just don't hurt her.''

Lexie turned a tear-stained face toward her, arms reaching out to her, imploring. ''Annie-Care!''

Claire took a step forward. ''Give her to me.''

The gun barrel shifted, nuzzling one of the bright blue geese on Lexie's little shirt. ''Stop right there,'' the man ordered.

Claire halted in her tracks, heart pounding as she raised her hands in the air, struggling to keep the fear she felt from seeping into her voice. ''It's all right, Lexie. I'm here. The man won't hurt you—will you?'' she pleaded, looking from the baby to the large, dark-haired man holding her.

Only then did she notice the familiar, Delft blue eyes—eyes that belonged to a dead man.

''Hello, Claire,'' he said. ''Surprised?''

''Michael!'' Knees threatening to buckle, Claire reached out to steady herself on a chair while a smile crept across lips she knew intimately. At the roots of his muddy brown hair, wheat-colored regrowth was beginning to sprout. She had seen more than a few bodies in her day, at crime scenes, on autopsy tables, and laid out in funerary caskets. None of those had shocked her as much as the sight of this man, who was supposed to be dead, but obviously wasn't. A few days earlier, she would have rejoiced at the miracle. Now, it seemed less a miracle than an omen for disaster, one whose outlines she had barely begun to perceive.

''Annie-Care!'' Lexie cried again.

''Michael, please—she's terrified, can't you see that? Give her to me.''

He studied the squirming baby as if she were no more than a minor landscape feature in some complex tactical attack strategy. ''I don't know if I can do that. Are you going to run? Because if you try, I'll have to slow you down the way I did old Gar here.''

''Gar?'' Claire spun toward him. From where she stood now, she saw what had escaped her before: he wasn't slouched in the chair, he was cuffed to it, his hands wrenched behind him, pulling him back and down at an uncomfortable-looking angle. Worse, a dark, wet stain on the left side of his denim shirt had spread and soaked its way down into the waistband and leg of his pants. Even as Claire watched, a tiny red drop splattered to the floor beneath his chair. Then another. "Oh, no, Gar! I'm sorry!"

He nodded wearily. "I saw him come up here. Called Sprague's house, told his daughter to get out, try to find you, keep you from coming back..." His voice faded to a whisper.

Lexie cried again, and Claire turned back to Kazarian. "I won't run, Michael, I promise. Just give her to me, please."

The cunning blue eyes shifted between her and the child. Finally, he bent his knees, an arthritic crack sounding as he set the toddler down.

Claire dropped to the floor and held out her arms. "Come here, baby, it's okay."

Her chubby legs scampered across the room, and Lexie threw herself into Claire's arms. "I want Mommy!"

"I know, sweetie, but Auntie Claire's going to take care of you for a little while." She held the baby close, rocking her while she fought back her own tears. "We're okay," she murmured. "We're okay."

''Sit over there,'' Kazarian ordered, waving the gun at the empty chair behind them.

Still holding tight to Lexie, Claire shuffled backward and pulled herself up onto it. ''Why are you doing this, Michael? *What* are you doing? Everyone thought you were dead.''

''Almost everyone—except Gar, of course,'' he added, his voice dripping with the caustic sarcasm of competitiveness grown lethal. ''Damn you, boy! You just never give up, do you? I could've been free and clear by now, with a bundle of cash in my pocket, but oh no! Every time I turn around, there you are again, sticking your nose in my business.''

''Your business hurts people, Mike. I should've turned you in long ago, but I never guessed how low you'd sink.''

''You *knew* he didn't die in that car-bombing?'' Claire said, turning to Doucet. ''But how? They said the body had been firmly identified as Michael's.''

''Found a body, all right,'' Doucet said. ''Pieces of clothing, personal effects—keys, bits of ID, his cross.''

Claire recalled the cross, a gold, double-barred Russian Orthodox icon that had swung on a chain against Michael's broad beam of a chest. It had belonged to his grandfather, he'd said, and he never took it off, even in the shower. "Then how—"

"Yes, please, do tell," Kazarian said, leaning back against the kitchen counter. "No way was there enough of that guy left for a check of dental or fingerprint records. He was my build and coloring. We even had the same blood type. I made sure of that in case they decided to type tissue remains. So how the hell did you know it wasn't me?"

"Never could believe it," Doucet said wearily. "You were a good agent, Mike, too good to be whupped by a penny-ante thug like Ivankov. I was so sure those weren't your remains, I was prepared to seek a court order for DNA samples from your parents."

"You exhumed my old man? Gee-*zus,* Doucet! You're a bloody ghoul, you know that?"

"Said I would have. In the end, didn't have to."

Claire looked down at Lexie, who was watching the two men with tear-stained eyes, one thumb in her mouth, her other fist gripping Claire's shirt tightly. "Then how did you know?" she asked, looking up once more.

"Bum knee gave him away."

Kazarian looked down at his legs. "My knee?"

"Like you said, nothing left after the blast but a few hanks of hair and bone. But among the bits and pieces that went back to Quantico, there was one perfect, intact patella."

"Patella?"

"Kneecap, *mon chum.* A right one, same as you smashed in that college game that kept you out of the pros. Except the one we found had never been damaged. We subpoenaed your old orthopedic X rays, to be sure, but that was definitely a younger, healthier bone the medical examiner had. Not yours."

"But there was a funeral," Claire said. "Even his mother thinks Michael's dead."

Doucet's shoulders attempted a shrug, but the movement made him blanch. He winced and held himself very still for a moment. "Seemed like the best way to lull them into a false sense of security," he said finally.

"*Them?* Who?"

"Not sure. I was betting on Ivankov. Mike had already been dealing under the table with the guy."

"I knew you were sniffing my trail in New York," Kazarian said. "I told people as much. Told 'em you were trying to make me look bad to get me out of the way, leave the field clear for you and Laurel.''

Doucet sighed in disgust. This was obviously an old bone of contention between them. Claire recalled Laurel's frustration on the same subject: trying to prove a negative in the kangaroo court of public opinion while mischief-makers stood by, quick to offer up facile innuendo and cruel half truths.

''OPR was on to you long before I came into the picture,'' Doucet told Kazarian. ''You'd been skimming, cutting unreported deals with Ivankov, not documenting other scams they knew about through independent sources. You compromised the whole investigation. By the time they brought me in, I figured you'd try something like that disappearing act. Only question was whether you had an accomplice. To be honest,'' he added apologetically to Claire, ''I thought at first you were in on it.''

''Me? Are you crazy?''

He gave her a melancholy smile. ''I surely am, *ma chère,* but that, as they say, is a whole 'nother story. But when you went to see Ivankov that day, so desperate to solve Mike's murder, I realized you didn't know he was alive.''

She turned to Kazarian once more. "But whose body was in the car?"

He gave an indifferent shrug. "Some homeless guy I picked out at a blood donor clinic. Took him under my wing, cleaned him up, gave him a new set of clothes—mine, of course. Guy figured I was some fruit looking for a date, but he was happy enough to go along for the ride—least, till I pulled the gun." He laughed. "You should've seen his face!"

Instinctively, Claire put a hand over Lexie's ear and pressed her head against her chest. "You sick—"

The weapon took a direct bead on her. "Don't say it. I am very disappointed in you, Claire—very disappointed indeed. I expected more loyalty, but instead of exposing my enemies the way you were supposed to, you went and turned that wife of mine into a bloody poster girl! Who told you to do that? There I am with a perfect plan to destroy them both, and you go and make her out to be goddamn Joan of Arc."

"That was the plan right from the start, wasn't it?" Claire said angrily. "You set me up to go after Laurel and Gar. Jesus, Mary and Joseph! You even used your mother in this sick scheme of yours, Michael! Do you have any idea how heartbroken she is, thinking her only child's been murdered? How could you do that to her?''

''Well, I'm very sorry, I'm sure. But at least *she* did what was expected of her—though it bloody well took her long enough to get around to it. Just goes to show, if you want something done right, you have to do it yourself.'' Kazarian stood. ''Laurel's next, soon as I finish with you two. She will not win. No way.''

''I should have known.'' Claire closed her eyes, sickened by her own self-delusion. ''Damnation, I should have known.''

''Don't feel bad, *ma chère.*''

She opened her eyes once more. ''I'm sorry I was so awful, Gar. I sensed I'd been wrong about you, but I don't trust my instincts anymore.''

''You're not the only one he fooled. Good people don't go around looking for evil, and certainly don't expect to find it in a pleasing package.''

''He's the *fifolet* you were trying to warn me about, isn't he?''

Doucet nodded, but Kazarian placed himself between them. ''Don't listen to him, Claire. He's jealous of me. Always has been.''

''That woman who provided your alibi for the night Theo died, Mike?'' Doucet said from behind him. ''She recanted.''

Kazarian turned to him once more. ''No way.''

''She thought you were dead. She had nothing to lose by telling the truth. I also found a credit-card trail in one of your aliases, proving you drove from New York to Virginia that day, then back again.''

Claire held Lexie closer. ''Oh no, Michael—it's true? You really did smother your own son?''

''Laurel was responsible. Not me.''

''You really convinced yourself of that, didn't you?'' Doucet said. ''You even had the polygraph machine confused. But you were the one who did it, Mike, not her. You killed Theo out of vindictive spite, and when you realized we were closing in on you, you pulled that disappearing act.'' Doucet paused, as if listening. He exchanged a glance with Claire, and she realized what it was that he was hearing: sirens, far off to the east of them, but coming closer. ''It's all over, Mike,'' he said quietly.

''You shut up!'' Kazarian raised a hand, looking ready to backhand his erstwhile friend, but then he froze. The sirens were close now, their screams ripping through the quiet afternoon.

''That'll be Sprague and company,'' Doucet said. ''I told his daughter, soon as she found

Claire, to call her father, say I was here. Took a little longer than I'd hoped, mind you.''

The sirens whined down into silence, and Bubba took up a frantic barking as tires crunched to a stop in the street outside. Claire glanced at Doucet, who had been steadily sinking lower in the chair, his strength ebbing into the growing puddle beneath it. Outside, the scratch of boots on asphalt announced what she knew would be a SWAT team moving into position. She turned back to Kazarian. ''It's finished, Michael. Whatever you had planned—for us, for Laurel—it's not going to happen.''

''I'm not going down for her,'' he said darkly.

''You were a SWAT instructor. You know you won't be allowed to walk away from this. Do the right thing and make it easier on yourself. Gar needs medical attention. And this baby—she never did anything to you. Give it up and let's all walk out of here, right now.''

''No, it can't end here! I'm not finished!'' He crouched in front of Claire, suddenly pleading. ''You believe me, don't you? I'm not the monster he says I am. You *know* that, Claire. It was her doing. She tried to steal my son and walk out on me. But she was nothing without me—everyone knew that. She was just this quiet, timid thing when I met her. How did she think she could get along without me?'' His expression darkened. ''How could she think I'd let her take my son away?''

Kazarian reached out a free hand to touch Lexie's cheek, but the baby recoiled from him, clambering higher on Claire's lap. Claire held her close, tempted to give him a swift shove with her foot. But she hesitated in the face of his shining eyes and the sight of his twitchy hand on the gun. When she spoke, she forced her voice to stay low and even. ''Whatever happened, Michael, we'll talk. I want to hear your side of it, I really do. But first, I want this child out of here, please.''

''I'm not a monster,'' he pleaded. ''This didn't have to happen. She had to be punished. The rest of them had to see she was a fraud. I knew it would take something major to get their attention, but I didn't want to hurt any of them, Claire. You have to believe me.''

''*Any* of them?'' Claire stared, dumbfounded, at the handsome, distracted face in front of her, ice water running through her veins as she recognized the words he was using—the same words she'd read in the taunting, angry notes from the Southland Snatcher. Horrified, she whispered,

''Michael—you? You're the Snatcher? You killed those *other* babies, too?''

But even as she asked, she knew it all fit, and understood at last the full, pathological horror of his treachery. The high-profile kidnappings, calculated for maximum terror. The knowledge of conflicting police jurisdictions, and how to defeat security surveillance. The hatred of a law enforcement community that had passed him by for promotion. The specific targeting of Laurel, whom he hated with a passion, not least because she seemed to be succeeding where he himself had failed to measure up to his own and everyone else's expectations.

She recalled Laurel's analysis of the different categories of physical and sexual abusers. Some were repressed types, who used children as a substitute for the adults they were incompetent to deal with. Some were fetishists, obsessed with fixed rituals that fed their sick psychosexual cravings. And then there were the morally indiscriminate, people who seemed superficially charming, but when push came to shove, were abusive in all of their relationships. Such was the son Alma Kazarian had raised and blindly loved.

She glanced over at Gar, who also watched, stunned, and she realized that he, too, had only just realized the full horror of what this man, once his friend, had degenerated into.

"My son was gone," Kazarian said dully. "It was her fault. She had to be exposed and knocked off her lofty perch. And him, too," he added, waving the gun at Doucet. "Everything would have been all right if he hadn't stuck his nose into my business. But I took care of old Gar, didn't I? He got the sack. But Laurel? Oh no! Not even suspicion of murder was enough to touch that snow-white reputation. All she got was a slap on that dainty wrist of hers and a transfer to goddamn Tinseltown. What kind of punishment is that?"

"Laurel and Gar were innocent, Michael. So were those babies."

"It wasn't about babies!" he cried. "Don't you see, dammit? I had to bring her down. If the crime was big enough, I knew the press out here would find her again. Only this time, she'd fall flat on her face right in front of them. She couldn't protect her own baby. She couldn't protect anyone's babies," Kazarian said, scowling. "You turned her into a big star again, Claire, but that's okay. The bigger they become, the harder they fall. It won't stop, you see. There'll be another snatch, then another, and then, they'll know she's a fraud."

Claire thought about something Laurel had said about the twisted internal logic of the psychopathic mind, and she realized that somehow this made perfect sense to him.

Suddenly, the feedback sound of a bullhorn whistled up from below. *''This is the FBI. This property is surrounded. Come out with your hands up!''*

''Michael,'' Claire said quietly, ''Gar is right. It's over. There won't be any more snatches because they won't let you walk away from here.''

''Doucet! This is Dan Sprague. Come on down.''

Kazarian turned, perplexed, to the wounded man. ''What's going on? Why are they calling you?''

''I knew Sprague would come if his daughter said I was here,'' Doucet said, his voice growing faint. ''He thought I was stalking Claire.''

''Doucet, come on out with your hands in the air!''

''He doesn't know you weren't really fired?'' Claire asked. ''That you've been tracking Michael?''

''He had no need to know.''

''But they've got a warrant out for your arrest!''

''What?'' Kazarian hooted. ''I love it!''

''Gar? It's Laurel. I want to talk to you.''

Kazarian's expression shifted from mirth to malevolence in a heartbeat. ''She doesn't know, either?''

Doucet shook his head. A tiny rivulet had begun to flow from the red pool next to his chair, revealing a slight defect of slope in the apartment's floor. His eyes seemed heavy, and Claire feared he was on the verge of losing consciousness.

''Michael, it's over,'' she pleaded. ''You can't possibly get away now. If you don't give yourself up, you'll die here. You, of all people, know that.'' A phrase ran through her mind: ''suicide by cop.'' It was the last defiant act of the arrogant outlaw. The question was, how many others was he prepared to take with him?

''Gar!'' Laurel cried again. *''Is Claire Gillespie up there with you? And the baby? Just tell me that, would you, please?''*

Claire glanced over at Doucet, but his head was slumped on his chest now, his eyes closed. She turned back to Kazarian. ''I know you suffered terribly, losing your son, but—''

''Doucet!'' Dan called. *''Send Claire and the baby down. I know you don't want to hurt them.''*

''Annie-Care?'' Lexie asked. ''We go see Unca Dan?''

Claire dredged up a smile for the frightened child. ''I think that's a good idea, sweetie.'' She looked up at Kazarian. ''Please, Michael, let us go. Do the right thing.''

He glanced at the door, then at Claire and her niece, then at Doucet, slumped in the chair. The clock on the kitchen wall ticked away long, noisy seconds. Finally, he seemed to come to a decision. ''Here's what I want you to do. Go to the screen door and call down to them. Tell them Doucet says he'll let you go, but only if Agent Madden comes up to talk to him. Understand? And Claire? Don't tell them I'm here. If you do...'' He turned the gun on Lexie. ''I'll have her in my sights every second. If you deviate one iota from what I've said—''

''I won't.''

''All right, then, let's do it. We'll walk slowly to the door. I'll be right beside you all the way, so don't mess up.''

She nodded and rose from the chair. ''Hold on tight to Auntie Claire, okay, sweetie?'' The toddler nodded and gave Kazarian a scathing look as her little arms locked around Claire's neck.

When they reached the door, he held himself

against the wall, out of sight, the gun on the child as his free hand held tight to Claire's shirt. ''Go ahead,'' he whispered. ''Tell them.''

''Dan?'' she called. ''It's Claire!''

''Claire! Are you all right? Is Lexie with you?''

''Yes, on both counts. He says we can come down, Dan.''

''That's good. Come on then. Nobody's going to get hurt.''

''It's not quite that simple. He wants Laurel to come up before he'll let us go.'' Claire winced as Kazarian's finger dug into her ribs. ''He wants to talk to her.''

There was a moment of silence from below, although Claire could imagine the frantic, whispered discussions that had to be taking place.

''Claire,'' Dan called, *''tell Doucet if he sends you and Lexie down, Agent Madden will be happy to talk to him. He can come to the window. She'll be right below, and he can stay up there till he's good and ready to come down. Nobody wants to rush him.''*

Kazarian poked her again, head shaking firmly. Claire watched his lips angrily mouth the words, ''She comes up.''

She started to protest, but he shook his head vigorously once more. She turned back to the screen door. ''He says no, Dan,'' she yelled. ''He wants her to come up.''

More silence, then Laurel's unamplified voice shouted, ''No problem, Gar! I'll come up!'' There was a hubbub below, and Claire knew Dan was reaming Laurel out.

Kazarian, meanwhile, scowled. ''Oh, yes,'' he hissed. ''No problem, Gar. I would *love* to talk to you, my sweet Gar. Bitch!''

Claire closed her eyes, trying not to shake. He was dangerously unstable, and barring a miracle, he was going to kill them all before Dan's people finally brought him down, as they inevitably would, no matter how long this standoff lasted.

Dan's voice came on the bullhorn again. *''Bring Claire and the baby out to the landing, Doucet, so I know you're dealing in good faith. Agent Madden starts up only when they start down. But she will come up, you have my word—hers, too. That's the deal. Take it or leave it.''*

''Yeah, right,'' Kazarian muttered. ''And how many snipers you figure are on the surrounding rooftops, ready to take me out the second you're out of firing range? No deal.''

Only the baby softness of Lexie's hair against her cheek and the feel of her trusting arms around her neck restrained Claire from screaming and pummeling him. ‘‘Michael, listen to me. I won’t go. I’ll stand in front of you the whole time. Just let me pass the baby down, please. I know you would never unnecessarily hurt a child,’’ she said, realizing full well that the road he was traveling had already gone far beyond considerations of mere morality or basic human decency, and that several tiny innocents had already been mowed down in his path. But she would do or say whatever it took to save the baby in her arms—the child of a sister who half seemed to be her own child after all the years she’d watched over Britty when their mother was preoccupied, first with Nicky, then with overwhelming grief at the loss of a husband too soon dead.

‘‘Doucet? Do we have a deal?’’

‘‘Please, Michael.’’ Claire said quietly.

He nodded. ‘‘All right. The kid leaves, but you and Laurel both stay. It’s better that way, anyhow. Now, let’s go.’’

‘‘Wait,’’ Claire said. ‘‘What about Gar?’’ He was slumped motionless in the chair—dying, Claire suspected, if he wasn’t already gone. Her heart ached at the sight of him. If not for the child in her arms, she would have tried to carry him to safety as well.

‘‘Don’t push your luck, girl.’’

"He's hurt."

Kazarian rolled his eyes. "Ask me if I care. Look, do you want to get this kid out or not?"

"Yes," Claire said hastily. "Absolutely." One thing at a time. First Lexie. After the baby was safe, there would be another opportunity to try to reason with him.

"Then let's do it," he said.

Kazarian dwarfed them both as he looped his left arm tightly around Claire's neck. She held Lexie close against her body, feeling the gun rest in the crook of her right elbow, looking down and shuddering at the obscenity of the muzzle pressed against one of the Mother Goose figures toddling across her niece's little shirt.

They stepped out onto the landing to a flurry of voices and movement below. Claire's eyes made a quick circuit of the area. Half a dozen people stood sheltered by the corner of the house. She could see the flashing blue light bars of cruisers in the street beyond the house and the black Ninja getups of at least three SWAT snipers: one on Dan's roof, one on his neighbor's and another in a tree along the Spragues' property line.

Kazarian obviously spotted them, too, because he kept the exposed side of his body away from them and toward the open apartment door, tightening his grip, ready to beat a hasty retreat and drag woman and child back in with him at the first sign of trouble.

''Ow!'' Lexie cried as the gun jammed her ribs, the hard metal pinching Claire's skin at the same time.

''Be careful with that thing!'' Claire snapped.

Bubba's frantic basso bark echoed between the buildings. Below them, Claire saw a police officer struggling to drag the dog, who was unhooked from the garage door but still leashed, down the drive. Possibly he was thinking to put the retriever into one of the cruisers, but with a hundred pounds on him and a low center of gravity, Bubba was mounting a formidable resistance.

''Okay, Doucet, send them down,'' Dan called.

But Laurel was peering up the stairs, her blond head shaking in confusion. ''That's not Gar Doucet.'' Then she cried out, ''Oh my God! *Michael?*''

Dan spun toward her. ''Who?''

''That's Michael Kazarian, my husband!''

Claire felt the strange sensation of the big man behind her quaking with silent laughter. ''Hello, Laurel!'' he yelled. ''Surprise, surprise!''

Laurel rushed to the bottom of the steps, a look

of pure hatred in her eyes. ''How can you be here? They said you were dead!''

''And a happy day I'll bet that was for you, wasn't it?''

''You'd better believe it. What are you doing?''

''I came to visit my dear friend Claire.'' Claire felt him crouch lower, moving his face next to hers. ''She's very special to me, you know, Laurel. Very special indeed.'' His lips brushed Claire's neck. ''I've missed you,'' he whispered in her ear. As he pulled her tight against himself, the gun's cold steel dug into her arm. Lexie shrieked in pain.

And then, pure pandemonium erupted.

Claire barely heard the cry from the struggling cop as Bubba ripped the leash from his hands. All she saw was a mass of golden fur flying at the stairs, the gentle giant suddenly transformed into the mad dog Cujo. When the dog barreled past Laurel, Claire felt Kazarian flinch with the realization that the snarling, foaming beast thundering up toward them had eyes for no one and nothing but him and his throat. Fangs bared, the dog catapulted himself vertically from a distance of at least five steps below where they stood.

Kazarian's gun bolted upward, and as the pistol flashed and the crack exploded by her ear, Claire was thrown off balance. One arm flailed to grab the banister as the other gripped the child. Bubba crumpled, midflight, as if some cruel finger had flipped a switch to cut the current that held him airborne. Plummeting to the steps, the dog slid and bumped back down them in a limp, furry mass of gold and crimson.

But before Kazarian could retract his gun arm—before anyone else had a chance to react—another roar sounded from behind. This was no animal, nor even the sniper's fire Claire had expected. It was, rather, a furious bellow of human rage.

Struck from behind, Kazarian lurched into the upper-landing rail, his big arm ripped from around her neck as the railing splintered and gave. The banister beneath Claire's hand wobbled but held. Clinging to it, she looked back in time to see a mass of legs disappear over the side of the broken guardrail.

A split second later, from the asphalt a dozen feet below, came the dreadful, queasy sound of soft tissue striking a hard and unforgiving surface, while splintered bits of wood clattered and tinkled a discordant tune on the pavement.

Regaining her balance, Claire held the sobbing toddler to her and peered over the banister. Two men and one of Bridget's kitchen chairs lay in a tangled heap on the drive below. On top was Doucet, not moving, still handcuffed to spindles at the back of the shattered wooden chair. Claire prayed that his fall had been cushioned by the big man lying beneath him.

The SWAT team swarmed in from every corner of the lot, weapons trained on the fallen men. One of the black-clad commandos kicked away the gun that had flown out of Kazarian's hand and landed on the driveway a few feet away, but the precaution was obviously unnccessary. Doucet lay prostrate and still across the other man, his eyes closed, his manacled hands still behind his back, palms up and defenseless.

Beneath him, big arms and legs akimbo, neck bent at an angle not recommended by the divine architect, Kazarian stared up at Claire, his eyes cold and unblinking. Even as she watched, their color began to change, from vivid Delft blue to the opaque, washed-out murkiness of death.

Epilogue

Christmas Day in Los Angeles: not exactly Currier and Ives material, Dan thought as he headed up the central, palm-lined walkway of Laurel's condominium complex. Temperatures were hovering near seventy-five and there was a six-foot swell at the beach—a gift from El Niño, appropriately—luring die-hard surfers away from wassail in favor of near-perfect waves. He turned his face to the sun, inhaling the odd, intoxicating combination of blooming roses and someone's roasting turkey. It wasn't so bad, just the same, he thought. A person could get used to the place.

An elderly, white-haired woman working in her garden directly opposite Laurel's front door peered up at him, and Dan gave her a festive wave. ''Afternoon! Beautiful day, isn't it?''

''Yes, it is. Are you here to see Agent Madden?''

''Yes, ma'am.''

"I haven't seen her today. I'm not sure she's home."

"I think she is. I spoke to her on the phone a while ago."

"Oh, well, then she probably is, I guess. She hasn't been feeling too well, you know, not since—well, since all the trouble."

Dan only nodded, turning up the walkway to the door. After cultivating anonymity for so long, it looked as though Laurel had become a neighborhood as well as national celebrity, an inescapable consequence of the *Newsworld* cover and subsequent bizarre ending to the TOTNAP case. Now this intensely private woman, struggling to recover from the treachery of the man she'd once loved, was forced to do so under the glaring light of a fame she'd never wanted.

At the top of the steps, he rang the bell, once, then again. The door finally cracked open after his third ring, and Laurel's face peeked around the edge, pale, swollen-eyed and exasperated. "Dan, I told you—"

"I know what you told me. I'm just not buying it. Now open up."

"No. I'm in my bathrobe."

He glanced around, then leaned close and whispered, "I've seen you in less." Her green eyes glared at him, but she didn't slam the door. Fine, Dan thought; he'd take his victories where he found them. "Come on. I've spent the whole morning wrestling a twenty-three-pound turkey into submission, and I have no energy left to kick in this door. Give an old guy a break, would you? Let me in."

There was a rustle on the sidewalk behind him, and Dan turned to see the elderly woman from across the way eyeing him suspiciously now, her garden-gloved hands gripping a nasty-looking digging implement. "Is everything all right, Agent Madden?" she called with a tremulous voice—a geriatric Neighborhood Watch, on patrol.

Laurel mustered a smile. "Yes, thank you, Mrs. Birnbaum. This is—" She hesitated. "This is a friend. Your roses are looking beautiful," she added as an obvious diversionary tactic.

"They are pretty, aren't they? It's the bonemeal, you know."

"I'll have to remember that."

"Well, I guess I should be getting back to them. If you're sure you're all right...?"

"Everything's fine, but thank you for asking."

The old woman peered not too subtly at Dan

once more, as if memorizing his face. Then she toddled back to her garden.

Laurel turned to him with a sigh. ''You'd better come in.''

''Thank God for Mrs. Birnbaum,'' Dan said as she stepped aside to let him pass. Once inside, she shut the door, pulling the robe tight around herself. He fingered her terry lapel. ''Have you got a hot date and don't want me to see what you're wearing under that robe? Is that why you're standing me up?''

''I'm not standing you up. I told you all along I couldn't come to your house today.''

''Couldn't or wouldn't?''

''Both. Dan, please, you've been wonderful. I don't know why, after all the trouble I've caused—'' Lips trembling, she looked away.

''You caused nothing. How many times do I have to say this? You're not responsible for another person's obsession.''

She began to cry softly. ''Those babies died because of me.''

He took her by the shoulders. ''Not because of you. Because of Michael. He was a sick bastard, and you didn't make him that way. You didn't make him arrogant and vindictive, or force him to believe he was God, with the power of life and death over others. You, of all people, know that, Laurel. A person like that always finds victims and whipping boys. If he hadn't had you to blame for his ugliness, he would have fixated on someone else. Michael was a pathological liar and manipulator. He confounded everyone."

"But he was right," Laurel said. "I didn't even protect my own baby. How could I be so arrogant as to think I could protect anyone else?" She shook her head. "I can't do the job, Dan."

He exhaled heavily. "I know how much you're hurting. Do you think any of us really knows for sure that we can beat back the monsters? We don't. All we can do is give it our best, day after day, using whatever skill and training we can muster. Don't forget, it was you more than anyone else who stopped this guy. You understood what it would take to flush him out of hiding, and you put yourself on the line to do that. Now it's over and he can never hurt anyone again, because Special Agent Laurel Madden did her job, regardless of personal cost." Dan folded her into his arms. "Don't give up now, Laurel. Don't let him win. We need you. *I* need you," he added quietly.

She hesitated, then slipped her arms around him, touching her forehead to his. "I love you.

But I don't know what good I can be, to you or anyone else."

"Maybe we can be good for each other."

"It'd never work. There's the job, to begin with. Even if I managed to hold on to it—"

"There's no question about that. The letter of censure will have to stay on your file. You should have reported what you suspected about Doucet, even if you were wrong. But censure doesn't mean the end of a career. And in this case, it's going to stand right next to a letter of commendation from the director for the work you did to close down TOTNAP."

"Even so, I'd have to transfer to another field office. How can we work—"

"I've already thought about that. It's not going to be a problem. We won't let it be. You report to Oz. Someone else will have to sign off on your performance reports. Beyond that, people know me and how I operate. Work is work, and off-duty is off-duty. But I won't skulk around, Laurel. I'm not going to pretend you aren't important to me. People will just have to deal with that." He took her face in his hands. "So will you."

"I don't know," she said dubiously. As she covered his hands with her own, a frown creased her forehead. She took his left hand and examined it. ''Your wedding band is gone.''

Dan studied the strange, rubbed-bare spot on his ring finger, an area of skin that, until yesterday, he hadn't seen in twenty-three years. ''Chris McCabe was telling me about the kids who come into the ER with all kinds of things stuck on their fingers and toes,'' he said. ''Lead pipes, washers, O-rings, God knows what else. He brought me this silicone lubricant they use to avoid cutting, and it worked.''

Laurel pressed her lips to the bare finger. ''I love that you didn't cut it off,'' she said quietly.

Dan pulled her close, kissing her deeply. They held each other, like two drowning people finding the same sturdy life raft in the midst of storm-tossed waters.

''What about your girls?'' Laurel asked. ''What do they think about this?''

''It's a change,'' he admitted, ''and it'll take some getting used to. But Erin wants to ask you about criminal profiling as a profession. Julie, meantime, can't believe her klutz of an old man actually found a woman without help. I think her exact words were, 'Wow, this is, like, weird, you know—but totally cool, Dad, really.' I'll take that as a blessing,'' he added wryly.

Laurel smiled—a real, unequivocal smile at last.

"So what do you say?" he said. "There's a huge bird just went into the oven back at the house. I think I've got the turkey and stuffing part of the operation down pat. Bridget and Claire are taking care of vegetables, but I'm a little unclear on the concept of gravy. Are you going to help me out here, or what?"

"Claire's invited Gar?"

"She's heading out shortly to see if they'll let him out of the hospital for the afternoon." Dan brushed his fingers through her hair. "Are you okay with him being there?"

"Yes, sure. I went by the hospital a couple of days ago. Claire was there."

"She's been up to see him every day, as far as I know."

"I hope that means something. My friend Gar is extremely smitten with your friend Claire, and I'd like to see him happy."

"He may have to be persistent. I think she's a little gun-shy."

"I know the feeling."

"So, we'll all have to be persistent," Dan said, pulling her close again. "She likes you, you know."

"I like her, too."

"Good. Now, are you going to put some clothes on, or do I have to take you to Christmas dinner in this bathrobe?"

Laurel pressed her cheek to his, lips at his ear, and Dan felt a shiver a desire run through him. "Tell you what," she murmured, "I'll go and change, if you'll come and help me."

"My pleasure."

Her hand floating above the repaired railing, Claire skipped down the steps from Bridget's apartment. At the bottom of the staircase, however, she pulled up short.

You're thirty-five years old, Gillespie, and you're skipping. Get a grip.

Moving at a more mature, sedate pace, she started toward the car. Suddenly, as it had so many times in the past week, the dull, heavy memory of Michael thudded down on her, and she found herself foundering under the recollection of what he'd done. Under a crushing weight of guilt, too, over the role she herself may have unwittingly played in feeding his revenge fantasies. If she'd been less distracted by the fresh pain of Alan's defection and the divorce—if she'd been smarter, stronger, more astute—would things have gone as far as they did? Night after night she lay awake, asking herself whether, if she'd only seen through Michael, she could have done anything to short-circuit his deadly scheming.

Climbing wearily into the Mustang, Claire reached for the ignition. But as she glanced into the rearview mirror, she saw a dark blue, low-slung Mercedes pull into the drive and roll to a stop behind her. "I don't believe it!" she cried, jumping out of the car and running back. "What are you doing? You're bandaged from head to toe, one arm in a cast, and you're *driving?*"

Doucet looked up sheepishly through the open window. "Well, the thing is, it's not so much the driving that's the problem, as the getting in and out. Think you could give me a hand here?"

Head shaking, she opened his door and leaned low to offer him her shoulder, maneuvering under the cast on his broken left arm, trying to avoid putting pressure on the bandages that cradled four cracked ribs, and also covered the incision where surgeons had gone in to remove his spleen, ripped apart by Michael's bullet after Gar cornered him in Bridget's apartment. They both groaned with the effort as he struggled his way awkwardly out of the driver's seat.

''Why didn't you wait for me?'' Claire protested. ''I told you I'd come get you.''

''The doctor came in early and agreed to a parole—''

''All you had to do was call.''

''—and I wanted to pick up your Christmas present.''

''Christmas present? Are you completely nuts? In the first place, you didn't need to get me a Christmas present. And in the second place, the only thing open today is the 7-Eleven, so what could you possibly get besides an extra-large Slurpee?''

He put a hand to his cheek in mock dismay. ''Oh no! You wanted extra-large?'' Slumping against the car, flushed and breathing hard, he tugged one of her curls. ''Here, wiseacre, take the keys. It's in the back.''

Claire went back and unlocked the trunk, only to find a sealed cardboard box addressed to Special Agent G. Doucet, c/o Los Angeles Field Office, Federal Bureau of Investigation. ''What is this?''

''Open it.''

She used the edge of the key to cut the packing tape, then ripped the box open. Reaching inside, she shuffled through piles of papers, computer diskettes and cassette tapes, not realizing at first what she was looking at. "Oh my gosh, my stolen files!" She shot him a suspicious glance. "Gar Doucet, you *swore* it wasn't you who took them."

"And that was the truth. I have never lied to you, *ma chère,* not once."

"Oh, right, except by gargantuan omission. And my files?"

"A couple of Ivankov's goons broke into your place while you were out in Brooklyn interviewing him that day. We'd been letting his operation walk after Mike's bomb stunt, trying to get as much solid evidence as we could to repair the damage he'd done to the investigation. Also, hoping to find out whether Ivankov knew where Mike was. But once the Russian had your files, it was diminishing returns. If he'd read your interviews, he'd have known we were onto him, and the jig would have been up. We took him down that very night. Your files were seized along with the rest of the evidence we carted away."

"And now I can have them back?"

"Well, I'd be lying if I said the U.S. Attorney's Office in New York hadn't given them a careful read before deciding to release them. They were inclined to hold on to them until after the trial was over."

"But that could take a couple of years!"

"I know. I argued that your files were essential for your livelihood, and they finally agreed to let them go. Frankly, we've got so much on Ivankov, from extortion and racketeering to murder, that one more break-and-enter charge isn't going to make much difference in the guy's ultimate fate. I'd say he's en route to Siberia by way of sixty years, minimum, in federal penitentiary."

"So I can still write my Russian-mob piece?"

"I don't see why not."

Claire stared at him, dumbstruck by his capacity to come up with one surprise after another. "Thank you," she said.

"Thank you? That's all I get for my incisive, heartfelt arguments on your behalf? Not to mention dragging my sorry butt from a hospital bed to go pick this stuff up for you?"

Claire spun his key chain on her finger, trying not to smile. "What else did you have in mind?"

Reaching out with his one good arm, he grabbed her sleeve and dragged her toward him. "This," he said. He wrapped the arm around her and kissed her full on the lips, a deep, wholehearted embrace that far exceeded the tentative canoodling they'd been doing in his hospital room.

Pity pecks was what Claire told herself she'd given him there. Admittedly, he turned out not to be the villain of the piece. He'd also, in all probability, saved her life—and Lexie's, for which she was eternally grateful. Except for distress over Bubba, the toddler had come through that horrible afternoon remarkably unscathed physically and emotionally, as far as they could tell. Bridget might even agree to let her sister baby-sit again one day—although probably not in the next decade or two, Claire thought ruefully.

But as for Gar Doucet, her mind was made up. Pity pecks were fine, but their paths were soon to part. After the bitter lesson of Michael Kazarian, she had no interest in casual dalliances, not even with a wing-clipped guardian angel who could set her feet to skipping, despite the weight of the guilt and anger she was carrying around.

Now, heart thumping in the heat of his kiss, Claire found herself reconsidering. Breathless, she pulled away. "Gar, this is not a good idea."

He put a finger to her lips. "Shh! I've got something else to tell you. I got a letter with that package, too. It's a job offer for an assistant U.S. attorney's position."

"That's wonderful—but would you leave the FBI?"

He frowned. "I said most of my goodbyes there a couple of months ago."

"That was a ruse, though."

"Was it? I don't know. A lot of people were pretty quick off the mark, ready to believe a lie. One way or another, it feels like a good time to move on, and this is a job I want, and a place I want to be."

"What place?" she asked, almost afraid to hear the answer.

"They want me to handle the Ivankov prosecution, for starters."

"In New York?"

"That's where the indictment's been filed, so I guess so. I'm just waiting for one more piece of information before I give them an answer."

"What's that?"

"Whether you're going to stay there. If my Dorothy's planning to blow back to Kansas, it puts a bit of a monkey wrench in my long-term plan." The dark eyes, suddenly very serious, studied her—always watchful, always thinking, Claire thought. "I'd tell you about that plan," he said, "but I don't think you're ready to hear it. For now, just tell me if this sounds like a good first step."

She leaned against the car beside him. "I don't

know what to say. I have no plans to leave New York—certainly not for Kansas. But this is so sudden.''

''To you, maybe. Not to me. Don't forget, I've been watching you for quite a while.''

Claire puffed up her cheeks and exhaled heavily. ''I don't know, Gar. I'm feeling really cautious these days. And with you—'' She shifted uncomfortably. ''It seems a little too weird and circular, you know?''

''Why is that?'' he asked. Then, apparently, it dawned on him. ''Because of Mike? And because you're still not certain whether there was really something between me and Laurel, is that it? Do you think that's why I'm leaving the Bureau?''

''It's none of my business.''

He took her hand. ''It is your business if I'm ever going to convince you I can be trusted. The truth is, there was a time when I thought I was in love with Laurel. It was before she and Mike ever met, and it lasted for about a week. We had one date, and when the end of the evening came, I did what you normally do, unless the date's been a total disaster, which it wasn't, exactly.''

''And?''

''Let me put it this way, have you ever kissed

your brother?'' He paused. ''Scratch that. You don't have a brother.''

''As you very well know.''

''That's true. But I have sisters, and it felt like kissing one of them. No chemistry. Not like this,'' he added, leaning sideways to give her another brief but decidedly nonfraternal kiss. Straightening again, he added, ''And speaking of things I know about you—''

''Don't tell me you found out about the time Sister Paul Ignatius caught me kissing Richard Mazursky under the bleachers.''

He swung his good arm around her shoulder. ''Oh, that's all right, I'm a very forgiving man. Actually, what I was going to say is, you haven't had a vacation in a long time. I'm supposed to be taking some R&R for the next few weeks. I have a buddy who runs a little hideaway down in the Yucatan called Inka'an—a little piece of paradise, with sun, sand, margaritas and Mayan ruins. And I was thinking—''

''You were thinking I'd just drop everything and run off to *Mexico* with you?''

''Yes, ma'am, I was. You could tell me about life in the Big Apple, I could tell you more stories about wizards and their *gris-gris* magic.''

Claire watched the mischievous dark eyes and

the lips that made her feel anything but sisterly, knowing full well who the real wizard was here. ''Well, maybe. We'll talk about it,'' she said cautiously.

''That's my girl.'' He bent to kiss her again, but just then the Spragues' back door opened, and Dan's daughters emerged, followed by Claire's sister and niece.

''All right, you two,'' Bridget called, ''how long are we going to have to wait at the window while you stand out here corrupting the youth of America? Poor old Bubba's going crazy.''

The dog squeezed past her, limping toward them on a splinted paw. With goodly portions of his body shaved and bandaged, he looked like a Civil War veteran with a bad case of poodle envy and the world's worst barber. Only his tail was unbowed, waving triumphant in the sun. Reaching them, he wriggled between Gar and Claire and plunked himself down.

Lexie scooted after him. Wrapping herself around Claire's leg, she peered shyly up at Gar. ''You got a boo-boo?'' she asked, pointing to his cast.

Gar smiled and nodded. ''Just like Bubba.'' He ruffled the dog's ears. ''We are not slain, only wounded, right, big fella?''

Lexie reached into the pinafore pocket of her Raggedy Ann dress and withdrew a Cheerio. "Bubba sick. I gotta give him a pill." The dog took it delicately between his teeth, gulping it down in a single swallow. She pulled out another one and handed it to Claire. "Annie-Care give Unca Gar a pill?"

Claire's face went hot, and she looked from Gar to a laughing Bridget and back again. "What is this, a conspiracy?"

"Out of the mouths of babes," he said, grinning broadly.

Bubba gave them all a drooling smile, tail thumping to a contented beat.

ACKNOWLEDGMENTS

My deepest thanks go to: *Special Agent Jack Trimarco,* FBI Los Angeles Field Office, whose impressive knowledge and experience are exceeded only by his amazing patience and generosity; *Larry Harris,* veteran consultant to the Orange County Sheriff's Search and Rescue Bloodhound Team, as well as his beautiful, talented, slobbery sidekicks, Duchess, Sable and Trace; *Lieutenant Mike Jackson* and *Detective Ken Cowell,* Newport Beach Police Department, fine officers who take duty seriously, but never themselves (what a delight); novelist *Patricia McFall,* who keeps my writerly spirits soaring, and all the other members of *Fictionaires,* Orange County's finest fiction writers; my good buddy and fellow novelist *Joyce Spizer* and her husband, *Harold,* ace P.I.s who cheerfully answer all my goofy questions; attorney *Virginia Landry,* who's always on call when I need a legal beagle's perspective; *Dr. Ed Friedlander,* the Internet pathologist; the talented, supportive folks at MIRA, especially *Dianne Moggy* and *Amy Moore-Benson,* editors extraordinaire (all the more extraordinary in Amy's case, given her superb double duty in marketing); also *Candy Lee, Randall Toye, Katherine Orr, Stacy Widdrington, Greg Sarney* and *Heather Locken,* for their constant support, Creative Art Editor *Krystyna de Duleba* and *Tad Aronowicz* for wonderful design work; and of course, *Alex Osuszek* and his terrific sales force, the people who bring stories and readers together.

Last, but never, *ever* least, love and thanks for their support and patience go to my dearest *Richard, Kate* and *Anna*—who will also, no doubt, wish me to acknowledge Toby, who's been a particularly great source of inspiration for *Random Acts* (an extra dog cookie is due).

The tale of the *fifolet* is from a wonderful collection, *Cajun Folktales,* gathered and retold by J. J. Reneaux (August House, 1995).

M282

From out of the ashes
arises an old and
deadly secret...

TAYLOR
SMITH

DEADLY GRACE

MIRA
THE INNOCENTS CLUB
TAYLOR SMITH
YOU CAN'T AFFORD TO BE INNOCENT...
IF YOU WANT TO STAY ALIVE
M291

JB
M322
MIRA®
ERICA SPINDLER
Only one man can uncover the secrets and sins
of three generations of Pierron women.
Tempted by the forbidden...
FORBIDDEN
FRUIT